Invincible, Indiana

Printed in the United States of America

First Printing, 2011

ISBN 978-0-9847624-0-8

Madison House Publishing
www.MadisonHousePublishing.com

Ordering Information:
Quantity sales. Special discounts are available on quantity purchases by corporations, associations, and others. For details, contact the publisher at the web-address above, or call 215-717-8302.

www.InvincibleIndiana.com

To Jerry James Dunlevy, Senior and Junior
For all the trips to Hinkle...
For all the hours...
For everything.

Table of Contents

Acknowledgments

I wish to thank the following people for their invaluable service to making this book a reality:

Deborah Dunlevy and Luke Dunlevy, for being my First Readers.

Brian and Tara Gornik, Rich and Jil Elledge, and all my friends at Madison House for all the advice, support, and hard work.

Matt Hasenbalg for his beautiful design work. Thanks for making art with me. I hope people judge this book by its cover.

Chad Braham for his creative assistance.

Rob Cullin, Bob Mangino, Nate Miller, and everyone whose input and encouragement helped to shape this book.

Jessica Tauber, my editor, for scores of great ideas.

Angelo Pizzo for writing the greatest sports movie not about sports ever written, and for helping to crystallize so many of the myths that define us as Hoosiers.

Bill Simmons, for his podcast episode about the Rick Pitino press.

The Harrison Center for Arts.

The 18to88 community for their endless encouragement. Your generosity of spirit amazes and empowers me.

Bobby Plump, The Big O, Larry Bird, Scott Skiles, Steve Alford, Eric Montross, Damon Bailey, Alan Henderson, Kevin Ault, Calbert Cheaney, Glenn Robinson, Chris Thomas, Eric Gordon, and the thousands of other young men who helped to build the legend of Hoosier Hysteria. You are all giants that will never be slain.

Thank you all,

Nate

Invincible, Indiana

The Indiana High School Basketball Tournament began in 1911. Crawfordsville was the first champion. Over the next eighty-six years, it grew to become the emotional centerpiece of Indiana sports. In the tournament, legends were made and legacies written. The tournament was famous world-wide and became synonymous with what it meant to be a Hoosier. The state finals were played at historic venues like Butler Fieldhouse, Assembly Hall in Bloomington, the Indianapolis Coliseum, and Market Square Arena. In time, the tournament outgrew them all, eventually moving to the Hoosier Dome in Indianapolis.

In the first eighty-six years of the Indiana high school boys' basketball tournament, there were eighty-six champions crowned.

In the first eight years the tournament was played at the Hoosier Dome, more than 450,000 people came to watch.

For eight years from 1990 to 1997, no fewer than 41,000 people attended the finals in any given year.

Six times the attendance exceeded 52,000.

Three times it exceeded 60,000.

In 1997, 55,125 people came to the Dome to watch four teams play the two sessions of the IHSAA Boys Basketball Finals.

Chapter One

Pink Houses

It wasn't the hiss or the static that drove him crazy. It was the Mellencamp. "Damn Jack and Diane!" he muttered as he turned onto County Road 12. Little flecks of gravel kicked up as he gained speed on the barely paved road. He could hear the sum total of everything he owned rattling together in the back seat: a few piles of clothes, a TV, VCR, and a few boxes full of VHS tapes. Fifteen minutes from a new life, and all he could hope for was not to endure *The Authority Song* one more time.

Despite the Cougar-intensive theme, the music helped kill the monotony. Few sights are as utterly uninspiring as an endless soybean field in early August. Aside from the random patch of trees or deer crossing sign, he could not remember seeing anything for the last hour and a half since he left Indianapolis. Not for the first time, Dale flogged himself for taking the job. "Ain't that America…" burst to life as he hit the search button on the radio. "Damn it, I'm about ready to put on the country station," he said out loud.

Just in time to save his sanity, he spotted a monolith rising from the bean fields. The sign in front read:

I.H.S.
1996-97 Registration
August 7-9
Classes Begin August 16

Invincible High School was impressive only because of the sharp contrast it offered with its surroundings. Its two stories towered over the soy fields, like an oversized silo. It was typical in every way, except one: the name over the front door. In most of rural Indiana, school consolidation had long since robbed small town schools of any individual charm or connection to a specific town or community. They wound up with names that came out like call letters for the dozens of Johnny Cougar obsessed radio stations that dotted the farm counties in north central Indiana. KCHS. TVHS. But somehow, despite drawing its students from several nearby towns, Invincible High managed to retain the name of the closest one: Invincible, Indiana.

I don't know if I'm up for this, he thought as he pulled into the parking lot. He happily snapped off the radio, and took a second to collect himself. He was the man. He was the boss. There was no one looking over his shoulder.

"This is what I want!" *Isn't it?*

"This is my place." *Seriously? This place?*

"Well, if it sucks, at least I'm still young." *Yeah, for how much longer?*

After collecting his breath, dignity, and briefcase, Dale Cooper stumbled out of his car and was knocked back by the heat. The blacktop had been baking in the August sun for about six hours, and now threatened to melt the soles off his shoes. He ran through the front doors of his new job with a fervor altogether unrelated to his enthusiasm for his new job.

Like most important moments in life, his first steps into IHS were completely anti-climatic. There was no greeting other than the cool recycled air pouring out of the vents in the main hall. He glanced to the left and noticed a huge banner stretching across the entry way.

WE ARE INVINCIBLE...FOUR NINE

Dale chuckled and headed in the direction of the home-made monstrosity that hung just slightly too low. *That'll be down by second period on the first day*, he thought. After a couple of lucky turns, he came across a glass corner office. The name plate above the door read,

Principal Hershey

Dale had arrived.

Jim Hershey, principal of Invincible High School, was an unassuming man. That is to say that he lacked any natural intuition that might enable him to make assumptions. He rose to greet Dale, stumbling slightly as the edge of his desk confounded him. He shot it a confused look before turning to make eye contact with his new coach. Squeaking in what seemed to be an unnaturally high pitched voice he said, "Mr. Cooper! I'm glad you made it! Um, did you find your way from Indianapolis without incident?"

"Well, I did confuse the school with that other two story building in town, but yes sir, I did," he said with a good natured laugh.

Missing the joke entirely, Hershey continued, "I'm glad we finally have the opportunity to meet in person. I did enjoy our phone conversation, and I'm sure you know we all have high hopes for our new 'hired gun.' Um, we haven't had a losing season in almost 50 years you know, so the pressure is on! Personally, I wouldn't have hired someone so young, no offense of course, but Superintendent Ericksen is, um, very persuasive. You'll be teaching government and US history, so you'll have mostly upper classmen. I understand that your classroom experience is quite limited; are you sure you can handle these classes." His question sounded more like a statement.

"Yes, Mr. Hershey, I'm sure I can manage. After all, not too long ago I was taking those classes, so I'm sure I can remember how it was done."

Hershey chirped, "Good, good. Um, well let me show you to your classroom. Classes start next Thursday, so that will give you a week or so to get settled in your new place and have your, um, lesson plans ready. If you have any questions about anything feel free to ask me, although I'm sure Miss Lawson, your department chair, will be much more helpful."

And so, without so much as leaving Miss Lawson's phone number or showing Dale which room she was in, Hershey waved him into a class room and bustled off to spend several hours staring intently at attendance reports.

High schools can be lonely places even when they are full of students and teachers, but during the summer, the isolation seeps through the cracks under every door. There is no murmur of students in the halls. There are no squeaking sneakers in gym. There is no dissonance from the band room. There is nothing but the reality that everyone else in the world is already someplace they would much rather be.

Dale did not need to feel more alone right then. Life had already done enough of that to him in the last few weeks. He was gripped with the urge to call someone. He even pulled his cell out of his briefcase and stared at it blankly, unable to think of anyone on earth that it would even make sense to talk to right then. It would not have mattered much; there was no service anyway. In Indianapolis, he had felt important because he had a mobile phone. In Invincible, it just served to remind him he had no one to call.

As he spread out the few papers and notes he had with him (most of them basketball related), he was chilled to realize that he would actually have to teach that year.

"You will actually have to teach this year, you know," said a voice from around the corner.

Dale started and quickly tried to quell the sick feeling he had. Her interruption of his private moment of doubt was as disturbing to him as if she had walked in on him reading Playboy. A weak "Excuse me?" was all he could muster in response to the pretty brunette with an ironic smile standing in his doorway.

"Dale Cooper? Hi, I'm Samantha Lawson. I'm your department chair." She smiled. He could tell that she was not much older than he was, but she was not quite as young either. "I'm just messing with you. Coach Anderson had a habit of…well let's just say that they kept a TV on reserve especially for him down in the AV room."

He stood up and shook her hand. "Yeah, ok, hi. Principal Hershey said you would be able to help me out. He was in a hurry to get back to…to the stack of papers on his desk."

She was quick and to the point. "Dale, if you are going to survive here, there are two things you need to know. First: Jim Hershey is an idiot, and second: he can't be bothered with details like students and teachers. He is a middle manager with an ed degree. I wouldn't expect too much out of him. I can help you out with whatever you need. I've been teaching here for five years now, and honestly, there's not that much to it. How was the last place you taught? You're from Indianapolis right?"

"Well, this is pretty much my first gig, as it were." Dale cursed himself silently for sounding like an idiot. "I'm from Indianapolis, but I was working as an assistant coach for Butler University. This is going to be my first year teaching."

"Ah. So you're just here to coach then? Wonderful. Invincible High, where excellence in education is about as common as excellence in anything else."

He scrambled. "No, no, no. Seriously, I'm glad to be teaching. I mean, I majored in it for a reason right?" He felt the need to earn her approval, though he was unsure why. She was pretty enough but wore a prominent engagement ring. He was driven more by desperation than attraction. At this wobbly moment in his life, he at least wanted an ally, if not a friend. She had an air of wry intelligence and confidence that might have put some people off, but not him. "I'm pumped about teaching…government." *Idiot.*

The smile returned. He had earned the benefit of her doubts. "Okay then. If there is anything I can do for you let me know. My classroom is right across the hall. I'm leaving in a few minutes, but I'll be in and out most of this week. Do you have any questions before I take off?"

"Yeah, what's the difference between a republic and a democracy again?"

Lawson showed the faintest signs of a grin before turning to go.

The drive through Invincible, Indiana was like a trip in the most boring time machine ever made. Main Street in Invincible was exactly like Main Street in any other Midwestern community. Anyone interested in small town life circa 1950 only needed to go as far as Northern Indiana to satisfy their curiosity. There was a diner, a bank, a minimart, a Dairy Queen, a gas station, and some 'antique' stores. Invincible was possibly the single most forgettable place on earth. The residents liked to compare it to a Norman Rockwell painting, but if it was, it would have been reminiscent of his early, forgotten 'velvet' period. Dale was choked by the profound normalcy of it all.

He completed the ten minute drive from Soy Field High (as he had already come to think of it), to the bustling metropolis of 2083 inhabitants and could not help but notice the giant banner that stretched from the light poles in front of BARBER SHOP and FIRST BRETHREN CHURCH. It read:

INVINCIBLE FOR FOUR NINE

The banner was weird to be sure. Just as odd was that there was no one on the streets. Only a few cars dotted the curb and there was no foot traffic. Dale checked his watch. It was 12:30. He figured someone had to be out getting lunch. As he passed the corner of Main (aka State Road 15) and Washington (pausing briefly as one of the two stoplights in town switched from red to green), he strained to read the street signs. Superintendent Ericksen had a place for him already rented. All he had to do was find 21 Oak Street. With only about 20 streets in town, Dale figured it could not be that difficult.

He was right, but not for the reason he expected. As he turned right off Main to Oak, he noticed a swell of people standing in the street in front of a smallish bungalow.

Invincible was out in force.

As Dale exited his car, he was accosted by the sound of a poor brass band playing what he would later decide had to be Hail to the Chief. A tall man in a checked sports coat and faded jeans strode toward him.

"COACH COOPER!" he boomed. "COACH, WE ARE SO GLAD YOU MADE IT! WE WERE EXPECTING YOU SOONER!"

Though Dale had not forgotten from their first meeting that Phil Ericksen shouted incessantly, he was still taken aback by the ferocity of the greeting. "Uh, yes sir, I stopped by the schoo…"

"YES, YES, OF COURSE YOU DID. THIS YOUNG MAN WANTS TO GET RIGHT TO WORK! NOSE TO THE OLD GRINDSTONE! EVERYONE, EVERYONE! LISTEN UP! I WA…"

"Mr. Ericksen would you like a microphone?" piped up a voice from his right. Dale was sickened that anyone would want to amplify the vocal chords already causing him permanent hearing loss. He noticed the sly grin on the young man's face.

"YES! TOM, THAT'S AN EXCELLENT IDEA!" As Ericksen took the mike from the student, Dale cursed the kid's idea of a joke. **"I JUST WANT TO TAKE THE TIME…** *He sounds like a damn foghorn…***TO WELCOME OUR NEW HEAD COACH OF BOYS BASKETBALL, MR. DALE COOOOOPER!** *I swear jet engines aren't this loud…* **LET'S ALL GIVE HIM A BIG CHEER!"**

Dale braced for a roar and resigned himself to being a permanent client of ListenAid, but instead was greeted by a smattering of applause and a few whistles. "**WONDERFUL! WONDERFUL! I'M SURE THAT...**

It should be impossible to drone on while speaking at a volume reserved for heavy machinery, but somehow Ericksen managed. Dale's mind wandered and he caught a glance of a young black man standing off to the side. He was studying Dale closely. Dale took note that he was the only African-American in the throng. **"AND WITH HIS HELP, I'M SURE THAT THIS WILL BE INVINCIBLE'S FIFTIETH CONSECUTIVE NON-LOSING SEASON!"**

This time the crowd did roar.

Dale shook a couple of hundred hands that afternoon. He had prepared himself for a couple of hundred awkward conversations as well, but those never materialized. Everyone seemed polite, without caring much to meet him. He had expected to answer questions about zone defense or motion offense, but instead just ended up saying, "Hi, nice to meet you, thanks!" enough times to choke a camel. Once the crowd dissipated he was left alone with the loudest man he had ever met and a teenager totally out of place in Wonderbread, USA.

"WELL DALE," Ericksen had mercifully abandoned the mike a half hour back. "I'LL LET YOU GET SETTLED IN HERE. HERE'RE THE KEYS TO THE HOUSE. I DIDN'T HAVE TIME TO GET IT TOTALLY CLEANED UP, BUT AS COMPENSATION FOR YOUR TROUBLE, I WON'T START CHARGING YOU RENT UNTIL JANUARY."

"Thanks, Mr. Ericksen, that'll be fine I'm sure. I'll get settled in and call you if I need anything."

"FINE! FINE, MY BOY. JUST GIVE A HOLLAR! HAVE A WONDERFUL DAY!" Ericksen then strolled off down the street, presumably to cause auditory damage to his loved ones over lunch.

Dale turned to size up the young man left standing there with him, but before he could even extend his hand, the teen spoke with determination. "Coach Cooper, I'm Calvin Turner. I want to win."

Dale laughed good-naturedly and said, "Calv—." but before the words were out of his mouth, Calvin was already gone, back turned, striding down the street.

Standing alone and more than a little confused, he took a hard look at the bright pink cottage and wondered just what the hell he had gotten himself into.

Chapter Two

1948

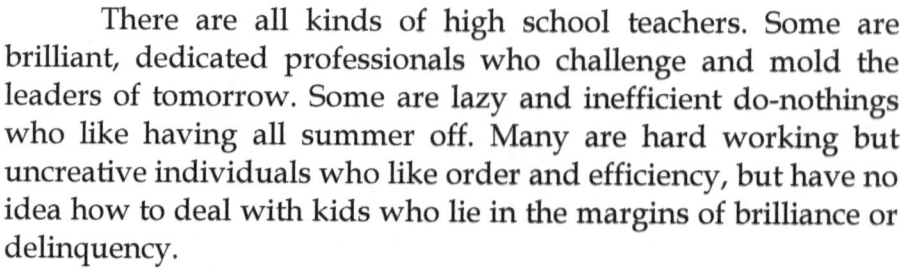

There are all kinds of high school teachers. Some are brilliant, dedicated professionals who challenge and mold the leaders of tomorrow. Some are lazy and inefficient do-nothings who like having all summer off. Many are hard working but uncreative individuals who like order and efficiency, but have no idea how to deal with kids who lie in the margins of brilliance or delinquency.

Then there are coaches.

In a sports crazy state like Indiana, even the best of men and women who teach and coach major high school sports like basketball and football struggle to keep up with the pressures of the classroom and the practice field. The work is demanding and the pay is not equal to the hours invested. They often gravitate to subjects like phys ed, health, and government. It remains unclear why teaching the Constitution of the United States of America is on par with lectures on acne control and the necessity of bathing every day, but in a great many schools it certainly is.

Invincible High was no exception. Dale's class load for the fall consisted of three hours of government: one "Special Emphasis" class for struggling students, one regular class and one Advanced Placement class. The administration was excited about offering it for the first time even though Dale's lesson plans were essentially identical for all three levels. IHS was small, and that made his class sizes miniscule. Throw in one hour of American History, two hours of Study Hall duty, a prep hour and for all intents and purposes, he was a full time basketball coach. He discussed it with Samantha over lunch the day before classes started.

"It's not that I'm complaining. But, I expected more somehow."

She smiled a tired smile. "Welcome to Invincible."

"Huh?" He routinely failed to have any intelligent reply when she spoke. She had a special way of making him feel like a moron.

"Dale, you are the head basketball coach. That's a big job in this town, hell in this whole state. Come on, are things really all that different in Indianapolis?"

"I don't know. I didn't teach there. I spent a couple of seasons playing in Spain after college, and then worked as an assistant at Butler. I basically just scouted high school games. I'm no idealist. I'm just surprised that I only have four real classes a day."

"Hey now, don't short change study hall. Taking attendance and writing bathroom passes can be a real bitch." She smiled, but he was unsure if she was laughing with or at him. He figured he would have to get used to it. "Don't tell me you're the sensitive type. You won't last long around here if you are."

"Yeah, well at least I don't have to work for a living," Dale replied.

"No, you just have to finish .500." There was a hint of disgust in her voice.

"Are you not a basketball fan, Sam?" She gave a little wince at the nickname, but he figured, screw it. She was not the only one who could be irritating.

"Dale," she said with emphasis, "I'm a fan of excellence, you know? I like things that are…that are quality and beautiful. I love basketball. I'm as much a Hoosier as the next girl. I get it. I know all about Wooden, and Bird, and…and Bailey. I like basketball. Just not in Invincible."

"Well, if you like excellent basketball, you're gonna have to start liking me."

"I hope you're right." She picked up her brown paper sack, wadded it up, and tossed it into the trash can in the corner. "I'm just not betting on it."

On the corner of Washington and Main sat Jack's Barber Shop. For generations, men have come together in search of a man who could make them look respectable without making them feel awkward in the process. Jack's continued that fine tradition without any variation from the standard themes. Pole. Mirror. Chair. Scissors. Clippers. It was reassuring.

A half a block away from a Saturday morning trim, Dale realized that he should have brought ear plugs.

"BUT REVEREND, I JUST DON'T THINK YOU…" boomed Phil Ericksen from inside of Jack's. The bellowing was interrupted by what Dale assumed was a second, more appropriately toned voice.

That day, Jack's was the host of an intense discussion that was also taking place in other small towns all over Indiana. The Indiana State High School Athletic Association had decided to abandon the traditional "one class" basketball tournament in favor of a four tiered system. The move was wildly unpopular among everyone except the principals of smaller schools who had maneuvered their way onto the board.

"YOU AREN'T BEING REALISTIC! IT'S BEEN MORE THAN FORTY YEARS SINCE MILAN. IT'S NEVER GOING TO HAPPEN AGAIN." Ericksen was apparently defending the school's decision to vote to abandon 80 plus years of tradition and adopt the new multi-class tournament.

As Dale entered the shop, he could finally hear the rebuttal. "Phil, it's about more than just Milan. It's about preserving a way of life, a dream, an ideal that our children and grandchildren can live up to." Dale did not recognize the man speaking. He was in his mid-fifties and wearing a shirt and tie. He gathered that he must be the 'Reverend' with whom Ericksen was arguing. "How can we turn our backs on the very essence of who we are as a state? This tournament is one of our most defining qualities, and we are going to abandon it? It's outrageous."

Phil Ericksen, who was sitting in the chair (there was only one at Jack's), chose his words carefully. Whether it was the influence of the man he was speaking to or merely the straight razor passing along under his chin, he spoke with a quiet voice for the first time in Dale's brief acquaintance with him. "More kids will have the chance to be champions. That means more kids will want to play basketball. THIS IS GOOD FOR THE SPORT!" A return to shouting was not enough to hide that he was unconvinced by his argument.

"Tradition matters. Phil, only about forty more kids a year will win a state championship under this new system. You are telling me that forty more kids a year is worth destroying 80 years of tradition? You are telling me that instead of boys all over the state dreaming of being Jimmy Chitwood, it is better that small town kids dream of beating some other small school, just so they can be named 1A State Champs? I know we haven't won around here in a long time, but I still like holding onto that hope. I've told my boy from the start that he should try to be the best. I didn't mean the best of the little guys. I meant the best of the best!" The reverend was getting through to his audience. The three other men waiting for haircuts murmured their assent, though the two elderly checkers players in the corner continued their game without comment.

"Well, I hope your son will be coming out for the team!" Dale had not planned to speak up but could not help himself.

"Coach Cooper! It's so very good to see you!" The reverend turned to Dale and extended his hand warmly, which was nice but unnerving. "I'm Greg Denton, Pastor of First Baptist Church. Wonderful to finally meet you." Dale resisted the urge to make a crack about whether there was a Second Baptist Church. It never pays to insult a minister in a small town. "My son Tom will definitely be playing for you this season," Denton continued. "Assuming he makes the squad of course."

"Well if he's one of the twelve best kids, I'm sure he'll help us having a winning season" Dale commented politically.

The other men in the room shared a chuckle.

"OH, HE'LL MAKE THE TEAM, SON. TOM WAS A TEAM CAPTAIN LAST YEAR. HE'S BEEN A THREE-YEAR STARTER. YOU KNOW TOM, DALE. HE'S THE THOUGHTFUL KID WHO HANDED ME THE MICROPHONE THE OTHER DAY."

Figuring he was finally in on the joke, Dale exhaled, "Ah! It's great to have senior leadership. Still, no one's guaranteed a spot, right? All the kids will have to earn their spots, fair and square. Sounds like the Reverend would be ok with that..."

Denton smiled warmly and said, "Wouldn't want it any other way. Like I said, I want Tom to strive for excellence. No one becomes great by having people hand him things. You have to work for them. I must say, Coach, it's encouraging to hear you talk that way. I especially like the part about a winning season."

The air went strangely cold. Dale guessed that not everyone in the room had confidence in his ability to deliver, and Denton had just poked a sore spot on the local consciousness. "I know you all have had a long tradition of winning here, and I will work my ass, um, butt off, sorry Reverend, to keep the streak alive for a fiftieth year. We will have a winning season. I promise." It rang false like pandering at a stump speech, but Dale meant every word.

Nothing could have prepared him for the gasp that followed from the men in the barber shop.

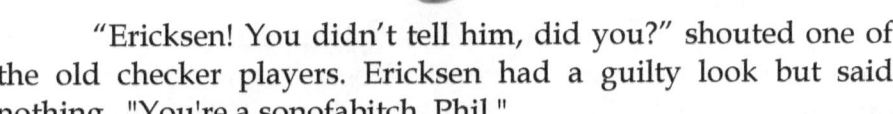

"Ericksen! You didn't tell him, did you?" shouted one of the old checker players. Ericksen had a guilty look but said nothing. "You're a sonofabitch, Phil."

Dale did not like the way this sounded. "Tell me what?"

"Boy," said the gray-topped man, "Invincible High has won exactly half of its games every single year since 1948. We have never had either a winning or a losing record since well before Koh-rea! This year will be the fiftieth straight .500 team. It's got to be some kind of record. Right, Bernie?"

His pot-bellied opponent in a John Deere hat and overalls chimed in, "Right, Barney!"

"Wait. What? What are you all talking about?" Dale was dumbfounded.

The reverend lowered his eyes. He felt sorry for the young man. "It's just what they said, Coach. For forty-nine straight years, our team has had neither a winning nor a losing record. Invincible High has finished .500 in basketball every year for almost half a century."

"Wait...wait...what?" He was repeating himself. It was all he could manage to say. They were pulling his leg. He expected to get invited out to a snipe hunt next. "Come on guys. It's not nice to make fun of the new guy. There is no conceivable way that a team could finish .500 for forty-nine years. That's impossible." He laughed nervously to encourage everyone else to give up the teasing and talk seriously again.

No one laughed with him.

Barney Robinson stared him down. "It ought to be impossible, but we've gone and done it! It's what we are most of proud of around these parts. It's no cause for joking! Right, Bernie?"

His friend replied in his usual tone, "Right, Barney!" Then he triple jumped his way to victory in their game.

Their assurance did nothing to diminish Dale's incredulity. "Seriously though. Does the team try to finish .500? You have to be doing it on purpose."

"NO!" came the unanimous shout from all corners of the shop. He had hit a nerve.

From under John Jr's scissors (old Jack had retired not long after Koh-rea, and his son had been running the store for over forty years), Ericksen finally spoke up. He covered his embarrassment by roaring, "ABSOLUTELY NOT! EVERYONE KNOWS THE RULES! WE CAN'T TRY TO FINISH .500. IT HAS TO HAPPEN NATURALLY!" Everyone but Denton loudly agreed.

Ever so slowly Dale began to accept that they were all serious, or seriously deranged. "Ok, so for forty-nine years, you've gone .500 without intentionally trying to…and you all are proud of this?" He tried not to sound judgmental.

He failed.

Barney angrily rose to his feet, upsetting the board in front of him. "Damn right we are proud of it! We ain't lost no more than half our games in foh-eveh'. It's a damn miracle. Imagine it! Fohty-nine years! Every season our boys hold their own against all the other towns. We even beat the big schools once in awhile. You had better believe we are proud! More than that, we are counting on you to bring us home for the fiftieth time. Right, Bernie?"

Bernie rejoined, "Right, Barney!"

Dale felt a mixture of nausea and anger pool up in his stomach washing away the fear and confusion completely. It was not that the town doubted he could win. They had no desire for him to win. What they wanted was what they had always had: the perfect stability of a .500 team.

Dale was not easily upset, but he had been made to feel foolish, and anger was a natural consequence. He was smart enough to understand that he was speaking in public with a man who could fire him. Still, with frustration growing into a simmering rage, he said, "We will try to win every game this season. My goal, the goal of every coach worth a damn, is to win as many ball games as we can while preparing young men for life…" The words began to flow freely as he recited the litany he had heard in the locker room at Hinkle so many times as a player. "Being a part of a team is a promise. Before we ever lace up, we promise each other that we will be great. We look each other in the eyes and promise that we will be one team with one heart. On the court we will play with one mind. We will have one weapon: work. We have one enemy: fear. We have one goal: victory. We have one reward: greatness!"

He knew the speech was cheesy, but somehow, in a barber shop that doubled as a window back to 1948, he found himself not just saying the words, but believing them, owning them. He did not mean to shout, but he could not help it. For twenty years he had been playing and coaching basketball. Coaching basketball had become his entire life. He had emptied everything else out. The dream he was chasing was all he had. He was incapable of talking about his goals as coach without his emotions taking over.

When he finally stopped, he felt the heat in his face, and realized what he had done. In the movies, such speeches are greeted with a slow clap building to cheers; in small town barbershops, they are greeted with slack-jawed shock.

The ice was mercifully broken by Denton. "Coach," he said carefully as Dale braced himself, "I hope my son makes your team." He gracefully put his arm around the younger man's shoulder and said, "Jack, will you save our spot? It's almost lunch time. I'm going to take Coach out for bite to eat."

Jack mumbled some assent, and the two men exited together. Jack appeared worried the coach might not return, and he would be out a customer. Barney, who was resetting the board for a rematch, noted his concern. "Don't worry Jack. He'll be back after lunch. Only a jackass would go all the way to Fort Wayne for a trim. Right, Bernie?"

Bernie agreed.

Pam's Homestyle Diner was one of two restaurants in Invincible, but the only one open for lunch. The Dairy Queen only served ice cream until four P.M. and even then only added hot dogs, burgers, and onion rings to its expansive menu of soft served treats. Everything at Pam's was either delicious or inedible depending on one's personal tolerance for grease. Reverend Denton sat down in the booth, warmly greeted the waitress and waited for Dale to finish looking over the menu before speaking. "So, they didn't tell you."

"No, they didn't." Dale said flatly. "I can't believe I just yelled at my boss in public."

"Yeah, you know what Coach? As a preacher, I've learned that sometimes people need to hear it loud."

The younger man laughed. "Please, don't call me Coach. It's Dale." He had never felt more alone or further from home, and this was someone he could trust.

"Well, Dale, I would normally shake your hand on that deal, but there are two reasons I'm going to keep calling you Coach. The first is that I have a feeling you are going to need some help getting respect in this town, and me calling you Coach all the time in public is going to help you with that. The second reason is that I'm one of your assistants."

Dale was not surprised. Denton was a tall enough man that anyone could have guessed that he had played at least some high school ball. "So you're a hoops coaching preacher. Those two things don't often go together, do they?

"Sure, why not? It does me good to get out of the study and be with people. Helps keep me young. Most of all, it gives me some time with my son. That can be hard to come by. I would have told you back at the barbershop, but I didn't feel it was quite the right setting. In a small town like this, there is a time and a place for everything. You would do well to remember that."

Dale recognized the gentle scolding and took it meekly. "I'm sorry I lost it like that, but I was shocked. I was clear in my interview that I want to win, and I wanted to go some place with a culture of winning. Ericksen went on and on about forty-nine years without a losing season, and how everyone was so proud of it. He made me feel like I was a good fit here."

"I think you could be a perfect fit here. Ericksen is a

political man. He's hired by the school board and wants to keep them happy. Deep down inside he's a good guy, but he's a bit of a coward. That's why I was giving it to him about this class basketball vote. He *knows* it's a terrible idea, but members of the board are for it, and he feels like he has to go along."

"Wait, why would the board be for class basketball if the school has finished .500 for a million years in a row?"

"Because they want to win too. They think that if the town can get excited about possibly winning a title, maybe they'll finally get behind upgrading the facilities and paying for a better class of coach. This town loves basketball, but it's a conservative bunch. It's hard to persuade people to invest in expensive buildings. They are tight with their money. This is happening all over the state. It's all about the money."

He continued, "In my opinion, winning is the right goal, but changing the tournament is the wrong way to get there. I believe that it is our holy duty as Americans to work as hard as we can to be as great as we can. Greatness is its own incentive, not pointless awards and trophies. That's why I found your little speech moving. Stupid maybe, but moving." He chuckled at his own dig. Years of ministry had helped him develop a warm, calming demeanor. He was a gifted man, able to correct and comfort at the same time.

Dale said, "I'm confused. If the plan was to push for class basketball so they could encourage the town to invest in the team, why hire me?"

Denton turned the question around on him. "You are young. You have no experience. Why do you think they hired you?"

He was too insightful not to know the answer. He said, "They expect me to fail. They want to break the streak without getting blamed for it."

Denton smiled a tired smile. "Your words, not mine. Some people feel you have to lose big before you can win big."

The waitress came over for their order, and they both settled on Farm House Fried Chicken. Denton continued after she left , "I'm not one of those people. I believe that you can win here, Coach." He said the first words quietly and the last word with emphasis so that the room could hear him. "But it's not going to be easy."

Chapter Three

I Want to Win

All lesson plans in all government classes across all of the United States of America on all school days include one of the following:

1. Memorize the Preamble to the Constitution
2. Learn the three branches of Government
3. Play videos about the JFK assassination.
4. "Make sure to vote"
5. Do a poster

It is amazing that this takes an entire semester of high school, but it illustrates the statistical fact that half of all people are of below average intelligence. Dale was no more thrilled by the subject matter than his students were. He got good grades in high school without being particularly motivated by academic achievement. Now on the other side of the desk, he found the Bill of Rights just as dull as when he was 18. Still, he was getting paid to teach so he felt a minor obligation to try to educate his students occasionally. Even so, he was relieved by his repeated respites throughout the day. He had all the time he needed to set up practice plans and a conditioning schedule.

He called for an informational meeting three weeks into the year. The announcement went out to the school that anyone interested in suiting up for the coming season could stop by his classroom after school on Thursday. Dale had no idea what to expect but was prepared for anything.

He was not serious by nature, but when it came to basketball, he managed to summon up an otherwise hidden intensity. The game mattered to him in a way that nothing else in his life could match. For most hours of the day, he was laid back, almost disinterested...as if he lived his life in a dentist's waiting room. His schoolmates and acquaintances were like piles of three week old People Magazines to him. When it was time for practice, whether as a player or a coach, something inside him would snap into place, and he was transformed. For the last twenty years of his life, he followed a daily ritual of Dr. Jekyll and Mr. Basketball. Until the day of the meeting, he had not realized how much he had been waiting to start the year. Something that had been caged up inside of him desperately wanted to break loose.

As he strode into the classroom after finishing hall duty, the air in his soul went flat. Twenty-five guys, several wearing letter jackets, lounged disinterestedly in the room. It was not the lack of numbers; it was not the lack of size. In fact, things were slightly brighter on that front than he would have thought. Several of the kids were at least 6-5, and one looked to stand 6-10 (even if he was only 170 lbs soaking wet).

What assailed Dale's spirit was a tangible sense of boredom in the air. There was no excitement. No one was horsing around. The kids barely spoke to each other. It felt more like employee orientation day at a phone solicitation service than the informational meeting for a high school basketball team in Indiana. Even Barry Kapler, his second assistant, sat in the corner half asleep.

"I'm Coach Cooper. Thanks for coming out. I want you all to know up front that no one in this room is guaranteed to make the team." He tried to sound stern and authoritarian. Objectively speaking, he should have been pulling it off quite nicely, but no one flinched or even blinked.

"I am going to work hard this year to bring winning basketball to Invincible High." That line garnered a smirk from several players. "And I expect you to work as well. If you want to play on my team, you will have to push harder than you ever have before." He passed out a schedule of after school workout days. They were not allowed to practice with a ball for a few more weeks, but they could meet to run and lift.

He would make them lift. He would make them run even more.

For someone as intense and passionate about basketball as Dale, the next half hour was pure torture. He did his best to fire up the troops while conducting introductions and laying out the key dates from the first practice to cut day, but only managed to produce about as much heat as two flint rocks and a pile of wet leaves. He was losing the room fast.

He had two equally risky options. He could pull back and accept their apathy, and later cut everyone who did not snap out of it (*ok, so we don't HAVE to have a JV squad,* he thought) or he could let loose with the big guns and try to win them over.

Dale Cooper was no coward. He cut off midsentence and gathered himself.

"I made a mistake. And I apologize." That got their attention. "I've been talking about tryouts and conditioning today, but there is something much more important I need to tell all of you. This is my first head coaching job, as I said, and I failed to tell you what my goals are for this year, and to make you all a promise." It was time for the litany.

"My goal is to win as many ball games as we can while preparing you men for life. I promise you that our team…" he paused, not so much for effect but so as to dredge up his own faith (in himself? in basketball? in Indiana?) to believe the words and to make his team believe them, "…we will work hard every practice. We will play hard every night. I promise you that we will be great. We will be one team with one heart. On the court we will play with one mind. We have one weapon: work. We have one enemy: fear. We have one goal: victory. We have one reward: greatness!"

Once again, there was no slow clap, no steadily rising cheer, but he did get a reaction. Most of the faces in the room were shocked, as if someone had come in and slapped them without warning. Some of the youngest guys were smiling. They wanted to believe what they were hearing. But there was one face Dale focused in on. A pair of dark eyes was burning. Calvin Turner sat in the back, and despite the fact they were in a small classroom with 27 people, he seemed ever so slightly separated from the others. He had been watching Dale the entire meeting, just sitting there, silently judging him. Now, Dale could tell that he had made up his mind about his new coach.

"Now that you know what I stand for," he continued after letting his words sink in for a moment. "know also that it will cost you to play on this team. You will pay in hard work. You will pay in floor burns. You will pay by touching endlines, after free throw lines, after midcourt lines. You will pay in thousands of free throws shot. If you want to play for Invincible High this season, you will pay. But you won't pay me. You will pay Basketball, and it is Basketball that will reward you. Now get out of here and spend the weekend deciding if you are up to wearing the colors of your school."

As the kids filed out, Assistant Coach Kapler gave Dale a half-hearted pat on the back. "Nice speech coach," he said, as he fell in line with the players leaving room. With surprising speed, the room cleared just as the late bus bell sounded. It was empty except for the occupant of the desk at the back.

"You told me that you want to win. I suppose now you know that you'll have to work for it." Dale did not mean to sound condescending, but did anyway. He was not a bad public speaker, but his personal conversations seldom started smoothly.

If Turner was offended, he did not show it. He extricated

himself from the desk and stood up, approaching his coach, looking him in the eyes. "You know now, don't you, Coach? These guys don't care. They are going to do just what their daddies did: wear a letter, knock up the homecoming queen, work at the soy plant or the grain elevator and not win. They ain't losers, but they ain't winners. They don't give a damn."

Dale paused. He knew the young man was right. It had not taken long to figure out what was going on in this town. He sensed the contempt in his player's voice, not just for the town he lived in, but also for his teammates. Calvin Turner was right, but Dale knew he could not bring that attitude to the court and still hope to be a winner.

So he changed the subject.

"I think you are the kind of person, Calvin, that I can ask a question to and get a straight answer. What are you doing here?"

"Why is a black kid going to an all white school, in an all white town? Is that what you mean?"

"Yeah. That's what I mean."

Dale was taking a calculated risk speaking that way to a student.

His faith was rewarded when Calvin answered, "Hatin' life." He was not offended by the question at all, but relished the chance to dive into it. "I'm from Gary. My dad was killed in the Gulf War. My momma couldn't afford for us to stay in the same neighborhood we used to live in. My new school was bad. So she sent me to live out here with my auntie who married a farmer. I tried to drop out so I could get a job and help her out, but she told me my dad would come back from the grave and beat me if he knew I was thinking about quittin' school."

"So you haven't lived here long?"

"I came second semester last year. I asked to try out for the team, and the coach let me. People around here are dumb, but no one is stupid enough to turn down a black kid who wants to play basketball for the school."

Dale laughed. "You're a good player. I've watched some tape on you. You have a nice stroke, but there are holes in your game." Never build a player up too much, too early.

Calvin bristled. "There are two problems with my game. One is that I want to win, and the guys that are lazy hate me for it. The second is that I'm black, and on this team, the ones that aren't lazy are racist."

Dale doubted that it was true, but engaging him on the issue was not likely to help anything. "No, I can see already that you have at least one problem that is bigger than that. You won't take criticism. You have some game. You could be a winner, but it'll cost you, kid. Greatness isn't something you are born with; you have to earn it. I told everyone in this room they would have to work this year. That means you too. You are going to have to work to stop blaming everyone else around you and start being accountable. Get out of here. Decide if you are willing to stop hating and start winning." He pointed to the door.

He had no idea if the eighteen year old who could look his 6′ 2″ coach square in the face would yell, or punch him or what. Instead, Calvin stared him down and said softly, "There is nothing I want more than to win." He grabbed his bag, and left.

Word spread through the town that the new coach was crazy, fiery, and stupid. Every once in a while someone even said it like it was a good thing. Dale's outburst at the barber shop combined with his lay-it-on-the-line approach at the organizational meeting had made him the talk of Invincible. The most common opinion was that the young outsider was going to ruin everything.

Most people were content to gossip behind his back, but once a day or so, one of the older citizens would shake his fist at him in public and yell something semi-coherent about "forty-nine years of tradition!" It did not stop at the school door either. Just weeks into the year, several members of the faculty held an impromptu meeting with Principal Hersey.

As utterly abhorrent of conflict as he was of critical

thinking, the entire affair was much too much for the principal to deal with. He assured the teachers that the decision to hire Mr. Cooper had not been up to him, and that yes, he would be sure to speak with him, and that no, he would not stand idly by and let him ruin the fifty year celebration. Meanwhile, the squeaky little man frantically calculated what course of action would allow him to sit idly by, regardless of its effect on the basketball season.

In the end, it was unavoidable. He would have to act. He was ill-equipped for action, but he could not have a mob of angry teachers distracting him from analyzing last year's ISTEP results. He called on Mr. Snyder, the oldest teacher in the school to talk some sense into the young coach.

P. William Snyder was seventy-five years old, and most schools would have long since asked him to retire. It was hard to get new teachers in Invincible, however, so no one was pushing him out the door quite yet. Besides, nothing new had happened in World History since 1945 anyway, so his knowledge base remained firmly up to date. Every year, the Greeks invented democracy, and the Senate offered the throne to Cesar anyway.

He came by Dale's classroom during his prep period and asked "for a word with him." He led the coach down the hallway outside the gym past the trophy case. It was filled with dusty conference title trophies with little runners or baseball bats and even a basketball or two on top. Dale wondered if Snyder was ever going to speak, as he had barely said a word since asking for one with the younger man.

"Mr. Cooper, I have lived in Invincible all my life," he finally wheezed. Apparently, he was a little winded from the trip down from the second floor. "Most every place has something that defines it, that it holds onto fervently. To this day, the Greeks are fiercely proud of having graced the world with democracy." Everything in Snyder's life could be traced back to the plucky Greeks and their invention of democracy. "Here in this town, we are proud of our basketball team."

"I know, sir. It's one of the reasons I'm so excited to coach here." Dale tried not to cut the older man off, but he was speaking so slowly, it was impossible to discern what was a comma and what was a period.

Snyder gave him an annoyed glance, and continued on his tortoise paced rant. "For forty-nine years, this school has won exactly half its games. Do you realize what a monumental accomplishment that is? Son, it's a record that could stand for years like the Coliseum of Rome! Frankly, word is getting around that you don't care about our tradition and heritage, and that you are barging around like a bull in a shop of Ming vases!" After almost a half-century of teaching world civ, he had incorporated so many such phrases into his daily speech that they just flowed out naturally.

"Mr. Snyder, I appreciate your concern, but nothing could be more important to me than keeping Invincible's string of, uh, non-losing seasons going. But let me ask you, wouldn't you like to have a WINNING season for once?"

Instead of answering, he strode down to the end of the trophy case where there were three framed photos. The first was a team photo with a player in the middle holding a ball with 1977 written on it. "That team, the '76-77 team, they were the miracle men. The streak had reached twenty-nine years, but it was going to stop. They were 10 -10 with one game left before the sectionals. The only problem was that that particular year, the Valley squad was how shall we say…not strong. They had several players get in a car wreck, and were down to just six warm bodies, all sophomores. They were an easy mark in the first round. Beyond that was a likely date with Plymouth in the second round. They had quite a good squad that year, and were ranked in the State. There was little hope of beating them. There was no possible way for Invincible to finish .500 with three games left." His story was paced with all the deliberation of his class room lectures.

"But then destiny stepped in. With the score tied at 48, and 10 seconds left, we in-bounded the ball and young Mike McAllister took a shot that would have won the game, but as the ball left his hands, as sure as Columbus discovered America, the transformer blew and all the lights in the building shut off. The game was suspended as a tie, and sure enough, the '77 Miracle Team finished 11-11-1. Later they found that a poor squirrel had made his way into the building and huddled in close to the transformer to stay warm, only to get burned alive and save our season." He bowed his head in honor of the sacrificial rodent.

Dale had no way to respond to the bizarre and rambling story, so he said, "Noble animal, the squirrel."

Snyder went on. "This picture is of the 1947-48 team. They were the first. We'd had several losing seasons, and were headed for another. They were 8-11 before the sectional, but won all three games and were sectional champs. They even won the first game of the regional before falling. They finished 12-12. They are the greatest champions in the history of Invincible."

Finally, Snyder pointed at the last picture; it was from 1939. "This was my senior year. We were the last winning team in Invincible history. We finished 19-1. The only game we lost all year was the first game of the sectionals. The town was crushed. Of course the war distracted most people after that, but the school had a string of losers before the Champs came together to save the '48 season."

"So you played on that team? Were you good?"

"Well, given that the scrawny one in front there is me, no. When we lost the sectional opener, it was the worst thing to ever happen to the town. I know that the 'Day of Infamy' came soon after, and I suppose that was worse in its way, but that loss left a scar on all of us. When the Champs rose from the ashes to redeem us, it set us on the path we are now. There hasn't been heartbreak in Invincible in a long time, young man."

Dale understood the message. The team meant a lot to people, and they were worried he would screw it up. "Mr. Snyder, let me ask you, who is remembered in history? Isn't it the conquerors?"

"Ah, we fill the history books with tales of their exploits, yes, but the conquerors never last. Someone else comes along to take their throne. The real strength in history is found in those who endure the attack without losing their identity. Dynasties come and go, but those that keep their sense of culture, of self are the true immortals. Greatness is not found in winning. It is found in enduring."

Dale was struck dumb. He was confronted with a colossal difference in understanding the nature of life. There was no way to reconcile his world view with that of Mr. Snyder. He thanked him for his time, and assured him that he understood the message. As Snyder left, Dale lingered a moment longer at the photos.

Before turning to go, under his breath, he said defiantly, "I want to win."

He had only been in Invincible for a month, but it was more than enough time to figure out that nightlife was not its strong suite. Most of the few twenty-somethings in town were already married with kids and not all that interested in tripping the light fantastic. He spent the first three or four weekends holed up in his pink bungalow fanatically watching all the game tape he could find. Even if he had no friends, at least he had work.

This was not the big leagues, however, and after a month, he had exhausted the stock piles of VHS tapes available for the past three years. He had a good handle on most of his returning players, as well as the other teams in the conference and sectional. He realized he was ready to have some fun. He decided to ask the only peer he knew for advice, so after the final bell on Friday he stopped in the door of Samantha Lawson's classroom

"Sam, what do people do for fun around here?" he asked, leaning awkwardly on the door frame. Around her, he only had two personas: retard or stalker.

"They drink beer, and then they go to the high school games, after which, uh, they drink more beer." She said. If she was joking, her face did not betray it.

"Okay, what do you do for fun?"

"Usually, weekends I either stay home and write my

fiancé and read books or I head out to Fort Wayne and visit my sister and hang out with her and her friends. Why? Are you starting to find small town life stifling?" she said, not bothering to look up from the papers she was stuffing in her bag.

"Well, there was a kick ass fish fry at the Methodist church last weekend, and I hear the firehouse is having a pancake breakfast this week. But, yes, I'm looking for something do to that won't involve a heart attack at age forty-eight." He managed to say that smoothly.

Samantha paused and looked up, but not at him, as if trying to decide whether or not to ask him the question forming in her head. Finally, out of pity she asked him, "Why don't you just head back to Indy on the weekend? Surely you have some friends there."

It was the first time in weeks that anyone had bothered to ask him a question that assumed he was a real person and not just a basketball coach. Still for such a simple inquiry, Dale realized that he did not have a good answer. "Uh. I…crap, to be honest I don't know."

She pressed him, "Invincible isn't a prison, you know. There is no warden and no lock. I get sick of this town as much as the next person, but I'm here because I choose to be here, and when I want to go, I go. Go home, see your friends. You have friends, right? Or family? There's nothing to do around here on the weekend once the game is over on Friday night, so take off."

The suggestion was obvious, but somehow it had never occurred to him to go back. Other than a couple of phone calls to his folks, he had not talked to anyone from Indianapolis since he left. He sat down behind one of the desks and considered why that was as he stared at a poster that read, "Welcome to Room 101" over the inside of the door.

Finally he said. "Do you know why colleges start classes after Labor Day?"

"So students don't take the long weekend to go home and not come back."

"Right. Maybe that's me right now. I don't want to head home quite yet."

She put down her stack of papers. "Dale, why Invincible? Why are you even here? What would posses you to move to a place where you don't know anyone, and aren't likely to meet anyone? There's no good reason to be here, unless it's already home."

He took a breath and gathered his thoughts before saying, "I'm here for basketball. All I have in my life is basketball. When I was at Butler, I traveled all the time, making recruiting trips, or scouting games. I had some friends, mostly guys I played with or coached with, but the ex-players have real grown-up lives now. The other coaches have spread out all over the place, and they are all busy as hell. At the college level, everyone is either a workaholic or unemployed. You have to choose basketball or everything else. It's not like I was that connected to people in Indy. I talked to my boss, Coach Collins, about where to go, and how to make the jump to the next level in my career. He told me to get some experience as a head coach at the high school level. When I was looking for jobs, the name of the town attracted me, and at the interview I was made to believe this place had a tradition of winning, and that I would have total control of the program. It seemed like a good fit. The school needed a coach, and I needed a stepping stone. So I came."

"And now you aren't so sure you want stay?"

"Should I be sure?" The frustration gurgled in his voice. "I'm sorry, but this town is freaky. Forty-nine years and the team finishes .500 every year? That's impossible, Sam. It's like they built the gym on an Indian burial ground or something. Everyone swears it just happens that way on its own, but I don't believe it. They can talk all they want to about jinxes, but it has to be a conspiracy, right? And if it is a giant scam they rig every season, what does that say about how they feel about winning? I saw Collins turn around the culture of losing at Butler; I think I could do that here too. But I've never seen a place so ambivalent to success. They don't have a culture of losing; they have a culture of not wanting to win. Winning isn't important to them, and that's something I can't fix."

Samantha felt like someone hearing an outsider describe

an annoying family member. She searched for the right way to respond without coming to the defense of a place that she spent most of her time belittling. "Different people have different ways of understanding success, you know? To everyone here, carrying on with life in much the same way their parents and their parents' parents did…that is victory. There are a lot of Amish around, and while nobody is going to give up the horseless carriage, they have influenced the way people think. People still feel the old ways are dependable, trustworthy, better. It's hard to hold the line against the world."

Dale was surprised that she took sides with the town. She had not said one supportive word about it from the moment he met her. He was not sure what she meant, but felt bad, knowing he had exposed a nerve.

After a pause, she said, "Never mind. Look, I'm heading to my sister's place after the football game tonight. Do you want to come with me for the weekend? She's single. It's just Fort Wayne, but it would do you some good to get out of town."

It had been so long since he had done anything that smacked of human contact that even a couple of days in Fort Wayne sounded like a good time. He quickly agreed, and left her office feeling simultaneously upbeat and pathetic. He was going to spend the weekend in Fort Wayne. And evidently that was a good thing.

When Harry Met Sally ruined it for everyone. If it was ever possible for men and women to be platonic friends without some degree of awkwardness, that movie blew it all to hell. Even if some men have not seen it, every woman on earth has, and most of them will believe anything Meg Ryan tells them. For there to ever be real friendship between a single man and woman, some sort of strict no-fly zone has to be in place. In the case of Samantha Lawson and Dale Cooper, that was accomplished by the ring on her finger. It was the modern equivalent of a chastity belt, and it helped to make Samantha exactly the right kind of unattainable. So despite the best advice of Mr. Crystal, Dale was pleasantly surprised at how well the two of them got along in the car.

The drive was helped by the fact that they did not know each other well. There was more than enough to talk about for the hour they had. Dale mostly kept Samantha talking. He figured he would not say anything stupid as long as the ball was in her court. He was especially careful to ask about her fiancée. Listening to Sam talk about getting married fascinated him. It was nice to envision that kind of settled, adult life, at least for someone else. He had never slowed down enough to consider any kind of existence away from the court, but for the first time, the idea of it almost sounded nice.

"Phil is in Germany right now. This is his last tour, and then he'll retire from active duty and take up a post with the Reserves. He's been gone awhile, but he's due home in six months. We were going to get married before he left, but when mom got sick, I just didn't feel like I could leave."

"So you guys are planning on staying in the area long-term?"

"Yeah, my mom needs to have someone around to watch out for her, and Phil's family farm is here, so it looks like I'm stuck."

Dale chuckled. "So you're back to hating Invincible?" he chided.

Samantha was irked because he had completely failed to understand the point she made to him earlier that day. "Do you know why I love Phil?" she asked. "He's incredibly brave. I know we aren't fighting in any major wars, but Phil is in the army anyway. He wants to be at the front edge of helping around the world. He's not content to stay at home and mind his own business. If there was a real war and America was threatened, every man in Invincible would try to join up. They love what is theirs, and they would die to protect it. That's natural, I suppose. But they don't care at all about what happens outside the boundaries of the good ol' USA. They barely care what happens on the other side of the state line. They love their home that much. Compared to them, I'm practically a traitor because I went to Michigan for college, but it doesn't mean I don't love my hometown…or the people in it."

"Sorry. I didn't mean to offend you," he said honestly.

"No, I can see how you would have been confused. I do criticize the way the town functions, especially when it comes to the school. I try to challenge my kids to expand their horizons, consider the larger world, leave home and explore a little, and for that some of the parents treat me like a pariah. Before teaching at Invincible, I wouldn't have thought that pushing a study abroad program would have been grounds for being burned at the stake. I want to grab the whole damn town by the shoulders sometimes and shake them awake. Towns are like sharks, if they don't keep moving, they die. Invincible has been floating belly up for decades now, and they are the only ones who can't smell the stench."

The street lights were almost constant, as they entered the Fort Wayne limits. Dale found them jarring. He enjoyed losing himself in conversation for awhile, but was now faced with the awkward reality of spending a weekend with two women he barely knew. He fought off the discomfort for a moment longer. "So what would it take? What could possibly happen to get this town to understand what is happening to it?"

Sam turned on Culver toward her sister's apartment and said, "A miracle. It would take a miracle, but these days resurrections are on short supply."

Chapter Four

Suicides

Attendance was strong at Tuesday's conditioning session. A few of the guys were missing because of football practice, but Dale figured they were working as hard there as they would be with him. The football team was not good, but at least there was no historically stupid record of non-achievement to burden them. High school sports of all kinds matter to towns like Invincible, and while basketball was the unquestioned king, there was still solid attendance at the football games. If nothing else, it gave people one more point of socialization.

Of the players who were there, most did just enough not to get yelled at. Dale had them run the halls for distance conditioning, and ran alongside his players. He set a good pace, and even encouraged Kapler to run as well. "Look at it this way. If anyone is slower than you, you get to yell at them," he told his assistant. With both coaches running the halls, it kept most of the boys together, but Dale suspected a couple ducked into the bathroom to avoid laps.

There was one encouraging sign. Turner passed his coach before the first turn and was out in front the entire run, marking a blistering pace. He was running as hard as he could, and it was only the first session. His effort did not have the effect on the others that Dale hoped for. He noticed glares from the other two seniors who did not like being shown up.

A veteran coach, well-established in his position could have responded in a conventional way. He could simply ass-chew the slackers and shame them into putting forth maximal effort or cut them from the team. Dale knew he did not have the cache with the team or the town to start throwing seniors off the team. He also did not want to undermine Calvin by turning him into a coach's pet.

Over the course of the next half hour, he ran a gamut of emotions. He was worried. He was irritated. Finally, he was furious. A lack of talent could be excused, but a lack of effort could not. No one had ever had to ask Dale Cooper to work harder. Even as a high school player he had put in the time and sweat to be his best. His players were disrespecting him, each other, and the game of basketball with their loafing. He was not going to stand for it.

"STOP!"

The runners were all too eager to oblige.

He thought he caught a glimpse of one guy slipping out of the men's room. "You make me SICK! Is there some place you would rather be than here, preparing to be champions?" His rage was dangerously close to igniting as he saw one of players lean over and whisper to a buddy. Still, he maintained control. *They are just kids. They need to learn.*

"Since some of you want to go home, I'll let you." He had their attention. "Three at a time you will face off against me. We will run suicides until you beat me. If you want to go home, you will outwork me. Otherwise, you stay. Seniors first." There was a palpable tension among the players. Turner, Tom Denton (who had become the focus of Dale's anger), and Sean Knorr stood forward.

Dale was going to punish these kids.

"ON THE LINE! Baseline to free-throw line and BACK! Baseline to half-court and BACK! Baseline to far free-throw line and BACK. Baseline to baseline and BACK! Beat me, and you go home. If I beat you, we run again."

Every player in the room knew what a suicide was, but Dale barked the instructions as if he was inventing some new kind of pain. As the other teens pooled along the back wall of the gym, Dale took his place alongside his 'senior leaders.' He hoped he knew something they did not, because it was clear that aside from the ultra-focused Turner, the other young men were not taking the situation seriously. The players were more curious than terrified.

Kapler took out a whistle and blew it, and the race was on. Dale's suspicions were correct. Calvin Turner was not only a hard worker but was physically gifted as well. He was blessed with great speed and the ability to cut and change directions with startling agility. He was going to win this race, and it would not be close. What the two slackers he was facing off with did not know was that twenty-seven is not old, and their coach was in pristine condition. Dale was a step quicker than the kids to the free throw line, and by the time race was over, he had thoroughly embarrassed the cut-ups.

"AGAIN!" he yelled. "YOU RUN UNTIL YOU BEAT ME!"

Denton and Knorr were shocked that they had lost to an 'old man,' and the other players clearly enjoyed their humiliation. They lined back up on the baseline with renewed determination.

Dale looked at Turner who was standing to the side. "You can go, Calvin. You beat me. You worked hard today. Great job." He knew already that his plan was paying off. Calvin was rewarded but based on his merits and not on the coach's favor. As for the others, they were about to get what was coming to them.

Turner did not leave. He stood, slightly apart from the

others, against the wall and watched as Kapler blew the whistle a second time. This time, the race was closer as Denton and Knorr clearly took it seriously. Close is not the same as winning, and while the margin was smaller, the result was the same. Dale dug deep and crossed the baseline two steps ahead of the boys. Without betraying how badly his lungs wanted to gulp down the air, he shouted "AGAIN!" and he immediately turned and stood on the baseline.

As the two young men slowly took their places, he gave a look to Kapler who read his mind and blew the whistle quick before Denton or Knorr were ready. Dale used his advantage to easily beat the boys a third straight time. His legs and lungs burned, but he had always had the ability to want his goal more than everyone else around him. He was not going to let these boys off. They would run again.

Dale prayed a fourth consecutive suicide with no break would be enough to accomplish his purpose. He suspected his players were out of shape, and could not take any more. He was right.

By the time they reached the far free throw line, they were completely gassed. Dale cruised to a victory and watched the boys standing back at the far baseline. Knorr had thrown up, and Denton had just given up. He stared at the two loafers as they slowly came back to join the rest of the team.

"When you are here," he said, carefully hiding the wobble in his own legs, "you are mine. We will work hard every second of every conditioning day and every second of every practice. We will be the best conditioned team in the state of Indiana. We will be the hardest working team in the state of Indiana. If you don't want to work, don't come back on Thursday. I don't want you here. We don't need you here. Everyone else, take the line." The other guys lined up along the baseline, and ran two suicides before they were dismissed. Turner stood and watched, but the other two seniors had long since departed to the lockers.

Normally, Dale would have ended with a team huddle and cheer, but not today. He let the players quietly file out. Turner was the last one left. He approached his coach.

"Coach, I know we can't practice, but I was wondering if I could shoot free throws for awhile."

"Calvin, state rules say that I can't be here while you have a ball, but the equipment room is unlocked. I have papers to grade, and will come back and lock up in awhile." He smiled. "What you do while I'm not here, I'm not responsible for."

The next conditioning session was disappointing. Reverend Denton joined Dale this time, so at least his son behaved. Still, while he was certain that no one slipped into the bathroom, the great energy level he naively hoped for was missing. His demonstration a few days back had brought law and order, but did little to ignite the passion of his team. Most of the kids were going through the motions, albeit a little faster and with less lip than before.

As the session wound down, Turner shot him a look, and Dale nodded. Dale brought a book because he had wound up waiting for three hours on Tuesday for Calvin to leave.

As he left the gym, the Reverend trailed back to Dale's classroom with him.

"Somber group today. Not a lot of life in them," he said to Dale.

"Yeah, I made sure there wasn't any screwing around on Tuesday, but I'm not sure how effective it was."

"Calvin was working hard."

"Yeah, you know he's in there right now shooting free throws. He kept me waiting for hours on Tuesday. But you know what? I don't mind."

"I wish I could get Tom to work that hard. He's not a lazy kid, but he could do more. I suppose all fathers think that about their sons, though."

Dale decided to step carefully. "I've watched a lot of tape on him. He's very talented. He needs a lot of coaching though. He runs the point fairly well, and keeps the ball moving. I wonder about his floor vision though. He seemed to have Turner open more often than he passed the ball to him."

"Oh, I agree. I kept telling him that he should keep Calvin active in the offense, but he would mutter about him shooting too much. He finally got so sick of me talking to him about it that I had to just drop it. Sometimes, you don't want coaching from your father."

"That can't be easy for you."

He sighed and ran his fingers through his hair, hesitating before responding. "It's scary, to be honest. Parenting is terrifying. You do the best you can to love and teach your kids, but they have to make their own choices. Tom has had his mind made up since he was a baby. He's been contrary all his life, but that doesn't stop me from trying to mold him and help him become as good a man as possible."

"Do you think he likes playing basketball?"

"He's a kid. He likes games. He hates work. He's your typical teenager. He wants to have fun. And to be honest, Coach, I don't know what you said to them the other day, but no one seemed to be having much fun today."

Dale bristled at the observation. "They weren't supposed to have fun. They come to conditioning to work."

Denton smiled. "Very true. I'm sorry. I wasn't trying to challenge your methods."

"No that's fine, Greg. I appreciate the feedback. You are always welcome to question anything you need to," Dale said, not really meaning it. This team was his life. He was in a new place; he knew almost no one, and he felt like he could only control one thing. He gave the polite answer, but in his heart he was determined to listen to no one when it came to the Invincible High Indians. Denton may or may not have been right, but Dale was in no frame of mind to hear him.

"How are you doing, Dale?" It sounded weird to hear his name from Denton. "You seem stressed."

In truth, Dale was under the worst kind of pressure. There was no release for his tension. He was wrapped up tightly with basketball, and there were still more than two months before practice could even start. With precious little to do but watch TV at home every night, Dale spent most of his time frustrated and bored. He had fun with Sam and her sister the previous weekend, but he needed more than a night out on the town with a platonic friend and her hot sister who never shut up.

Things were tough, but he was not so low as to be ready to bear his soul to a minister. So, he lied.

"Oh, yeah, it's just my first year teaching and all. Every day is a new set of lesson plans…it's all pretty challenging." He was not convincing. *Damn. Next time I need to lie to a preacher, I have to remember to think it through first!*

To his credit, Denton did not press him on it. "Sure, Sue had a really tough time her first year. It can be a lot of work."

A connection flickered in Dale's mind. "Ooooh, of course, Mrs. Denton the Spanish teacher is your wife!"

The older man chuckled, "There you go. You probably haven't talked to her much, have you?"

"No, she's on the other side of the building."

"Well, she's seen you around and thinks you look too thin. She's wanted me to invite you over for some real food. Would you like to come to dinner tomorrow? Or if you have plans this weekend, we could do it next week." Denton posed the invite in such a way that Dale knew he would have to accept.

Not that he had any reason to decline. He liked the Reverend well enough, even though his frustrations with life made him anti-social. Refusal would not be possible, so he said he would come the next night.

Denton was pleased and after giving Dale directions to his house, glanced suddenly at his watch. "Ooooh. I'm late! There's an AA group that meets in the church basement on Thursdays, but only if I get there to unlock the door. It's amazing, but for a town with no bar and liquor store, we have a lot of drunks. Sorry, Dale! I have to run, I'll see you tomorrow night!"

Dale said goodbye and focused his attention on his lesson plan for the next day. It would not take long to arrange, and he would be left with a lot of time to kill.

Calvin Turner shot a lot of free throws.

On Fridays, most government teachers find a way to disguise time wasting as learning. Dale instituted "For the People Fridays." Any student who wanted to bring in a current event article remotely related to the government in action could present the topic and lead a brief discussion on it for extra credit. Considering what a great time waster it could be, Dale was surprised that no one bothered to do it for the first couple of weeks. Finally, Sean Knorr came through with an article.

"Coach, I have an article. It's about the state legislature and basketball."

"Ah, great topic, Sean. Let's hear it. Come to the front of the class and lead the discussion." *While I kick back and relax!* He decided that maybe he could get to like teaching.

"Well, they don't want the guys running basketball to screw up the tournament, because of Hoosiers and stuff. Some guys want to pass a law to make them keep the tourney the way it was instead of going to four classes." His voice trailed off.

"Ok, good. Now lead a discussion. Ask the class questions about the topic."

"Uh, what do you guys think about that?"

No one responded. It is the solemn duty of the student to never respond to a question asked by any person in front of the class, especially if that person is a fellow student.

Dale stepped in and bailed a visibly sweating Knorr out. "Ok, what are the issues here? For one, the IHSAA wants to move to a multi-class basketball system. Sean, can you tell the class what that means?"

Knorr responded, "It means that when it comes to the state tournament, all the big schools will play each other and all the small schools will play each other. Then we will have four state champions instead of one."

"Great, now class, who can give some advantages of that?"

"It gives everyone a chance to win," said a girl in the

front.

Dale was bothered by the answer, but did not show it, "Yes. It gives smaller schools a better chance to win a championship, because they will only play schools with similar resources and enrollments." His subtle correction was lost on most of the class. "So what are the disadvantages of a multi-class system?"

"Tradition" Tom Denton spoke forcefully. "There's no reason to change something that isn't broken. We have the best tournament in the world, and people want to go screwing with it."

"Ok, but tradition alone isn't a good enough reason. We can't let 'that's the way we've always done it' become a barrier to change. Is there something that is fundamentally wrong with the idea?"

"If you don't whip everyone, you aren't really a winner," Calvin said from the back of the room. "Only the best is the real champ. This is just a stupid way to make losers feel better about themselves."

Sometimes all it takes for a debate to erupt is for someone to go and say something utterly over the top. This was no exception.

Knorr replied defensively, "What's so bad about giving people a chance? There are schools in Indianapolis that have ten times as many students as we do. They have more players, more money, more everything!"

Calvin fired back, "So what? This is America. Nobody gives you nothin'. You work hard, and you beat down anyone who tries to stop you from gettin' what you want. If they beat you to it, then it's theirs."

Dale grinned. It was hard not to love the kid.

The other students were bothered by his reasoning. "That's not true! America is built on fairness and equality. We even make special laws to make sure of it. You should know that better than any of us!" The voice responding to Calvin belonged to Jil Somethingoranother in the first row. It occurred to Dale that he really needed to get around to learning everyone's names.

He braced himself for Turner to unload on the girl, but instead it was Denton who angrily shot back, "That's bull! You have to earn what you get! It's that kind of talk that leads to stupid ideas like giving incompetent black people and women jobs that a better qualified white man should have."

The words hit Dale like a two-by-four to the head. He instinctively shot his eyes over to Turner, but Calvin was unfazed. He sat icily still and without comment. The class stared at him waiting to gauge his reaction. Dale regained his equilibrium and took back control of the floor, redirecting the conversation.

"Well this is the issue, isn't it? What does fair mean? Does fair mean equality of opportunity or equality of outcome? Some people want there to be more sectional and state champions. They want a more equal outcome. Others say that it doesn't matter how things finish up, only that everyone gets an equal chance at the start. So, do small schools have an equal chance to win under the current system?"

Knorr spoke up, "No. We don't. We don't have the number of players; we don't have the money. The game is set up against us." This argument carried most of the class. Denton backed off, not wanting to scrap with his friend. Calvin had not moved since the earlier barrage.

Dale posed another question to the class, "Since this class is about government, and not basketball, let's talk about what the article is about. The IHSAA is a private organization. It isn't tax payer funded. Does the legislature of the State of Indiana have any right or authority to tell a private organization what to do?"

It was a good question, but the students were all firmly back in their shells. The earlier tensions still rested heavily in the posture of several kids. There would be no more discussion. He was disappointed, but not surprised. He encouraged the kids to consider the question for future classes, and resumed his regularly scheduled lecture on checks and balances.

The dismissal bell rang and the students happily filed out into the hall for another of the day's welcome five minute reprieves from their teachers. Dale grabbed Tom Denton by the arm as he made his way for freedom. "Can I have a word with you, Tom?"

Denton froze. His gaze fixed straight ahead at the door and he replied, "Yes," without emotion.

"Do we have a problem, Tom?"

The student's face was fixed in a scowl that declared, "I don't want to be hassled." He said, "No, sir," in just the wrong way.

Dale could tell the kid was angry. It was never far from the surface with Tom Denton. He decided that an aggressive stance would only serve to increase the tension. "Tom, I've heard you're a great player. Everyone in town has talked to me about you." He saw the muscles in the boy's face relax. He was proud, and it clearly mattered to him what people thought of him on the court. "I know you were team captain last season, but if we are going to have a good year this year, I need more out of you. I need you to be a leader in conditioning. You have to show the younger kids how to work."

For a moment, Tom was changed. His defenses were down, and he engaged with his coach, facing him for the first time. "Yes sir. Sean and I will get in line. I'm sorry. I'll do better. I want to lead the team."

This was progress. "Good. I know I can count on you." Dale went for the second and more disturbing issue. "But, I have another question. What you said in class this morning, don't you think it was insensitive?"

The words left Dale's mouth and died. Whatever thaw Tom Denton had shown froze over instantly. He turned back to the door. "I'm going to be late for trig."

Dale knew then that they did, in fact, have a problem.

Chapter Five

Rutabaga Days

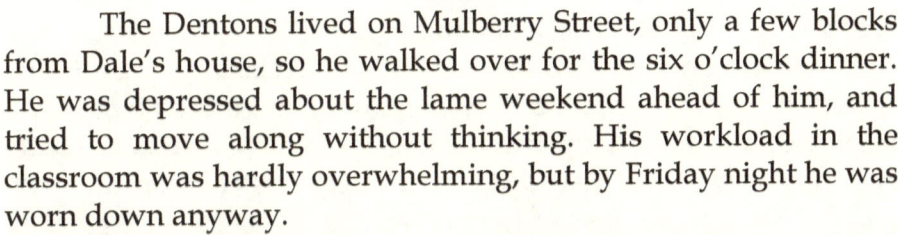

The Dentons lived on Mulberry Street, only a few blocks from Dale's house, so he walked over for the six o'clock dinner. He was depressed about the lame weekend ahead of him, and tried to move along without thinking. His workload in the classroom was hardly overwhelming, but by Friday night he was worn down anyway.

There were people out in their yards as he meandered vacantly down the street. He smiled and nodded at the ones who said hello. He passed under the shadow of a new banner strung up across Main Street. It trumpeted proudly:

RUTABAGA DAYS
SEPTEMBER 27-29

I'll be sure not to miss the fun, he thought. He then chuckled to himself as he thought about the implications of living in a town where the best way to communicate with everyone was to string banners across the street. The possibilities were endless:

TRASH DAY IS THURSDAY

NO LEAF BURNING

WILL MILDRED SIMON PLEASE KEEP HER GATE CLOSED BECAUSE HER DOG IS CRAPPING IN EVERYONE'S YARD

In a matter of minutes, he arrived at the Dentons' home. It was a modest two story farmhouse. The land had long since been parceled off, but they had a good sized yard with a creek running through the back yard. The interior was warm and informal. The walls were covered in family pictures and the mantel was filled with trophies. It was a welcoming house, and Dale felt comforted by it.

Sue Denton invited Dale in and led him out to the back deck where Greg was grilling steaks.

"I hope you are hungry! How do you like your meat?" Denton asked him as they arrived.

"Well done," Dale replied. Then he noticed the steaks. "Holy crap, look at those! They're huge!"

If Denton took offense to Dale declaring feces to be sacred, he did not show it. "My neighbor slaughtered a cow last weekend, and gave us plenty of meat. We have a freezer in the basement." He then placed the four massive steaks on the grill. Each one had to be close to twenty ounces.

In the background, they heard the front door slam as Tom arrived. "We're out back, son!" Greg called to his only child. He came out and joined them on deck, greeting Dale with a flat, "Hi, Coach." He did not address his father at all.

They made small talk as the meat cooked. Tom was obviously uncomfortable with his coach's presence, and spoke only when directly spoken to.

Greg enthusiastically shared grilling tips with Dale. "The key, Dale, is indirect heat. You don't want the flames to lick the meat. The slower you cook good meat, the more tender it will be."

Grilling was his hobby, and he took great pride in his grills and wide assortment of grilling paraphernalia. His guest was more impressed than his son.

As they sat down to what could conservatively be described as a feast, Greg said grace. "Father God, we thank you for the food we have to share tonight. We thank you for bringing Dale into our community. Amen." Dale was impressed by the simple straightforward way that Denton prayed. He lacked any pretension.

"Sue, the food looks wonderful!"

They chatted pleasantly throughout the meal, and Dale had to admit that it was good to eat a home cooked dinner. The steak was amazing, and there was no shortage of anything. He enjoyed getting to know the Dentons, who were surprisingly well traveled, having spent time in Spain and the Middle East. The entire evening was perfectly comfortable aside from the glaring silence of Tom.

Dale, concerned about Tom's state of mind, attempted to get him involved in the conversation. "We had a fascinating discussion in government class today about class basketball. Your son spoke in favor of the current system."

Denton sensed what Dale was trying to do and grabbed the chance to drag his son into the flow of things. "Yeah, Tom? What did you have to say?"

Tom was irritated by the thinly veiled attempts to engage him, but having been backed into a corner, he had no choice but to participate. "I just said we have the best tourney in the world, and there's no reason to change it."

"Well, there's no argument here. I think it's sad that we live in a day where people are afraid of a challenge. When we measure ourselves against the best, we come out better for it, win or lose," the elder Denton said.

Dale spotted an opportunity. "Tom, what did you mean by the thing you said later? I was a little unclear as to what you were getting at." He was not at all unclear, and Tom knew it.

"I was just saying that America has gotten weak because

the best people don't get hired for jobs and have a harder time getting into schools, because everyone makes allowances for the weak." Tom understated his position.

Dale pressed the issue, "How so?"

Tom was silent for a minute, deciding how proceed. "Jil said that America was all about giving special opportunities to people who don't deserve it. I think that's what's wrong with this country. I don't like to see people get what they don't deserve." There was a bitter edge to his voice.

His father replied, "Tom, you are totally right. You have to earn things in this world. But don't be ungracious. God lets the rain fall on the just and the unjust alike. We all get things we don't deserve in this world. There's nothing wrong with helping people who need it for whatever reason."

His son's face had "Whatever" written on it, but aimed the look at the wall rather than directly at his father. Dale understood that it was time to let the conversation drop. Whatever mixed up ideas Tom had, they did not originate with his parents. There was tension in the house, but it was one sided.

Dale was relieved. It was clear that Tom was one of the players Calvin had tagged as "racist." From his comments in class that day, Tom certainly qualified as young and stupid at the very least, and the game tape that Dale watched showed that Tom was loathe to dish off to Turner. Even so, Dale was sure he would not have to worry about having an assistant coach who hated his star player. The Dentons were too cultured and too kind to have taught their son to hate blacks.

As dinner wore down, Tom was excused for the evening. Dale decided to raise the issue gently with the boy's parents. "Sue, Greg, I want to ask you something about your son. He made some comments today in class that were pretty insensitive to other students—"

Denton stopped him mid-thought, "Let's see, he probably spouted off about how blacks and women get all the breaks."

"Yes, that was exactly it."

Denton sighed. "I guessed as much. We've talked to him about it before. This all started a couple of years ago. He used to spend every summer in Alabama with my father on his farm. My dad is…not a modern man, let's say. I knew that he was filling Tom's head with nonsense, but we always worked hard to counteract it. I thought we had taught him well, but he's worried about college and how to get in and how to pay for it. Recently, he's started complaining all the time about affirmative action, and 'why people who don't deserve it get ahead.' It troubles me, but I'm sure it's just a phase."

Sue defended her son, but her eyes revealed her distress. "Tommy is a good boy. He is under a lot of pressure. Do you want us to talk to him about it?"

Dale paused and said, "No. No, I'm sure it's nothing. Please just keep emphasizing the right things with him, though. Not to sound shallow or anything, but my main concern is for the team. If we are going to have a good season, there can't be any issues between my point guard and my shooting guard. I need to know I can trust Tom to evenly distribute the ball."

The implication surprised Greg. "He'll make the right plays. You can count on him."

The last thing Dale expected on a random Wednesday was a look-in by the school's resident bureaucrat. All first year teachers in Indiana were to be evaluated twice by the principal. He had to visually check that the teacher was performing competently and give an evaluation with suggestions for improvement. Often in smaller schools desperate to fill classrooms that guideline was quietly ignored, and Dale had heard rumors that Principal Hershey rarely, if ever, ventured from his office.

Just before the bell for his third period class, Hershey arrived at Dale's open door and knocked. He immediately stepped inside and interrupted a conversation Dale was having with a student. "Good morning, Mr., um, Cooper," he clipped at an upper octave.

"Uh, yes, hi, Mr. Hershey, what can I do for you?" Dale

replied, unnerved by the sudden interruption from his boss.

"I'm here for your first semester evaluation, Mr. Cooper. Um, I'll just sit at a desk in the back and take notes. Forget I'm here. But I must say, I'm already a little, um, disappointed. The school handbook clearly states that all teachers must maintain a presence in the hallway during passing periods. It's a very important time to connect with students as well as to, um, maintain order in the halls."

Dale did not respond well to criticism, and when it was grossly unwarranted he found it difficult to maintain his calm. In this case however, the bird-like delivery of the critique almost made him laugh and helped him keep his cool. "Mr. Hershey, my apologies. Dan here had a question about the test I'm giving this period, and we stepped inside so he could hear my answer. It's noisy out there. Are you sure you want to stick around? I'm just giving an exam, and there won't be much to see."

He could see the wheels turning in Hershey's head. It took a lot to rouse him from his nest-like office, and once he was out, he was determined to fulfill whatever job requirement that dared force him away from his precious piles of forms and papers. After a moment's thought, Hersey replied, "No sir. Tests are an important part of being a teacher. A *very* important part. No, no. Your evaluation will, um, continue."

For the next fifty minutes, Dale tried to avoid eye-contact with Hershey. He was terrified that he would laugh or crack a smile. He explained the exam, waited out the slowest students, and when everyone was done, he instructed them to read chapter four in preparation for their next class. When it was over, Hershey approached him.

"Fine job, Mr. Cooper. Fine job," he squeaked out. "I like that you maintained control of your classroom, and took, um, advantage of the extra time after the test to encourage the students to read ahead. Nice work." Without waiting for a response, he turned and made his way back to his office downstairs.

Dale sat down, slightly dazed. The hour had been high pressure absurdity.

Samantha broke him from his haze without warning. "Don't you think you should be monitoring the hallways," she said, weakly suppressing a laugh. "Jim Hershey just stopped me and advised me, as department head, that you are a fine teacher, but that I should make sure you are in the hallways between periods."

Dale groaned. "What was that? I wasn't expecting an evaluation from him at all, and then when he came, he just sat in the back and watched me give a test."

Sam laughed. "Oh, that's priceless! No, he would normally never bother with a teacher review, but I made an extra point to remind him of his duty in your case. I leaned upon his encyclopedic knowledge of the school handbook to convince him to come down to give you a once over."

"What? Why would you do that?"

She laughed. "Get back out into that hallway and do some monitoring before Hershey catches you!"

"What are the odds he's going to climb those stairs twice in one day?" Dale quipped.

"Good point. I suppose you're safe. Did he really just sit back there and watch a test period for an hour?"

"Oh, yeah. He took copious notes."

Sam shook her head and left. She almost said, "I don't believe it!" but he would have known that was a lie.

Most every small town in Indiana has its own festival every year. Whether celebrating covered bridges, popcorn, marshmallows or even the regal rutabaga, Hoosiers love a chance to get together, hold a parade and eat fried food. In Invincible, the festival continued in 1997 in the same way as it always had. Dale was astute enough to assume his attendance was mandatory. Everyone in town was there.

Local farmers had produce stands, and women's church groups from all over the county had tables of baked goods. In the parking lot of the Brethren Church there were a few inflatable games for the kids, and a clown or two wandered by. The high school band gave a concert on Main Street on Saturday, and there were hay rides at night. The weather was immaculate, and it was just cool enough at dusk that the patrons happily donned jackets. Everywhere on every street of Invincible, Indiana, there was good food and friendly people.

Despite himself, Dale had fun. He ran into Sam and her mother on Saturday. They meandered through the booths together. Everyone treated him with a warm inclusivity that he had not experienced before. He began to feel at home in the oddly painful way that made him realize how much he missed his real home.

"You know, Sam, I realize that this is just a glorified block party, but it reminds me of the State Fair when I was kid," he said as they passed the 4-H winners at a table displaying various ribbons that had been awarded in Indianapolis just a few weeks before. "Even though I was a city kid, it always made me feel some connection to the rest of the state. Now I know why."

Sam smiled. "I can see that. I mean, who doesn't enjoy a spin on the Tilt-a-Puke or a delicious Heart-Attack-on-a-Stick?" Her mother gave her a disapproving look for saying puke. Sam rolled her eyes and waived her off toward a flock of grey haired ladies standing behind a large table of cakes.

He took note of the subtle reminders of the town pride in their forty-nine years of .500. Most every table sponsored by a local group had a baked good doubling as a hint of the town's expectations. The Ladies Foreign Aid Auxiliary was raising money for wells in Africa by selling sweets, and every price tag ended in .49. The Future Homemakers of America club from the high school was selling cupcakes with the number forty-nine on them. Any of a number of other families and groups had forty-nine on their signs or emblazoned right on to the food they were selling. It was too weird for Dale to let it go without comment.

"Everything is always forty-nine instead of fifty?" he asked Sam.

She rolled her eyes. "Everyone in this town believes in fate. I know you think everyone must be in on some big conspiracy to make the team finish .500, but people are too scared to try anything like that. I can remember back to '77. Everyone started chalking up another .500 season before it happened. There were banners about thirty years this and that. I was little, but I can remember it. Once it became clear that the team wasn't going to finish .500, the town held a pep rally. The principal at the time came up with the idea that everyone would burn one thing 'as a sacrifice.' It sounds creepy now, but it was just a cheesy stunt. The idea is that the town would appease fate by making up for the fact that everyone chalked up the thirtieth year too early. Then, the night after the bonfire, the game was tied..."

Dale broke in, "Oh, right. Dead squirrel, blackout, season saved. ...the Miracles they called them. Yeah, I got a nice lecture on the history of basketball at Invincible already from Mr. Snyder."

Sam found this hilarious. She composed herself and continued, "So these days, everyone is terrified to jinx this season. Destiny is a funny thing. Everyone believes that as long as they don't make too big a deal of the fifty years, it'll happen and nothing can stop it. But the minute they think too hard about it or if they do anything to try to hit the .500 mark, something will go terribly wrong. The Miracles 'proved' it."

"So it's fate; it's certain, but pride can undo it all? Come on. That barely makes sense. This has to be some big joke that everyone is in on but me."

Samantha sighed. "I wish it was a joke. I wish it was all made up. Just remember, things around here don't have to make sense. They are how they are. And if the town has any say in it, they'll stay that way for a long time."

The festival marked a turning point for Dale. He saw a new warmth and openness in the people of Invincible that he had not previously known. It made him want to belong for the first time. He decided to attend a service at Greg Denton's church. Dale was not a religious man, but everyone in town went to church somewhere, and since there was nothing to do late on Saturday night, he got up early and headed down to the First Baptist Church.

Though it was a small town, Invincible had seven different churches. Actually, there were eight, but Dale did not think that attending the Amish service in German was a realistic option. There were the Brethren, the Grace Brethren, the United Methodist, the Free Methodist, the Presbyterians, the Mennonites, and the Baptists. First Baptist was the 'big church' and teemed with 300 people on Sundays. He was relieved at the size of the gathering, because despite his yearning for connection, he still wanted to remain fairly invisible. He slipped in and sat in the back row.

The service easily met Dale's expectation of what should happen at church. Pastor Greg, as he was called by the congregation, spoke with energy, and would have been easy to listen to if he could have kept his remarks to a half an hour. He rambled on twice that long leaving Dale glassy eyed.

There was one highlight: 'special music' by a woman named Anita Walker. She was beautiful, in her early forties, and had a powerful voice. Dale was unfamiliar with the Christian pop song she sang, but was intrigued because she happened to be Calvin Turner's aunt. He wondered about it as soon as he saw her because hers was the only black face around. He did not want to assume that just because she was a black woman she must be related to the one black kid in town. But as she made her way back to her seat, he caught a glimpse of Calvin, slouched next to his uncle in the pew. He was a big kid, but somehow managed to make himself look small. His body language screamed that he would rather be anywhere but in the church.

The scariest part of visiting a strange church is the awkward time when the service ends. In a large meeting, people stream out without too much connection. In a small gathering, there can be a protracted period of painful chit chat. In a medium sized church, like First Baptist, anything is possible. Dale decided that he was there to meet people, and since the morning had been painless, if not pleasant, he stood up with the goal of talking to at least one familiar face. It was easily met. Denton was stationed just beyond the back door of the sanctuary that led to the main foyer of the building. He saw Dale exit and made a beeline for him.

"Coach! Wow, it's great to see you!" he effused.

Dale smiled, "Thanks…Pastor Greg." The words came out awkwardly. "I just thought I'd get a feel for where you work."

Denton was obviously pleased that he had come. "Just call me Greg, please! Although, Pastor beats 'Reverend' any day." A line of people waiting to talk to him was forming behind the two men.

"Well, I'm glad I came. You have a very nice church. I'll get out of your way," he said, gesturing to the line.

Denton squeezed his arm and said, "Thanks. It's great to have you, Coach." By now there were quite a few people within earshot. By again calling him 'Coach' in a loud voice, he had accomplished the unintentional aim of siphoning off people from his line and transferring them to Dale.

Up until that morning, people in town had treated Dale as an outsider: a curiosity at best, a threat at the worst, but ignored by most. At the church service, however, Dale was amazed by how many people introduced themselves and greeted him warmly. He even had the chance to talk X's and O's with a couple of the men. It felt good to think that people were genuinely interested in the team, if not him. He was glad that he had come.

He was thrilled when the Walkers came up to him. Anita was accompanied by her husband, but Calvin was nowhere to be seen. Dale greeted them and thanked Anita for her song.

"Thank you," she said with an easy grace. "It's a joy to meet you. This is my husband, David. I'd say we had heard so much about you, but Calvin isn't much of a talker. I know he likes you though. When I asked him about his new coach, he said, 'He's ok.' Coming from him, that's gushing praise! Tell me, Mr. Cooper, would you like to join us for lunch this afternoon?"

The clock was rolling up on 12:30 and Dale was not

anxious to get home for a frozen pizza, so he readily agreed. He wanted to get to know Calvin and see him away from school. Turner was no more comfortable at church than he was at Invincible High. Dale followed the Walkers out of the building, stopping to shake a couple more hands along the way.

The Walkers lived about fifteen minutes outside of Invincible on a farm off of county road 930. They owned a large home, and the property contained an elaborate complex. As they pulled into the dusty driveway, Dale understood how a worried mother could send her son to live there. Compared with the mean streets of Gary, it must have seemed like a paradise, more Amish than Gangster's. The corn was high and ready for harvest, and the barns were painted red. The small patch of sugar maples that remained after the land was cleared more than a century before was exploding with red in the October sun. There was a cement slab to one side of the main barn with the obligatory hoop attached to it. He guessed that the small plot of ground was Calvin's one touchstone to his home. It struck Dale as an incongruous place to find a tough black kid with lightning quick feet and a smooth jumper.

Dale was excited about another home cooked meal. Mooching off the residents of Invincible was a habit he could get used to. Upon arriving at the Walkers' Calvin approached him, "Coach, do you want to shoot hoops while Auntie gets dinner ready?"

David Walker, who barely spoke five words at the church, chimed in. "Coach, I've got an extra pair of shorts if you need them."

"I appreciate the offer, but I always carry a gym bag in my Taurus," Dale replied.

The three headed inside to change clothes, but were sternly reprimanded by Anita. "Calvin Turner Jr., get back in this house! I don't want you men going and stinking yourselves up before Sunday dinner. It'll be ready soon enough. I already put the roast in this morning. Go watch football or something. We have a guest, and I am going to have a civilized Sunday meal." She was not a woman to be ignored.

None of the men were football fans, and the only game on was the Colts at Bills. Sports served its usual role of allowing men who do not know each other to coexist happily. Calvin was relaxed and comfortable for once. He was a different kid than the brooding intense one from school and altogether transformed from the shy, miserable one Dale had seen just that morning at the church service.

Lunch was served before half-time. The food was delicious and the conversation was constant. His perspective on Calvin changed and improved as he got to know his aunt and uncle. They met at Purdue where he studied Ag and she was an engineering student. They enjoyed small town life and managed to be successful both with the farm and Anita's job with a farm equipment manufacturer. For a town like Invincible, they stuck out in every conceivable way. Dale found Anita fascinating.

Though the Walker's story was unusual, the bi-racial farm couple in which the woman was an engineer was not the most surprising aspect of the afternoon. The change in Calvin impressed Dale the most. He was at ease, even jovial with his aunt and uncle. He was painfully polite, which one would expect from the son of a soldier, but his good natured joking with his uncle and obvious pride in them as they told Dale their story, was unexpected. From their brief talks and watching him attack conditioning, Dale had formed a mental image of Calvin, but in a few short hours, whatever notions he had of understanding the young man were shattered.

After clearing the dishes against Anita's insistence, Dale asked if Calvin was still up for some hoops, and in minutes the two were out on the court. There were worn spots on the concrete at regular intervals around the three point arc. The two shot around for a few minutes before agreeing to a game to ten, win by two. "I have to tell you, Turner, I had a great time with your aunt and uncle today. She's a great cook."

Calvin checked him the ball and said softly, "They are

good people." Dale drove to his left and stepped back for a quick jumper. Swish.

Dale retrieved the ball, and checked it up to Calvin. Already the happy kid from lunch was gone, replaced by the intense one Dale was accustomed to. Turner tried a power dribble and clearly expected to use his quickness to blow past the older man. Dale had spent the last 10 years of his life playing against college caliber players, and was much faster than Calvin realized. Still, he managed to draw contact and hit a difficult layup.

"By the way, no blood…no foul, Coach," he said, without humor.

Dale took the check and tried another jumper, but this one was grazed by Turner's long fingers. It fell woefully short. Calvin hurried for the rebound, and Dale got the sense that his blood was already in the water. Turner quickly ripped off three straight hoops before giving up a tough banker from sixteen feet to his coach. The afternoon was comfortably cool, but Dale could already feel himself sweating. Calvin Turner was a much better player than he had realized.

Still, he was not invincible. Dale tried to get in his head by asking him, "So what did you think of church today? You didn't seem to be enjoying yourself." Calvin took the ball, stepped back and drained a twenty-three footer. "5-2," he replied icily.

Dale took the ball and gave a head and shoulders fake, followed by his best cross over. He slipped past his player and cruised for a layup, but Turner made him pay for it with a hard foul. "Was it something I said?" Dale asked forcing a laugh. His shoulder hurt.

"Don't mess with me on the court, Coach" was all the response he would get until the game was over. Calvin had a switch inside of him. When it was off, he was a likeable happy young man. With a ball in his hands, he became an assassin. Dale was a good ball player and still in practice, but he was no match for this kid. The final score was 10-5, and he walked off the court with his body more bruised than his ego.

"Cal, I've watched all your games on tape from last year,

but you've improved. How much time are you spending on your shot?"

"I shoot 1,000 free throws a day. I spend at least three hours every night just shooting jumpers from every spot on the court. I told you, I want to win. My dad used to tell me 'great victories are won on small battlefields.' Don't hold me back, Coach, and I'll take this team as far as I can." There was never any equivocation in his words. They were forceful and direct.

Dale looked his player in the eyes for a long moment. "I won't hold you back, but you still have a long way to go. You have an elite game; I can see I might have underestimated your ability. You have the will to dominate your opponent, but winning takes an entire team. We have a lot of work to do."

"If there is one thing I know," he said, checking the ball to his coach to reset their match, "it's how to work hard."

Dale stepped back, letting fly a twenty-one-footer. "1-0," he said.

Chapter Six

Bored of Education

"Mr. Cooper, can we get extra credit if we attend the town meeting on Saturday?" said the flannel wearing kid in the front row. It amused Dale that farm kids managed to be accidently trendy. He wondered if grunge knew how much it owed to John Deere.

Saturday night in the gym there was going to be an official meeting of the school board to field questions and hear arguments about the school's vote for multi-class basketball. The debate was raging all over the state as ardent supporters of Hoosier Hysteria desperately sought to reverse the inexorable march toward the destruction of the State Tournament.

Dale seized on the question. "Sure, anyone who wants to attend AND write a two page position paper arguing for or against the change can get...twenty points of extra credit if turned in on Monday." The amount was arbitrary. Any of the students engaged enough to do the work were probably going to get an A or B anyway. "But let's talk about the government's involvement in this discussion. What levels of government are in play here?" Silence. "Ok, come on. What are the three levels of government?"

"Legislative, judicial, and executive," said the brown-noser who had brought the whole subject up in the first place.

"No, Jay, those are the three branches. The three levels are federal, state, and local. Where does this controversy land?" Again, there was no answer, but after two months, Dale had learned not to expect one. "State and local, right? How is local government involved?" Still no answer. Some mornings, teaching was enough to steal his soul. "The school board is a form of local government. They were elected here locally from among your parents and their friends. They hire the Superintendent of schools, Mr. Ericksen, who hired Mr. Hershey who votes with the IHSAA. So now, SOMEBODY tell me where the State government comes in."

Mercifully, a girl in the back bailed him out. "They pay for things."

Dale was relieved the class showed faint signs of life. "That's right. The State of Indiana helps pay for schools especially with lottery money. In this case though, athletics are funded privately, no tax money can go to fund sports. Except…?" he trailed off indicating that he was looking for an answer.

The same girl replied, "The gym is part of the school, and the state helped pay for it."

"Ding. The state has helped with building projects, and therefore has helped indirectly to fund the gyms that our teams play in. Tom, what is it that the state wants to do now regarding class basketball?"

Denton answered, "The legislature wants to force them to keep the tournament the way it is."

"Right. There are two problems here; one is a question of law… what recourse do people have if they don't like what their elected officials decide, and does the state have the right to tell a private organization that benefits from indirect state funding what to do? So, Calvin, tell me one of the options people have if they don't like the decisions of their elected officials."

He responded quickly, "Vote them out of office."

"Good. The problem is that the principal isn't elected. He's selected by a person who is selected by the school board, and has many responsibilities beyond just voting in the IHSAA. So even in towns where the people don't want to change to class basketball, the principal is often only distantly responsible to the citizens of the town. So the other option people have is to complain to their state officials. Why would the state officials care?"

Jesse Herr, who was what passed for a stoner in a farm town, responded, "Because they love to jump on things that are popular but don't matter. Like outlawing pot!" His deadpan delivery and gratuitous mention of drugs drew a laugh from the class. His mission was accomplished.

Dale was amused, and tried to ride the very small wave of energy. "Very good, Jesse! You are correct…about the legislature, not about pot." The class laughed again. Piggybacking on a pot joke was weak, but he was desperate. Teaching had a funny way of murdering his shame reflex. "The state has no reason to get involved in this, but it's a topic that people feel passionately about, and it is an opportunity for a senator or representative to make a name for him or herself by talking a lot about something people are paying attention to, without doing any real governing. It's a win-win for everyone!" He delivered the last line with an ironic tone, but there was no laugh from the class this time.

He knew it was too much to ask.

On Friday afternoon, Dale's prep period was interrupted by a knock on his door. Superintendent Ericksen asked to come in, and was followed immediately by Mr. Hershey. "MR. COOPER, MAY WE HAVE A WORD WITH YOU?" There was nothing more incongruous than a man asking for a private conversation at the volume of a jackhammer.

"Of course," Dale said. He closed his door behind the men, but he did not think it would make much difference. If anyone in the building cared to hear the contents of the conversation, they certainly could. In fact, they would have to try not to.

"AS YOU MAY HAVE HEARD AROUND TOWN, THERE IS A LOT OF PRESSURE ON US TO CHANGE INVINCIBLE'S VOTE REGARDING THE STATE TOURNAMENT. HERSHEY AND I WERE HOPING YOU COULD LEND US YOUR SUPPORT TOMORROW." Hershey looked bored with the whole issue, though officially, it was his vote to cast.

Dale did not know how to respond at all. These men were his bosses but he absolutely disagreed with their position. He chose his words carefully. "Of course, I support the school and your right to judge as you see fit as representatives of the community."

Hershey smiled at Dale's response, but Ericksen's face flashed concern. He was a loud man but not a stupid one. He said, "YES, YES, THAT'S FINE. BUT YOU KNOW THAT'S NOT WHAT I WANT. ARE YOU WILLING TO GIVE A SPEECH TOMORROW LAYING OUT THE REASONS THAT CLASS BASKETBALL WILL HELP INVINCIBLE HIGH SCHOOL?"

It would be easy to resent the power play being worked on him, but Dale respected sound strategy, even when applied in inappropriate ways. "Sir, I think you know that I don't approve of class basketball. I don't think it is good for the state or the school, and I think it is terrible for the kids." He was punting. It was not an overt refusal, but if Ericksen wanted to push him, he would have to give Dale a direct order.

"PRINCIPAL HERSHEY AND I DISAGREE," he said loudly, but without conviction. "MORE IMPORTANTLY, THE BOARD DISAGREES." Ericksen was going to twist Dale's arm to speak for them but was not man enough to take responsibility for it. It was all the board's fault.

"What do you want me to say, sir? This is a horrible plan,

and I'm not willing to stand up in front of the whole town, including my students and players and lie about how much I love the worst idea in state history. What can I do?"

Ericksen was visibly irritated. "The board wants this, son. They will not support it publicly, but they want it. They have made it clear to me that jobs are on the line." He spoke softly, almost at whisper, and his change in demeanor left Dale cold. The man was under more pressure than Dale realized.

There was no point in arguing. The government teacher knew when politics were being played. "I'll consider it," he said. At least he could buy time while he figured out what to do.

Ericksen was not satisfied, but sensed that this concession was the most he was going to get for the time being. He switched the charm back on, "FINE, FINE, MY BOY. WE'LL SEE YOU TOMORROW NIGHT AT THE MEETING. Think hard about what is best for the school, and for your career." He spoke softly, but so firmly that a deaf man could have heard him.

"See you tonight, Mr. Cooper!" Hershey chirped. Dale wondered if Hershey had followed any of the subtext of the conversation. The man was a few desks short of a seating chart.

After the final bell of the day, Samantha came into his room. "What was all that shouting this afternoon? I was trying to teach, but it was impossible with Ericksen yelling in here. I couldn't focus on what he was saying, but he didn't sound happy."

Dale slumped in his chair. "They want me to speak in favor of class basketball at the meeting tonight. I'm not sure why it even matters to them. It's not like I have any credibility in this town. I think that everyone is just trying to avoid the blame. The board wants to push for this but doesn't want to risk being voted out. So they are making Ericksen do the dirty work. Now he's leaning on me to back him up."

Sam was disgusted. "Figures. The school board is a bunch of weasels. I know all three of them. They have one concern: keeping taxes down so they can get reelected. I'm sorry they are pushing you. That won't be a fun speech to give."

"That's just the thing, I'm not going to give it. I hate class basketball. I don't think the town wants it. But honestly, what matters the most to me right now is that if I give that speech it'll send the wrong message to my team. I want them to aim high and believe that they can beat anyone. What will it say to them if I come out and say, 'oh yeah, you can beat anyone! Unless of course their enrollment has 500 more kids than ours, in which case there's no chance in hell we win.' I don't know what I'm going to do, but I won't support their idiot plan."

Sam took hold of his arm. "Well, they can't fire you. Not from your teaching job at least. The union would back you. Your best bet might be to just skip the meeting and tell them you came down with the flu. I'm not sure this is a fight you really want to join on either side."

Dale feigned a sneeze.

A Saturday night meeting of the school board would not normally generate interest. Unless a referendum to raise taxes was on the docket, most people in the consolidated school district were more than happy to let others tend to the tedious business of making educational choices for their kids. But on this particular night the topic was basketball, and in Indiana that always drew a crowd. Dale made his way over to the gym with a hint of bitterness. Students hate coming to school on Saturdays, but teachers hate it even worse. It was not like he had other plans; he just hated it on principle.

The gymnasium was packed. Extra chairs had been set up on a tarp that covered the hardwood floor. The bleachers were filled. There was an uneasy buzz in air. The room was uncomfortably warm. In about a half an hour, it would be hot enough to thoroughly irritate everyone present. The extra emotion would not be welcome. Dale did not have the flu, but he already felt sick. He could not bring himself to take the coward's way out; he had to come to the meeting. He still did not know what to say. He took solace in one thing only. *This place will be hell on the visiting teams.* For a few seconds he felt like a coach and not like a pawn in some silly game of small town political chess. He was glad for it.

His spirits were squelched as he felt a strong hand grab him by the back of the arm. "COACH! COME UP HERE WITH US!" Ericksen said. He ushered Dale into his worst nightmare. If the forty-year-old gym was channeling the spirit of the Roman arena, Dale was being forced to sit in the center of the ring, with as many lions in the stands as in the pit with him. There were six chairs in the middle of the floor, three on either side of the half-court line. In the first three sat the school board behind a heavy folding table, while the second three were completely exposed and reserved for Ericksen, Hershey, and Cooper. Sitting quietly in the back was not going to be an option.

The meeting came to order sharply at eight, with board president Ben Gordon thanking everyone for attending and launching into a long winded speech about the importance of basketball as a tool for training young men. Knowing the entire proceeding was a sham made it all the harder for Dale to listen to. The board had already made up its mind about how Invincible would vote; it was just a matter of convincing the town to blame someone else for it. The format would allow for open comments from the floor via two microphones stationed at either end of the bleacher stairs. Anyone could speak for two minutes. At the end of the session, Superintendent Ericksen and Principal Hershey would address the meeting and explain the decision. The board would then comment and hold a vote of confidence in the ruling.

As the evening unfolded, it became apparent to Dale why the board felt the need to let the town vent its frustrations. There was over-whelming sentiment against changing the tournament. Invincible was slow to embrace any kind of change, but change involving basketball was an impossible sell. Throughout the evening there was a smattering of support for class basketball, but it was drowned out by the angry disdain of a town that had no argument better than "But we've always done it this way!" Dale was embarrassed to hold a position associated with such an ill-informed group of supporters.

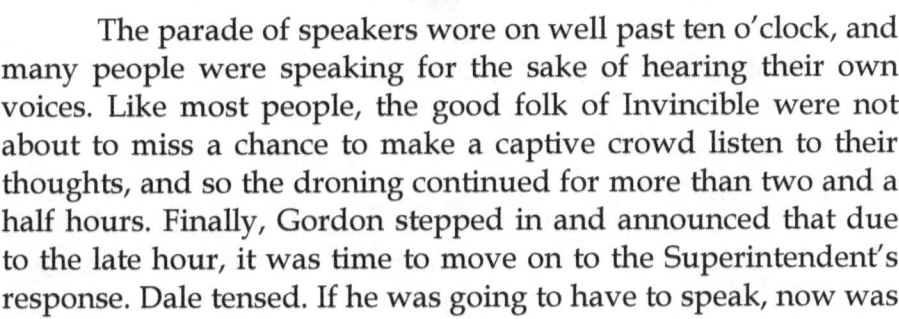

The parade of speakers wore on well past ten o'clock, and many people were speaking for the sake of hearing their own voices. Like most people, the good folk of Invincible were not about to miss a chance to make a captive crowd listen to their thoughts, and so the droning continued for more than two and a half hours. Finally, Gordon stepped in and announced that due to the late hour, it was time to move on to the Superintendent's response. Dale tensed. If he was going to have to speak, now was the time.

Ericksen stood up and boomed a greeting into the mike. The combination of heat and speaker feedback blaring from his "LADIES AND GENTLEMEN OF INVINCIBLE..." was enough to convince Dale that he had died and gone to hell. Fortunately, whoever was working the sound wisely hit the kill switch, which eliminated the feedback and saved everyone sitting in the first three rows.

"IN EDUCATION, IT IS OUR MISSION TO PREPARE CHILDREN FOR LIFE. THE IHSAA HAS TAKEN THIS MATTER INTO DEEP STUDY AND HAS CONCLUDED THAT CLASS BASKETBALL WOULD DRAMATICALLY RAISE BOTH THE PARTICIPATION RATE AND QUALITY OF PLAY IN OUR STATE BY GIVING MORE STUDENT ATHELETES THE OPPORTUNITY TO EXPERIENCE THE TANGIBLE BENEFITS OF SUCCESS!" The more he shouted nonsense the angrier Dale became. He roared on about the importance of fairness and rewarding hard work. Every word made Dale's blood boil. He tried to calm himself down, but was reduced to praying that he would not have to speak.

Mercifully, Ericksen wrapped up his remarks and turned the microphone over to Principal Hershey. It was his job to announce the decision. "In my judgment the best course of action is to, um, support the IHSAA's conclusions that class basketball is in the best interest of our students. Invincible High will be voting in favor of a move to four class basketball, to be effective in the 1997-1998 season." He read his statement from a sheet of paper, with all the enthusiasm he would give a Monday morning announcement of the week's lunch menu.

Dale was infuriated by the whole night, but was grateful that it looked like he was going to avoid having to talk. The board would publicly disagree with the decision but give a vote of confidence to Ericksen and Hershey, and the whole drama would be forgotten.

He was not prepared for the reaction of the crowd when Hershey finished reading his statement, however. There was anger. Real anger. The community did not appreciate being crammed into a gym, steamed like lobsters, and bored by their neighbors only to have a stiff in a suit announce that he would vote against their expressly stated wishes. A cascade of boos and 'Nooоos' washed down on top of the embattled group in the middle of the floor. The room turned overtly hostile, and the scent of violence was in the air. This was no time to stay silent.

Dale stood up and approached the microphone. He had no plan, no strategy. He was just trying to buy time as he searched for a way to calm people down. He raised his hands and said "Ladies and gentlemen" at least three time before the din subsided enough that he could be heard. "Ladies and gentlemen, I am not from Invincible," he said, as people slowly sat down. "I am not from Invincible, but I am a Hoosier, and I LOVE INDIANA!"

As he shouted, he could feel an internal momentum building, and he knew he would find the right words. He summoned up the echoes of a lifetime of pregame and halftime speeches by all the coaches he had ever had. The room grew small in his mind. Instead of hundreds, he imagined a dozen people sitting on a locker room bench. Part of what he loved about coaching was the opportunity to inspire others to action. The room was hanging on his words, and he felt right at home.

"I believe that we have the best tournament in the world, and that it should never change!" The crowd cheered his declaration. He could not afford a glance behind him, but he could feel a hole burning in the back of his head from the death glare Ericksen was surely shooting at him.

"I want to prepare my players for life. In life, you have to compete with everyone, big and small. I want them to never settle for less than the best. In this world, there will always be obstacles. There will be others who have the deck stacked in their favor. I want every young man who plays for me to graduate knowing that if his will is great enough, he has everything he needs to trump whatever life throws at him. If we start seeding the basketball tournament, we are not only destroying our State's great treasure, but we are telling our children that it is ok to stop reaching for the top, to stop trying to be the best! Being small does not make you weak. Being out-numbered does not mean you are defeated!" The crowd applauded every line. Dale's own sense of self-preservation kicked in, and he knew he had to choose his next words with care.

"In spite of how I feel, I have talked with these two men behind me. They are good men who care about your children. They work hard to do what is best for the community. We can argue their decision, but we owe it to them to do it with civility, recognizing that they are serving us and our kids." The room quieted.

"I hope there is something that we can do to let those in authority know how we feel about their decision. We can't ask these men to vote against their conscience, and we certainly can't ask the school board to fire the men who run our schools over a single vote against the tourney. What we can do is this: we can let them know they are wrong. I ask everyone to stand up. Let's show them how we feel. Indiana is our home. This tournament is our home! We have to do something to show them we want it back."

From the stands, a voice yelled, "Let's sing 'Back Home Again!'"

Dale laughed, but he had no better idea, so he said, "Ok, then. Let's sing 'Back Home Again in Indiana' together, and leave. There's no need to hear the vote. It won't go down the way we want. Let's leave together, showing them that to ruin our tournament is to destroy a piece of what it means to be from

Indiana."

He stepped back from the microphone, and began to sing, "Back home again, in Indiana…" The chorus was immediately joined by the crowd. With one voice they sang,

Back home again in Indiana,
And it seems that I can see
The gleaming candlelight, still shining bright,
Through the sycamores for me.
The new-mown hay sends all its fragrance
From the fields I used to roam.
When I dream about the moonlight on the Wabash,
Then I long for my Indiana home

When they all finished, Dale turned and left the gym. He could hear the footsteps on the bleachers ring out behind him. The song brought tears to his eyes, and he was glad that no one would see them. He could have left that night feeling any number of emotions: relief, pride, empowerment, even fear for his job. But the only sensation he had was heartbreak. The handwriting was all over the wall, and no matter how Invincible voted, the papers had already reported that there were more than enough votes to install multi-class basketball. The tournament was dead. Knowing that it was something that no one wanted made the inevitability all the more tragic.

He did not know what was waiting for him at school on Monday. He kept a low profile all weekend, and other than a couple of supportive calls from Samantha and Denton, his phone was quiet. Sam stayed long enough to watch the board react to the walk-out. They passed a 'resolution of unity,' entering in the minutes their solidarity "with the people of Invincible, the State of Indiana, and the Superintendent and Principal." They stated publicly that while they felt it was a mistake to abandon history and tradition, "they would not presume to ask anyone to violate his conscience in this important vote." Ericksen and Hershey would "receive their full support no matter how they chose to vote." In other words, they were gutless, but Dale already knew that.

The only issue left unsettled was how the ax would fall on Dale personally. There was little commentary about Saturday night in his classes, though he did receive a half dozen extra credit reports on Monday. He glanced through them on his prep period, and was gratified to see that all of them were against the change. Whether or not they were just sucking up to the teacher did not matter. He was glad for the affirmation anyway. The day slowly passed without a hint of repercussions.

Dale worried it was a bad sign. As he made his way to the car at the end of the day, he turned a corner and almost ran over Principal Hershey. A head-on collision was not the ideal way to meet, but Dale was grateful that it forced a conversation. He was shocked when the Principal greeted him warmly.

"Ah, Mister Cooper! I was hoping I would run into to you." It was not a pun; he was not quite bright enough to make that joke. "I just wanted to, um, tell you how much I enjoyed your speech and that song on Saturday night!"

Dale stared at him in wonderment. He knew there was not a sarcastic bone in Hershey's body. "Uh, thanks" was all he could say.

"Yes, yes, I love 'Back Home Again.' I always look forward to Jim Nabors singing it every year, um, before the race. I just love him, don't you? They just don't make television like the Andy Griffith show anymore. Do they?"

Dale had no idea what he was getting at, but agreed. "No, no they don't. At least we still have the reruns, huh?"

"Quite, quite! Anyway, um, I thought it was a beautiful speech, and it got me thinking. Ericksen told me the board wanted Invincible to vote for multi-class basketball, and whatever the board says is fine with me, but then, um, they changed their minds and said I was free to vote however I wanted. Well I faxed in my vote to IHSAA today, against the, um, change. You were quite persuasive!"

"What? Are you serious?" Dale was elated. "What did

Mr. Ericksen say?"

"Oh, I haven't discussed it with him yet. I'm sure he won't care. The town was against it, and the board said they were too, but that I could do what, um, I wanted. I can't imagine that he will care one way or another. Anyway, wonderful job." With that he stepped past Dale and walked off down the hall humming the Andy Griffith theme song.

Dale laughed out loud. All the scheming and plotting by the board had been summarily undone by their most clueless pawn. Hershey took all their posturing seriously. He was always only following orders. Once he felt he was free to vote his mind, his mind voted happily for Gomer Pile. No matter how the other IHSAA schools voted, Invincible High would go on the record as voting against changing the tournament.

Dale went home happy, even if he knew it was Pyrrhic victory.

Jim Hershey may have been one of the simplest men in Invincible, Indiana, but there were still hundreds of high school principals even more stupid than he was. Change was coming, like it or not.

Chapter Seven

Practice Makes Problems

Though it had only been two months since he arrived in Invincible, Dale was exhausted. The days before the first official practice of 1996 ebbed along at a glacial pace. He keenly felt the kind of nervous exhaustion that comes from waiting too intensely for too long. He sailed right past elation at the impending start of practice, and spent a solid week jittery and irritated. He pushed harder than ever at the off-season conditioning sessions.

He was unlikely to face any fall-out for his stunt at the previous month's school board meeting. Ericksen had to let the issue go because there was no way to punish him at this point. He could not suspend Dale for anything, and firing him just before basketball season would create more problems than it would solve. Dale was temporarily untouchable.

After his first practice, he was glad for that. He only had

two weeks to select his team, install a new offense and defense, and get ready for the opener against Whitko. His first mistake was hoping to accomplish all of it on the first day.

Practice started at three, and Dale's goal was to have the final whistle blow at 5:30. He favored quick paced, efficient practices. It only took about ten minutes to realize that high school kids were not college kids.

At three, fifteen players gathered at center court. The bulk of the freshmen who were trying out were absent, and no one seemed to know anything about where they were. After a few minutes, they all came out wearing water soaked shoes. Someone, Dale guessed Tom and Sean, had stolen all their sneakers and tossed them into the girls' locker room showers. He did not ask how they got them back. He was more concerned with the water they tracked all over the gym floor. The stunt wasted a half hour of his precious practice time. Unfortunately, it would also prove to be the highlight of the first day.

Dale's strategy was to alternate drills with theory. He split his players into three groups of eight, rotating them between the three coaches. Invincible only had one gym, and that gym only had two baskets; there were no fancy retractable hoops in the small school. He gave Kapler a free throw shooting drill. Through their preseason talks, he came to understand that Coach Kapler was a nice man, but his concept of basketball strategy only went as far as "shoot when you're open." Dale considered replacing him, but did not know anyone better, and knew he could at least count on him to take orders well. It was Dale's goal to get his kids to shoot free throws at a 70% clip. Kapler would spend a total of twenty minutes of every practice working on one end of the floor with players on their technique.

The second group occupied the other half court with Denton working on passing drills. Dale was thankful for his presence on the staff. Greg was a smart man, and quickly captured what Dale wanted out of his team. His only misgiving about working with the reverend was the giant blind spot he had when it came to his son. Dale knew that the team would never be successful unless he managed to get Tom Denton on board. He was the second best player but the most difficult to coach.

While the first two groups did drills, Dale worked on game theory in the entry way of the school, in front of the main stair case. He wheeled out the wipe board, and it just barely provided enough room to do some limited walking drills used to show floor positioning. He favored a motion offense that he knew would be complicated for the kids. He simplified it as much as he could but had little expectation that most of them would fully grasp it before February. His best hope was that Denton and Turner would catch on fast enough to cover up the ignorance of their teammates.

The second hour was slated to go much like the first with the groups focusing on ball control, defensive drills, and defensive theory, with a half hour left over for conditioning drills. There was no time in the first week for scrimmaging. There was too much to teach, and it was critical that the players be well grounded in the system and in the fundamentals. Dale planned that by Saturday's all day practice the team would shake out enough that he could divide up the players into A and B teams and make any necessary cuts. After the first day, he was ready to cut the whole squad.

Aside from the mild hazing issue, the lack of attention by the players drove him crazy. Turner constantly hustled and focused for each drill and lecture. The freshmen had developed a healthy terror of the coach, but the other players loafed around. They took the free throw shooting seriously, but most of them gave the passing work half-hearted effort. Dale's theory sessions were a loss. The players' faces read "This is way too complicated" even on the most basic concepts. It was as if they wanted it to be too hard, so that they would not be responsible when it failed.

Dale responded with the only weapon he had on the first day. He made them spend the last 45 minutes of practice running. They ran stairs. They ran lines. They would have run all night, but Dale needed their legs to work hard the rest of the week. He finally waved them all to the lockers, and stormed back to his office.

Everyone responds differently when faced with obstacles: frustration, anger, displaced aggression onto loved ones, even despondence. Dale was blessed with the rare ability to get creative when blocked by circumstance. He was angry to be sure, but his first true challenge in months lit up parts of his mind that life in a small town had lulled into atrophy.

As Kapler and Denton piled behind him into the small office just off the locker room, he grabbed a small plastic ball off his desk and quick flicked it to the reverend. "Greg, you first. What are we going to do?" With that, he swiveled in his chair to the white board behind him and grabbed a marker.

If Denton was surprised by the quick change in the coach's demeanor, he did not show it. "I think we have to sell these players on why practice matters. They have to care about working hard." He tossed the ball back to the younger man.

He wrote MAKE THEM CARE in capital letters on the board. He set the marker down and pitched the ball to Kapler. "Barry, what about you?"

Kapler stared at him blankly. He was not the observant type. He liked the young coach, but thought Dale was a bit of a hard ass. "Well…free throw shooting was solid today. Some minor form corrections are going to take time for the freshmen, but mostly, they did alright. Tom was mouthy as usual, but that's nothing new…sorry, Greg." Denton just chuckled. "Honestly, coach, I don't think the kids had fun today. They have to want to come to practice." He did not throw the ball back to Dale when he was done. He had not picked up on the role it was serving in the session.

Dale absorbed the rebuke hidden in the comment. He was magnanimous with the marker in his hand, so he wrote 'have more fun' underneath the first line on the board. His use of lower case letters was the extent of his passive-aggressiveness.

"We're going about this the wrong way guys. Practice can't go like that again. I blew it," Dale admitted. "The whole shoe prank got the afternoon off poorly, and I didn't recover. We have to make these kids see that hard work is the only path to victory."

Kapler laughed involuntarily. Dale asked him coolly, "Did I make a joke that I wasn't aware of?"

Kapler sat thoughtfully for a second and finally spoke slowly, "But coach...you don't....really...think they can win, do you?"

Dale said, "What?" as he stared ice shards at his assistant.

"Look, Coach. This team has finished .500 for forty-nine years. Do you think you can change that? Do you really want to change that?" Kapler, oblivious to the emotional consequences of his words, continued on, picking up steam as he spoke. "I think our job is to get these kids to play together and have fun. We'll teach them some skills, and do our best to win our half of the games we play. Do you have to make it all about winning?"

After a beat, Dale said, "Yes."

The next day, practice had a different tone from the start. Dale was energized by the challenge placed before him, and his spirits were high. No one showed up with wet shoes; Denton had dealt with that issue quietly at home, and there would be no more hazing rituals. As the players made their way to center court, Dale greeted them with a smile. He had been plotting his course all day. Whatever tone he chose to strike needed to be consistent with the one he had already spent two months laying down.

He had wheeled a TV unit into the gym. Without a word, he pressed play as Denton killed the lights, and they let the images wash over the kids. It was a tape of celebrations. Ben Davis winning the tournament. Damon Bailey hugging his mom. Keith Smart lifting the Hoosiers. Even Hickory over South Bend Central. He had spent all night raiding his tape collection and pieced it together using a couple of VCRs the night before. The tape ended with a shot of the RCA Dome in Indianapolis with the words "Every Team's Dream."

Dale spoke clearly and firmly, "Being a part of a team is a promise. Before we ever lace up we promise each other that we will be great. We will work hard every practice. We will play hard every night. We look each other in the eyes and promise that we will be one team with one heart. On the court we will play with one mind. We have one weapon: work. We have one enemy: fear. We have one goal: victory. We have one reward: greatness! We are Invincible! Now…let's get to work."

It was a cheap ploy, but the collection of teenaged farm boys was not the most discerning audience. The result was positive, if not entirely successful. The boys still lacked intensity, in spite of Turner who had it to spare. Dale met with too many blank looks during the theory sessions, but at least he felt like players were trying to understand. He would have to find new and engaging ways of teaching them, but that was something he could deal with. Their size and skill was reason for optimism, but the team remained a far cry from the standards he had set. He ran them hard again to close practice.

After speaking with the staff and changing clothes, Dale stepped out the office and headed for his car. Calvin stopped him at the back door of the school. "Coach, can I talk to you about the offense?"

"Of course Calvin."

"It won't work, coach," he said.

Dale was almost speechless. "What's the problem?"

"I get the stuff about ball movement and screens. I can move with and without the ball. I understand the sets. I know you think it works, but it won't."

"Why is that, Calvin?"

"You are tryin' to run an unselfish offense with a ball hog point guard. Denton won't swing the ball like you want. He sure as hell won't swing it to me."

Dale was annoyed. He did not like facing imaginary problems. The team had not even scrimmaged for the first time, and already Calvin was complaining about touches. "Listen. You do your job. You are going to be our starting two guard. You work on understanding how to get open and how to make good decisions with the ball. My job is to make sure everyone else does their part. I saw the tapes from last year. I know Tom doesn't like to give up the ball, but he will, or he'll sit. Let me worry about him; you have your own game to work on."

Turner did not like the answer, but to his credit he took it like a man. "Yes sir." he said with no trace of emotion. He was only eighteen years old, but he already understood loss, sacrifice, work and authority. To Dale Cooper, that was admission to the club. He promised himself to never treat this player like a child. Calvin deserved more than that.

As Calvin walked away, Dale called after him, "I appreciate how hard you are working, Turner. You are a real leader out there."

Calvin stopped cold and turned to look at his coach. "You ain't leadin' if no one is followin'," he said.

Progress was slow all week. Players put forth minimal effort. Dale was satisfied with the freshmen and sophomores. Because most of them were competing for a spot on the JV team, they hustled and worked hard. It was a young squad, with only three seniors among the twenty-five players who were trying out. Invincible teams were often young. It was common for players to drop out after two or three years. With no goals to shoot for, many kids got bored. Among the juniors, it showed up the most. They were not lazy as much as disinterested.

Dale was in crisis-mode all week. What little there was of life was put on hold. He devoted all his waking hours trying to devise ways to motivate his team. It was obvious that a healthy portion of the team was not buying into the ethic he demanded. He needed a dramatic demonstration to get their attention, but in the few months he had been in charge, he had been high on drama and none of them were moved by it. He lay awake until three in the morning every night running each sloppy practice over again in his mind. The more he tried to draw out his players, the more withdrawn he became from the world around him.

Finally when he could not stand the lethargy any more, he picked out one of the laziest juniors, Mark Fey, and made an example of him. He was not particularly talented and was one of the players Dale frequently caught ducking into the restroom during conditioning. If he had any desire to work at all, Cooper could have made a player out of him. On Friday, he called him into his office after practice and told him not to come out on Saturday. He was cut.

It was never pleasant to cut a player, but Dale found this occasion distasteful because of Fey's reaction. Official cuts were not supposed to take place until Monday, but when Fey heard the news he was cut early, he shrugged and strolled back out into the locker room without a word. He was not putting up a front; he honestly did not care if he was on the team or not. Dale should not have been surprised, but he found himself angered by the young man's apathy. It was as if he had been purposely wasting everyone's time. He had not taken his spot on the team for granted nor had pride made him lazy. He was a kid who did not care about any of it one way or the other.

Saturday's practice was critical to the development of the team. He started by announcing the cut. He got no reaction from the upper classmen, but the freshmen and sophomores were unnerved. Dale announced he was going to keep eighteen players for the two teams and that cuts would be posted on Monday morning. This would be their first chance to scrimmage, and practice would last six hours with three in the morning and three after a break for lunch. After warm ups, they would play fifteen minute quarters with a running clock followed by a cool down/instruction time. He split the players up into four groups of six, rotating in subs and allowing each team to sit a quarter.

He placed his five best players on one team to start. Normally he would have spread them out to increase the competition but they had seven days to prepare for Whitko and they needed every second to build cohesion in the new offense.

Turner, Denton, and Knorr took the floor with the 6'10"

bean-pole sophomore Steve Thompson and junior swing man Linus Aldridge, who despite having a name straight out of Motown, had the palest complexion ever seen on a basketball player. For a small school, they posed a formidably tall line-up. Denton was the smallest player on the floor at 5'11." They might have trouble inside with some of the biggest schools, but that was not Dale's concern at the moment. Today, he just wanted some glimmer of hope that the players understood the offense.

The first scrimmage was a disaster. The B team, consisting mostly of juniors, was lethargic. This was annoying but not surprising. What worried Dale was that the failure to hustle by the B team masked the fact that the A team was not running his offense. More specifically, Denton was not running it. Calvin dutifully ran his cuts and rubbed off screens, but would only see the ball one out of every four times he was open. Tom Denton would not distribute the ball to him. Dale was unsure if the other coaches noticed because they were too busy getting on the B team for their lack of hustle. Calvin proved himself to be a force anyway by playing suffocating defense and grabbing every loose ball while soaring for rebounds. He was not playing against motivated competition, but his improvement as a player was on full display.

When it came time to switch out to the C and D squads, Dale let the other coaches run the scrimmage while he grabbed the younger Denton and pulled him off to the corner of the court. "I've asked you this before, and this will be the last time. Do we have a problem, Tom?" He asked him. "Is there a reason you don't want play point guard for this team?"

Tom glared defiantly and said, "No sir."

Dale said, "Then this conversation is over. Pass the damn ball to the open man, or I'll find someone who can." He turned back toward the court, but not without hearing Denton mutter, "Good luck" under his breath.

The coaches' meeting that night was understandably tense. After one solid week of practice, the only two players that had any idea what was going on were Turner and Tom Denton. He knew Calvin understood the offensive and defensive plans because he was always in the correct position. Dale knew Tom understood, because only someone with an excellent understanding of how to run his sets could so effectively and systematically avoid passing Turner the ball. If Tom was just confused, he would have managed to hit his open teammate a few times out of dumb luck. As it stood, they had three seniors (two of whom did not get along), a handful of juniors who did not give a damn, and a pile of underclassmen who were scared out of their minds of the new coach and had no clue how to play basketball.

As they sat in Dale's bungalow, he waited for Reverend Denton to speak. He was furious with the man's son and could not find any diplomatic way to start the conversation. The team was sunk unless they could convince Tom to include Calvin in the offense. Finally, after sitting together for an uncomfortable five minutes, Denton said, "I'm sorry. I don't know what's wrong with him. But I'll take care of it."

"You have to, Greg. If you don't, I have to cut him. I can't have him undermining the team that way. He's practically daring me to throw him off. He's a good player, but if he won't pass the ball to our best man, how can I play him? I'm out of ideas. I've run him. I've pulled him aside. I've embarrassed him. I've yelled at him. I've encouraged him. If you can't get through to him fast, he's done. Do you understand? I've only kept him around this long because he's your kid."

"I'll take care of it," was Denton's terse response.

The rest of the meeting was lighter, but the cloud never completely left the room. The round of cuts was not contentious. There was some raw talent, but as usual a couple of the worst players were the hardest working. After significant discussion about what to do with them, they all agreed that Riley and

Phelps could stay with the team, practice, and sit in dress clothes in JV games if they also served as team managers. Ben Hanagan was a 5′7″ freshman who simply had no game at all. He was a smart kid though. He managed to go the entire week without missing a free throw, which was strange because from any other spot on the floor, he was not an adept shooter. The coaches agreed to offer him the position of statistician.

Dale was pleased with the list. The only kids who would be disappointed were the ones who had done the absolute least. He wanted to reward the young ones who were hard working and still trying. The final squad had the three seniors, four juniors, seven sophomores, and four freshmen. They were young, thin, did not understand the offensive or defensive sets, and the two best players hated each other.

As the coaches headed home for the night, Dale doubted if he would have his team ready to play in seven days. *I don't know if I could get a win out of them if I had seven months.*

Chapter Eight

The Opener

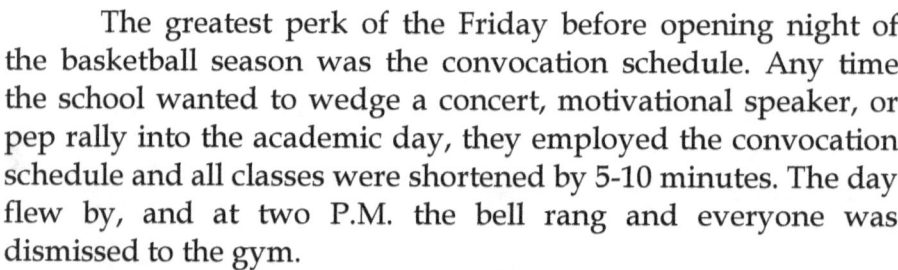

The greatest perk of the Friday before opening night of the basketball season was the convocation schedule. Any time the school wanted to wedge a concert, motivational speaker, or pep rally into the academic day, they employed the convocation schedule and all classes were shortened by 5-10 minutes. The day flew by, and at two P.M. the bell rang and everyone was dismissed to the gym.

The varsity players were permitted to skip their last class of the day and head to the locker room to dress. They changed out of their shirts and ties and donned the red and gold trimmed home whites of Invincible High. Standing in the locker room, waiting to be introduced by their coach, was a moment of true joy. The six hundred students and teachers were clapping in rhythm, and the pep band, meager though it was, alternated between the two songs they knew. One was the Invincible Fight song (which had been stolen from the University of Illinois), and the other was Go Team Go. For just a few moments, the young men in the locker room looked at one another and felt like a team. They absorbed the love of the school, and it made them strong.

In the coaches' office, Dale Cooper felt sick. The second week of practice was not an unmitigated disaster, but neither was he pleased with the team's progress. Denton managed to knock some sense into his son (literally or figuratively, Dale could not be sure), but his cooperation was never more than begrudging. Dale started running more drills with Calvin working with the second team, just to see what would happen. The advantage was that it allowed him to see what good defenders his two stars really were. They matched up against each other, and their battles were intense. Though he favored a trap zone defense, the thought of putting two tenacious man defenders on the floor together made his eyes sparkle with possibility. There was potential for a suffocating full court trap, fast break style, but that could never become reality as long as Tom Denton persisted in his stinginess with the basketball.

Dale tried to soak in the moment and prepare himself to rally not only the school but his players behind him, but he could not generate any enthusiasm. Having a team that refused to be excellent was torture. He would have preferred to switch places with Barry Kapler who was responsible for coaching the JV games. The young kids were not great, but they were visibly improving every day. He threw back his third Mountain Dew of the afternoon and waited for his cue. He could not muster any authentic excitement but he was not above resorting to a performance enhancing drug.

In the gym, the students were loud and enthusiastic, their numbers swelled with community members filling in the visitors' bleachers. A line of cheerleaders held hands with dress shirt wearing JV players to form an archway for the players to run under. For most of the freshmen players, holding hands with the cheerleaders was a dream come true. Unfortunately, the height differences made for an ugly tunnel, and because the players were unwilling to let go of the hands of the girls, they built a human barricade. At center court, Principal Hershey, ineptly tried to quiet the crowd. The managers stood underneath the baskets preparing for the layup drills.

Finally, someone managed to get Hershey's mike loud enough that he obtained the attention of the room and proudly introduced "Your 1996 Invincible Indians!" Dale led his players through the gauntlet of hormonal underclassmen and out into the bright lights of the gym. As the players peeled off to begin layups, Dale mustered all the hyperactivity in his sugar soaked system and clapped his hands together rhythmically over his head. Miraculously, the crowd joined with him. Dale got a welcome boost from Turner who grabbed the toss from Pete Riley and threw down a violent dunk. The room erupted in a collective gasp, followed by wild cheering. Dale was speechless. He knew Calvin had elite physical skills and a developing game, but he had been saving that particular talent for just this moment.

Turner had rendered anything else that would be said or done that afternoon meaningless. Cooper introduced the varsity squad one by one and gave a short speech about how they would uphold the best tradition of Invincible, but no one was listening. The buzz in the room never quieted, and all eyes were fixed on Calvin Turner.

The first game of the 1996-1997 Invincible High season was at Whitko on Saturday night, November 22nd. Dale was glad it was a road game because it meant there would not be as many Invincible fans present to be disappointed. It was a forty-five minute drive from Invincible proper to South Whitley along two-lane state roads. Dale had the team arrive at school at three p.m. for a walk through of the offense and a light pasta dinner prepared by Sue Denton and a couple of the other mothers. Then they boarded the bus so as to arrive for the JV game by 5:30. A modest caravan accompanied them, but most would follow along later.

Whitko had won the sectional last season. They had lost

some talent but Dale figured them to be at least a middling club. They provided an excellent opening game test. Dale had his players watch the first half of the JV game, before spending time in the locker room going over the offense and defense again, using plays from the first half as teaching points. The Invincible JV team was thoroughly outmanned, as they leaned heavily on freshmen. Invincible was not large enough to field three teams, so most of the JV players were matched up against guys a year or even two older. They held their own for a quarter plus, but by half time the rout was on. Dale just hoped that they would keep playing hard in the second half.

After he finished diagramming plays on the black board in the visitors' locker room, the team dressed and prepared for the game. Spirits were high; they were loose and ready. Only Turner was quiet. Just before it was time to take the court, Dale addressed his players.

"This is not our first step in this journey," he said. "We've been working hard together for a few months already. I've seen enough from you to know that this team has the talent to play with anyone. But not yet. This Whitko club is solid. They won't beat themselves. Go out there tonight and play hard. Right now, look each other in the eyes and promise that we will be one team with one heart. On the court we play with one mind. We have one weapon, work. We have one enemy, fear. We have one goal, victory. We have one reward, greatness! We are INVINCIBLE!" His delivery was constant, rhythmic, and hit a perfect crescendo.

As they had arranged, Denton picked up as soon as Cooper finished his litany. "Let's pray, boys. God Most High, we honor you tonight with our play. We ask that you would protect us and our opponents from injury. We ask you to bless our efforts with success and to allow us to play to the best of our ability. Most of all, we ask that you would find pleasure in us tonight as we play with honor. Amen"

Tom stood up and motioned the team into a huddle. "Indians on three!" he yelled. All hands rose and fell as one; they left the locker room and took the court.

The locker room is a sanctuary; the court is chaos. From the confines of the dressing room, a team can hear the echoes and rhythms of the crowd and the band as they prepare for the arrival of the players. The dull thumps and muted cheers are promises of the glory that waits outside. They say there are no atheists in foxholes, and there are few in Indiana high school locker rooms. When immortality stoops so near that it can almost be grasped, even vain young men stop to beg for divine assistance. Then, as one, they march out together. For many teams, this trek before the first game of the season marks the last time they will ever be truly united. For others, the bond deepens as the weeks pass. From the twilight of the lockers, the team breaks into the dawn of the court. The burst of sound and color that washes down to the floor bathes the body in a rush of adrenaline unmatched outside of sport. If there was a heart so hard that it was not pounding before, emerging to the adulation or ire of the fans in any of the hundreds of gyms in Hoosierland is enough to quicken it.

The moment was simultaneously glorious and ridiculous because of how much gravity it possessed.

It was basketball. It was Indiana. It was real. It mattered.

Warm-ups completed, Invincible sent its starting five to center court. Cooper lined up Denton, Turner, Knorr, Aldrige and Thompson. Whitko was a typical high school team and posed no real matchup problems for Dale to unravel. He knew his squad was more talented, but even though Denton had behaved himself that week, he could not be fully trusted. Dale did not care if they lost by thirty, not this time. All he wanted was for them to play hard and run their sets. He was not convinced they would.

Despite standing more than a half foot shorter than Thompson, Calvin was to take the tap. God may have made

Thompson 6'10", but He had not yet taught him to jump. Turner easily slapped the ball to Knorr to start the game. Knorr flipped the ball off to Denton, and they ran the offense.

Turner was moving frenetically without the ball. He flashed open three times on the opening possession, before Thompson saw him open. Calvin forced home a layup. The opening quarter flew by as both teams struggled with their shooting. Turner managed 6 points but only because he hit a couple of free throws, and picked off a pass for a layup going the other way. Denton passed him the ball only when he was not open for a shot. Calvin was frustrated, and forced a couple of contested jumpers. The score settled in at 10-10 through one.

Cooper staggered the rests for Turner and Denton with the dual purpose of not taking both his best players off the floor at the same time, but also so that he could evaluate the team without the animosity between his stars clouding the picture. Turner sat first as the second quarter opened, and while the offense ran more smoothly, it did not generate any more points. Henry Adams, the junior guard who replaced Calvin, did not have the same skill set. Denton fed him the ball when he was open, but he was hesitant to shoot. When Adams finally uncorked a couple, it was obvious that his hesitancy was well advised. Predictably, with Turner on the bench the over-all energy level of the team lagged, especially on defense. Whitko opened up an 18-12 lead in the three minutes that Calvin sat.

Dale called a timeout and made almost wholesale substitutions. He left Adams in, and paired him with Turner. Dave Jones, Phillip Stevens, and Al Alberts all came off the bench as well. The biggest problem with the second string was a serious lack of height. No one was taller than 6'4", and Alberts was only 5'10." He was a fast little guard. Only a sophomore, he was one of the hardest workers on the team and a decent ball handler. Dale was determined to let him run some point despite his inexperience. With the second squad in, Invincible played with four guards.

Turner, rejuvenated by his time on the pine, came out firing and immediately drained an eighteen-footer off a nice feed from Alberts. Unfortunately, even the return of Calvin's energy on the defensive end was not enough to slow down the bigger Whitko team. The young players on Invincible were not versed enough in their matchup zone to close down passing lanes and allowed too many layups. Even as Turner caught fire from the floor, the deficit kept growing. The starters returned and played an even, if unspectacular final two minutes together. The Indians found themselves down ten at the half, 35-25.

Dale saw no point in yelling. If anything, the team had performed better than he had feared, though they did not play the kind of defense he demanded. He spent the brief half time going over some individual techniques with players, but as the team headed out, he grabbed Turner by the number on his jersey and held him back. "Stay within yourself and within the offense. I know you could do more, and if you did, we might win this game, but it would cost us down the line. Do you understand me, Ten?"

Calvin stared at him without response and then turned and headed for the court.

Turner was miserable, but managed a quiet kind of brilliance throughout the rest of the game. He was smart and efficient with his shots, making a difference with offensive rebounds and put backs. He silenced Whitko's best scorer on the other end, taking him so completely out of the game that the coaches would later notice on tape that he only had three touches in the entire second half. Even as Denton continued to ignore him in the offense, he dutifully ran his cuts and worked to get himself open. The result was good looks for his teammates, as Whitko collapsed and doubled down on him never noticing that Denton was not giving him the ball. Invincible climbed back into the game and found themselves down only a basket headed into the fourth quarter.

Whatever modest goals Dale had set for the game beforehand were washed out now by his competitive nature. His first win as a head coach was within his grasp, and it was tempting to turn Turner loose to go and get it for him. He sat Denton for a rest, but Whitko responded by posting up Alberts and exploiting any trap for an open shot. No matter what lineup he played, the problems were always obvious. Down just four points with the ball and two minutes to play, he finally returned his starting five to the floor. Without wasting much time, Denton actually hit Turner with a perfect feed off his drive for an open three. Calvin buried his 22nd, 23rd, and 24th points of the night, but Whitko still led 57-56.

There is no shot clock in Indiana high school basketball, and it can make the end of games tedious. A trailing team rarely has any option but to foul if they want to get the ball back. Invincible was already over the limit, but it had not hurt them as Whitko was only a mediocre free throw shooting team. As the clock passed under a minute to play, Thompson put the Wildcats on the line. A lanky seventeen year old stepped to the line in his home gym. The crowd was silent, and the pressure was palpable.

He missed both shots.

Sean Knorr, who had played well, collected his eighth rebound, and as the team came across half court, Dale called for a timeout to set up his offense for the final shot. Some of the players were nervous, but Dale was calm. He was having fun coaching for the first time since he came to town. He called for the base offense, figuring that it had been run correctly so infrequently that day that Whitko would not think to look for it, and would not recognize it even if they did. Knorr was to set a high screen for Turner who would take a jumper with about eight seconds to play. Dale wanted to leave time for a rebound and put back.

With a peace that came from knowing the real fight was still ahead of him, Dale watched his kids take the floor. Every high school game regardless of the sport has the potential to provide a young person with the greatest moment of his sporting life. Nearly everyone can remember that one time he hit the game winning shot or struck out some poor kid with the bases loaded. This day was no exception as someone was going to remember a made shot, a big stop, or a key rebound for the next several decades. It did not matter that it was just the first of many games that year. On the basketball court, immortality comes in all shapes and sizes, and it grows with age.

Invincible worked the clock down under twenty seconds, and Whitko was happy to allow it. As poorly as they had shot from the charity stripe, they had no intention of entering into a back and forth with the Indians.

Finally, Denton brought the ball up to the top of the key, and Turner glided to his spot as Knorr took his place to screen off Calvin's defender. Unfortunately, just as Turner was coming open, Steve Thompson's man flashed out to double, and Denton instead went inside with the pass. Whitko had set up the opening, and Knorr's man dropped down and deflected the pass as the clock wound down. Aldrige dove for the ball, knocking it back to Denton who put it on the floor before pulling up for a ten-footer just before the buzzer.

There are dozens of reasons why a shot does or does not go in the basket. The angle can be wrong, and the ball will still tap off the glass and go. The rotation can be perfect, but the air compressor in the gym, triggered by the heat from the fans, can click on at the wrong moment and cool the air just enough so that a shot that would have found the bottom of the net just minutes earlier spins off the rim and out. The shooter feels like he has control, but it is just an illusion. At the moment of release, the ball leaves his hands and chance and probability take over. The same shot that makes a hero on one court, on one rim, can glance harmlessly away on another court, another rim.

On this court, on this rim Tom Denton let the ball fly and it glanced off the back of the iron as time expired. Tom looked around for a call, but there was no whistle. The game was over. In the first game of the season, Invincible was defeated.

Chapter Nine

Thanks for Nothing

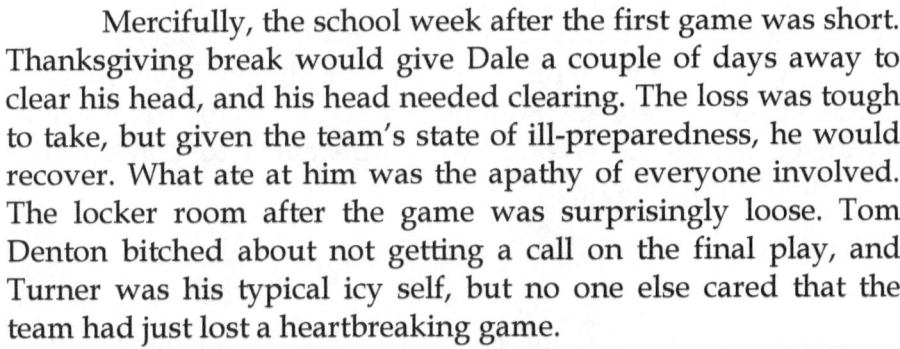

Mercifully, the school week after the first game was short. Thanksgiving break would give Dale a couple of days away to clear his head, and his head needed clearing. The loss was tough to take, but given the team's state of ill-preparedness, he would recover. What ate at him was the apathy of everyone involved. The locker room after the game was surprisingly loose. Tom Denton bitched about not getting a call on the final play, and Turner was his typical icy self, but no one else cared that the team had just lost a heartbreaking game.

At school on Monday, several people mentioned what a great game it was, but no one was perturbed by the loss. It was eerie. The school and the town clearly cared about the team, but a tough loss in the opener garnered no reaction whatsoever. Dale tried to use the defeat as a motivator at Monday's practice, but got no reaction from his players. It was as if Saturday's game had been a scrimmage or a youth league game where no one kept score and everyone just 'had fun'.

Unnerved but undaunted, Dale took aim at the weekend holiday tournament. Invincible was to play at the Fort Wayne Coliseum in the Summit City Classic. It was a brief mini-tournament featuring two Fort Wayne area teams and two teams from the outlying counties. There would be a morning and an evening game, win or lose. Invincible was expected to show up and be a sacrificial lamb for Fort Wayne South, one of the strongest teams in the state. Their first game would be televised in the Fort Wayne area, and he hoped that would help provide some motivation to his boys.

Unfortunately, the loss had no effect on Denton's attitude. While some of the younger players were showing signs of finally understanding their roles in the offense, Denton continued distributing the ball to everyone but the one guy who knew what to do with it. He got Calvin the ball just often enough to avoid getting yanked off the floor. Dale wanted to pull Denton off the point, but his only other option was Alberts, who was growing in his understanding of the offense but was a terrible shooter.

Tom was popular with his teammates. He, not Calvin, was voted team captain by the players. Turner did not complain or even react. He treated every practice like a battle, and took every slight as an added weapon in his arsenal. He was increasingly creative with and without the ball, learning to optimize every touch. His play coupled with the steady improvement of the second string threatened to make Dale's team downright average.

As he navigated the back roads that would lead him to Indianapolis, it struck Dale that his trip home was far from the usual. People typically abandon the cities during Thanksgiving and Christmas and head back out to the country where their parents still live. Dale Cooper, on the other hand, was leaving the 'farm' to head back to the familiar comforts and urban intimacy of a city of hundreds of thousands of people.

He could not stay long at his folks' place. The team had practice Friday night. He regretted making the boys miss out on a long weekend but understood that was part of the sacrifice of sports. Basketball players in Indiana receive many perks and much attention, but it comes with a price. While other kids are goofing off and taking family trips over winter break, the ball players are practicing and playing games. After not seeing his folks for several months, Dale realized what a loss it was to sacrifice time with family.

Of course, he could have gone home several times that fall, even just for a weekend, but he had not. Men who return home want to boast of their accomplishments and victories. Dale did not have any yet, and it kept him away. When he could not bear his mother's insistence any more, he agreed to go home for Thanksgiving, even if just for a couple of nights. Now that he was on the road, he was glad for it. He was lonely. He was frustrated. He needed home. He needed someone to be glad to see him.

His time with his parents was short and uneventful. There were hugs and food. Other than the few obligatory questions there was not much talk about his job or the team. For a few hours at least, Invincible was as invisible in his life as it was on most state maps. He sat with his dad and watched the Lions and Cowboys; they did not talk except when the action called for it. His mother made way too much for three people to eat, and at night they watched the Pacers take down the Kings. It was simple; it was quiet; it was home.

There was no time to see friends. There were none to see. He had to leave by noon on Friday to make it back for practice that night. Mrs. Cooper packed her son a cooler full of leftovers and lectured him about how thin he was. He kissed her goodbye, shook his father's hand, and hopped back in the Taurus, fresh with the security that they loved him even though he had not yet conquered any new worlds or achieved any lasting victories. As he headed out of town, it occurred to him that if things did not work out in Invincible, he could always go home again.

The thought terrified him.

The weekend tournament was a disaster. South Side was talented and well coached and throttled the Indians by twenty-five. The game was especially disappointing because Dale felt that his team could eventually compete with them but was not ready yet. Calvin pressed, and the team took too many contested shots. The late afternoon consolation game was more competitive, but the offense routinely stalled out. Turner led an inspired defensive effort on tired legs, but an inferior Adams Central team eked out a close win. With December on the way, the team was sitting at 0-3, and frustration should have been mounting.

From the players and fans there was none.

Usually, when a team starts out poorly, players either buckle down, lash out, or realize they are not a good team and become complacent. To Dale's astonishment there was little reaction from his players, the parents, or the people of Invincible. He ate at the diner on Monday, and the patrons were downright pleasant to him. He got a few "we'll get 'em next times" and several "hi Coaches," but there was no panic or anger in anyone's voice. If anything, people were glad about how the team was doing. He had expected more criticism, and for once he was grateful for everyone's low expectations.

His gratitude did not extend to his players. Other than Turner, who internalized not only every loss but every possession of every game, there was no indication in any of the other boys that the team had even played, let alone lost three games. Dale struggled to stay positive as their apathy ate at him. The home opener was Friday night, and the team was unreasonably confident. The first string showed no improvement, although the younger players were rapidly gelling. Dale's frustration with Tom Denton was volcanic, and Tom's father noticed.

Friday's night's game provided a flash point. Columbia City visited Invincible's gym. The Indians jumped out to an early lead, and appeared destined for their first victory of the season. They led by twelve at the half, and Dale was confident that if they maintained their effort level, they could cruise in the second half. The Eagles were outgunned, especially with a red-hot Turner posting sixteen first-half points on 8-9 shooting.

Without warning the wheels fell off in the third quarter. Tom Denton instituted his first full-on freeze out of Calvin since the first team scrimmage weeks before. He effectively kept Turner from touching the ball for the first five minutes of the third quarter.

Dale responded by emphatically asking for a timeout. "Denton!" He screamed before the players had even arrived at the bench. "What the hell are you doing? Are you my point guard?"

Tom said nothing, so Dale continued his rant. "That was the worst damn stretch of guard play I've ever seen. What is wrong with you? I know you aren't stupid. Pass the damn ball, Tom! If you don't shape up fast, you'll never see the court again. Disgusting. That was just pathetic. Sit here the rest of the game and think about how terrible you played!" The words rolled off his tongue. He had not lost control of his senses, but he enjoyed berating Tom Denton more than he should have. He refused to even look at the player the rest of the night.

With Tom on the bench, the offense picked up thanks to Calvin's own personal magic, but the defense was out of synch. Alberts had not played many minutes with the starters, and there were several breakdowns which led to easy buckets the other way.

Even as Columbia City took the lead with three minutes to play, Dale refused to reinsert Tom Denton in the lineup. Defeat was snatched from the jaws of victory, and Invincible remained winless.

That night, Coach Cooper took his first phone call from an angry parent. It came from Greg Denton who had been too angry to speak with him after the game. Denton's voice trembled as he yelled into the phone, "I've never been so upset with a coach in all my years watching my son play sports. How could you yell at him like that?

Dale said nothing. Denton was wound up, and the best strategy was to not interrupt until he got it all out.

"I know something isn't quite right with Tom, but have you ever considered he's doing the best he can? Sure early on, Tom didn't give the ball to Turner, but we talked it out. Tom assured me that he would do better. He's playing his best! Frankly, your constant disapproval of him is insulting! The boy needs some coaching! Instead of blaming him, maybe you should look in the mirror! You expect him to master a complex offense in just a few weeks? You rode the boy too hard tonight! You humiliated him in front of the whole world. What's worse is that I had to sit and watch you do it. You back off my son, Cooper. I won't stand for it again!" He did not wait for a response, slamming down the phone and cutting off the call.

The loss was discouraging enough, but having to defend himself against the charges of an upset father hurt Dale. His assistant and nearly friend questioned his impartiality and ability to coach. Denton's tirade gave new life to all Dale's private self-doubts. But despite the call and the questions Denton raised, Dale could not deny the truth. Tom Denton was killing his team.

He could not understand it. With four consecutive losses out of the gate, the Invincible faithful should have been ready to crucify him, but Dale was suddenly everyone's best friend. Other than the Dentons, the rest of the town embraced him more readily now than they had before the season. His players showed up for practice on Monday loose and amicable. It was more than odd; it was unnatural.

He stopped by Samantha's classroom during her prep period on Tuesday to ask her about it.

"Hey Dale, what's up?" She was focused on grading papers and spoke with a hint of impatience. Lawson, unlike a lot of teachers at Invincible, worked hard, so at first she was not thrilled to have him interrupt her work.

He ignored her tone. His day was littered with study halls, and he knew it gave him more flexibility than most teachers had. He did not blame her for being annoyed, but neither did it stop him from pestering her regularly. "What's up with this town, Sam? We go out and stink up the joint four straight times, and now everyone loves me. I don't get it."

She put down her pen and looked at him. "They are probably relieved." His expression suggested she needed to continue. "When you came into town talking about excellence and winning, it bothered people. Not only did you imply that things were going to change, which no one likes anyway, but in a way, you condemned what they are most proud of. This community takes comfort from knowing that harvest is in the fall, Indiana always votes for a Republican president, and that the Invincible Indians will finish .500. They want things to stay that way. They *need* them to stay that way."

"So why is everyone happy that we are losing?"

"Because they know it'll even out in the end. This town believes it's the destiny of Invincible High school to win exactly half its games. A fast start just means a string of losses at the end of the season. But a slow start means that wins are right around the corner. The worse things are, the better they'll get."

"Sam, that's insane. There are no guarantees in life and certainly not in basketball. My team is a mess. It's a talented bunch, but they have a long way to go. I can't promise they are going to finish .500."

She sighed and shook her head at him. "You don't have to. It's out of your hands. All you've proved in the last two weeks is that you aren't going to make this team a winner. If you can't make them a winner, everything will be fine. I bet your players are pretty happy right now too."

"We had our best practice of the year."

"Dale, they think they are about to go on a winning streak."

"This place is nuts. It doesn't work like that."

She had no energy to argue the point. There were too

many essays tests to score, and besides, she knew he was right. The whole conversation bothered her in a way she could not quite identify.

She wanted to defend people for their superstitions, or at least make Dale understand them, even though they irritated her. Her complaints about the town and its inhabitants were innumerable, but they were hers. As long as she held them, she was the superior insider. Now an outsider voicing the same complaints was forcing her to pick a side. It disrupted her sense of balance. Life on the fence was a comfortable one. She did not want to be one of 'them,' a citizen of Invincible just like any other, but in an undeniable way she was. She responded to his question with a defeated tone.

"No, I don't suppose it does."

Game five was the next day. A strong team from Muncie rolled in and back out again leaving the Indians at 0-5. The home crowd was enthusiastic for most of the game, but Invincible's offensive problems grew worse. Tom Denton was no more generous with Turner than he had been the previous game. In spite of his conversation with the boy's father, Dale held fast, and benched Denton for the final three quarters. Little Al Alberts was not only ineffectual but completely exhausted from seeing so much floor time. The game got away from them early. Turner scored whenever he touched the ball, but the kids from Muncie doubled and even tripled teamed him in order to deny him. Alberts was perpetually left unguarded but could not buy a bucket, finishing with four points on two for ten shooting. The only bright spot of the night was that the JV club won its first game and looked excellent doing it.

No one else cared much about yet another loss, but it did not surprise Dale to find Calvin waiting for him after the others left. He had sent his aunt and uncle home and asked Cooper for a ride. He wasted no time in stating his mind. "This isn't working, Coach. What are we going to do?"

Spoken so bluntly, the statement and the question carried fresh weight. His team was a broken motor. The parts did not fit together. On top of everything else, the tank was full of unleaded, but the engine was a diesel. Without a major overhaul, this ride was going nowhere fast.

"I'm sorry, Ten. You deserve better," he said.

The confession was no consolation to the player. "My father always told me that life is not about what you think you deserve. It's about what you earn. I don't feel sorry for myself, Coach. I just want to win. What I want is to know what you are going to do to make that happen?"

At that moment, Dale felt a spark of encouragement. He had to admire the young man in his car. He had become one of the best high school players in a state full of great players, and no one knew it. He worked tirelessly on all aspects of his game. He was tenacious in pursuit of his goals and refused to allow the ignorance and cruelty of others to deny him. Dale owed this young man his best effort. Calvin Turner Jr. deserved it. He had earned it.

Dale spoke frankly. "We have two obstacles. The first is Tom. He's a talented player, and if he would get on board we'd be better. The second is that no one cares that we are losing. The players don't care. The school doesn't care. The fans don't care. They are convinced that we'll just rally and turn it around. If we can't change these things, we can't win."

"How good can we be, Coach? Be honest."

Holed up in his 750 square foot pink bungalow for the past three months, Dale Cooper had watched more tape of high school basketball games than any man in the state. He knew every one of the top ten teams in the state. He knew their talent levels; he knew their coaches. He knew he had the most complete player with the most devastating will to win in Indiana. He knew exactly how good his team could be; it was the very thing keeping him up at night. Dale Cooper was not a coward, but his stomach tightened at the thought of saying the thing aloud. Calvin deserved the truth, but what the truth implied was more than Dale could admit. He could not bring himself to do it just yet.

"I don't know," he said. "But if we want to find out, I have to bench you."

Chapter Ten

A Merry Little Losing Streak

December was half gone, and Christmas break was just over a week away. On Dale's radio, *Have Yourself a Merry Little Christmas* had mercifully vanquished the Mellencamp, if only for a few weeks. The joy of the season manifested itself in blinking cascade lights on porches and plastic reindeer dotting the lawns around town. Dale liked Christmas well enough, but the kitsch did nothing to improve his mood. He was not happy about what he had to do.

Fortunately, he had all day to figure out how to tell the team. He still had to navigate the little matter of actually having to teach that day but figured he could mumble his way through something about a bicameral legislature and assign the students the questions at the end of chapter sixteen. He could let them work on it in groups for twenty minutes, and skate through the day on maybe an hour and half tops of actual instruction. Dale was not proud of his prowess as an educator, but in his defense, he had only shown one video the entire semester.

At practice, he assembled the players at center court before drills. "We are not playing up to our capability," he told them. "That much is obvious. Everyone is going to have to work harder, and no one should feel like he is entitled to playing time. I'm changing up the rotation for Saturday's game, and practice the next two days will reflect that. I am moving Adams and Stevens to the starting lineup and letting Turner and Aldrige work with the second unit. I want to see where these new matchups take us."

The news generated smirks from Tom Denton and Sean Knorr, but the rest of the team looked surprised. The Stevens for Aldrige swap was a lateral move, but Calvin's demotion was patently unfair. Tom Denton cast a long shadow over the other teenagers, however, and everyone saw the decision to bench Turner as a vindication for the team captain.

While he and Greg Denton ran the practice, Dale assigned Coach Kapler to spend the first hour working with Alberts and a couple of the freshmen on shooting. If they could make him a threat to score, he had a shot of becoming a viable point guard. As things stood, he was too great a liability to be on the court in a close game. He shot a sort of knuckle jumper that floated toward the hoop with almost no rotation. It was a horrifyingly ugly shot, and Dale hoped it could be salvaged.

To end the workout, the first and second units had a series of five minute scrimmages, with short breaks to let the JV players get floor time. Dale was tempted to place Turner on Denton, but he knew it would undermine his long term goals. The second unit of Turner, Alberts, Aldrige, Jones, and 6'1" junior Chet James was hurting for size, so Dale instructed Calvin to guard the 6'10 Thompson. Calvin was drastically undersized for the job, but he played longer than he was because of his vertical. Dale was determined to help Turner develop all aspects of his game, and working against a much taller player would force him to think creatively about defense and not allow him to only depend on his quickness.

From the start, it was obvious that Turner's presence with the second team would upset the natural balance. The unit had not worked together much, but on the first day, the first unit only outscored them by five. Dale stopped the action regularly to freeze his players in position and show them new options with the ball. He did this most often when Turner would face a double team trap. This kind of heavy ball pressure on the other team's best scorer was Dale's favorite strategy against teams that depended too heavily on one player, and he patiently instructed the second squad on which spots on the floor would stay in Calvin's vision. Double teams mean open players, but the inexperienced players did not always know how to make themselves seen by the man with the ball.

As the team made its way back to the lockers after practice, Turner stopped his coach. "I can front Thompson sometimes but can't defend him from behind without fouling him. If Denton has enough room for the entry pass, I can't stop him no matter what I do. What's the best way to keep a bigger man from scoring?"

Dale was amazed. On a day in which he had been humiliated by a demotion, even if he'd expected something of the sort to happen, Calvin Turner's only concern was solving a defensive problem that he would likely never face in a real game. His interest was how to be the best, most dominant player possible.

Dale said, "You'll give up baskets from time to time. First, you can't let that bother you. The other man has an advantage, and unless he's stupid, he will be able to exploit it sometimes. There are some things you can do. A player like Thompson is light, so move him off his spot with the body as much as you can. You don't have bulk, but you are stronger than he is. Use your feet and try to make him move as much as possible, if you can wear him down, you may give up some points early, but not late. You can also try and use your speed to play to the side and pick off any lazy passes that come to him."

Turner shook his head slowly and processed the information. "I won't try that last trick against Denton. He doesn't throw any lazy passes...not to Thompson. Thanks coach." He jogged off.

At that moment, Dale was sure of what he had suspected for weeks. For three more months, he was coaching the best player in Indiana.

Dale unveiled a new tactic for the Huntington North game. Instead of staggered substitutions, he opted for a more wholesale approach. He let the starters play most of the first quarter. Without Turner in the lineup, Denton played his best game of the season. He distributed the ball well enough, but on most possessions he ended up with the shot. Despite his best efforts, the overall difference in talent between the two teams was noticeable. Huntington opened an early lead.

With a couple of minutes left in the quarter Dale played the entire B team together. There was a method to his madness, but the results were ugly. Calvin singlehandedly kept the score close, but with a small lineup and the painfully slow Chet James on the floor, North's lead kept growing. The best news was that Alberts hit his only shot. The starters retook the floor down eight points, which grew to a 32-20 deficit by the half.

The second half brought more of the same. Dale again played the second squad four minutes bridging the third and fourth quarters. Turner caught fire and finished with thirteen points in just eight minutes of total floor time. The Indians' first team took the floor with 6 minutes to play down only six points. The fans were subdued and the game was within reach. Tom Denton spoke up in the huddle just before the A squad was to reenter. "They got it close for us, guys! If our bench can take it to them like that, let's show them what our best players can do!" The team broke huddle and made its way back out onto the floor.

Dale could not believe his point guard's arrogance. There is a difference between leadership and self-aggrandizement that eighteen-year olds rarely understand. He glanced at Greg

Denton, who shook his head unhappily. It was their first moment of mutual understanding in the last week. Dale wondered how he was going to coach the kid to see the error of his ways but decided that North was doing a good enough job of that for him.

Denton was a mess in the final six minutes. He missed four shots, turned the ball over twice, and committed two fouls. The A squad never found its rhythm, and North went on a 20-2 run to end the game. What promised to be a barnburner, devolved into a massacre. The spectators were delirious.

After the game, Dale met the Huntington coach on the sideline for the post-game hand shake. George Ross was in his late sixties and had been coaching against Invincible for many years. He shook his head as he greeted the young coach. "Son," he said, leaning close to make sure Dale could hear him over the still blaring pep band. "Why in hell aren't you starting that number ten? He's a demon. Are you punishing him for something?"

"No, there're just some problems with the team dynamic, that's all. He's a special kid and a great player."

"Well, I've coached a lot games, but I don't think I've ever seen a coach try as hard to lose a game as you did today. I'd thank you for letting us win, but quite frankly, it's embarrassing. Respect the game, boy. Black, white, or blue, he's a player. If you can't understand that, find a new line of work and stop messing up kids." He did not offer his hand to Dale but turned back toward his team.

The rebuke did not have its intended effect. Dale was not concerned that others would assume that race was the reason Calvin was on the bench. Soon enough he would showcase the young man to the state. He knew Turner merited every opportunity to show off for the scouts. Dale was sure that the benching was in his best long term interest. There was something else in the old coach's words that caught Dale's imagination. He filed it away and led his team into the locker room.

Dale did no screaming after the game. There would be no extra running of the stairs when they got back to the gym. That ship had long since sailed. He spent a few minutes teaching and instructing individual players on points of improvement, and was about to address his squad as a whole when Tom Denton stood up to speak to the squad.

It took six losses before someone finally got mad. Unfortunately, the anger was misplaced.

"We were better than those assholes!" Denton shouted. "Get your heads out of your asses and play!" He was red hot and began to call out Knorr and Thompson for not setting screens. He blasted Stevens for taking a couple of contested shots. He ranted for a solid five minutes, criticizing everyone in the room except for himself and Calvin, whom he completely ignored. With any self-awareness at all, he would have realized that every second he ripped his teammates, their animosity toward him grew.

Finally, Dale stepped in. "That's enough, Tom. Sit down and shut up. Everyone on this team is going to have to work hard in the coming weeks if we are going to meet our potential. Go home, look in the mirror and decide if you want to get better, or if you like losing every night."

The bus ride back to Invincible was quiet.

Christmas was in the air, but it was beginning to feel a lot like Groundhog's Day. Despite the sixth consecutive loss and Tom Denton's ill informed fit in the locker room, there was no urgency from the players at practice. Christmas fever had set in and with only one game left before the holiday break; perhaps total focus was too much to ask of a bunch of high school boys. Most of Dale's players were more excited about what presents they were going to receive for Christmas than they were about representing their community through the game of basketball.

Dale stopped by the barber's after practice on Thursday night. He was going back to his folks for Christmas, and then taking a trip to the Bahamas, so he wanted a trim. Even though it was only 5:30, winter darkness had already set in on Invincible. Still, there were a couple of the old regulars sitting idly in the warmth of the small shop. They greeted the coach with the kind of warm smugness generally reserved for an admonished child.

Barney Robinson, still engaged in an endless checkers match, smiled at him with calm assurance and said, "The boys are gonna win this Fridah, Coach. Right, Bernie?"

"Right, Barney!" came the familiar refrain from his opponent.

Dale appreciated the support, "We certainly expect to. It's been a rough start, but there is a lot of talent there. Things are about to turn for us."

Robinson replied, "Well, no one around here is too worried. The boys just need to go 10-4 from here on out. We've done that scores of times. The 1984 team went 8-2 to close the season. The wins are about to start commin', I can feel it. Right, Bernie?" Bernie agreed.

His confidence baffled Dale. "The boys have a lot of work to do to be as good as they can..."

Bernie Keys abandoned his usual agreeability, "This is the fiftieth year. Work ain't got nuthin' to do with it! Those boys are going 10-4!" He was not interested in hearing any discussion on the topic. In his mind there was no other option. John Jr. and Barney Robinson nodded in agreement.

"Well, I certainly hope we can go at least that. I have to say, I doubt any winless coach in history has been treated as well by a town as I have!" Dale said.

Barney eyed him suspiciously. "We aren't worried about the wins, Coach. They'll come soon enough. Our boys will come through. They know our way. You just see if you don't get some real fight out of them soon."

Dale's eyes narrowed as he began to make sense out of the lethargy that gripped his team. He chose his words carefully. "I doubt any of them would want to be part of the team that let the whole town down, would they?"

"Hell no!" Robinson said. "I expect every kid on that team knows how much is ridin' on them, except maybe that colored boy, though he seems to be a fine player. No, sir, they'll have a fire lit under them soon enough. They'll nevah hear the end of it if they don't."

"We'll do our best to do even better than everyone expects. I'm working the kids hard, and we should have something for Churubusco on Friday."

"'Busco is for shit, son. Y'all will wipe the floor with them. As for what we expect, it's ten and four. I don't care if you win the damn championship myself. All I want is my ten and four." With that, Robinson turned back to the checkerboard, just in time to watch the old man jump him to end the game. He glanced back at Dale as if he was to blame for the loss, before saying, "Let's run it back, Bernie. I'll get a split out of you, yet."

Bernie chuckled. "Right, Barney."

'Busco was for shit, as Barney Robinson predicted, but it did not stop them from sending Invincible down to defeat for the seventh time in seven games. The fan support was intense, and a group of students had red and gold shirts made up that said INVINCIBLE on the front and 10-4 on the back. The game itself was a heartbreaker, with the boys from Turtle Town coming out on top in overtime.

Despite not putting Turner and Denton on the floor together all night, Dale felt he had to put his best five out for the extra period. Turner never saw the ball and Steve Thompson missed three of five free throws in the final two minutes. Any hope for victory was extinguished as the Churubusco center muscled home 10 points in the period. As the players walked to the locker room, the crowd gave them a standing ovation for their effort.

Dale scrounged up a small hope that he would find genuine disappointment or anger in the locker room. Instead, the players jovially teased Thompson for his misses at the line and laughed it up. Christmas break was finally upon them. Losing in overtime was not enough to dampen their mood. Only Turner and Denton, at opposite ends of the row of lockers were unhappy. Turner glared into his locker without a word, while

Tom angrily tossed his uniform into his bag.

Not knowing what else to say, Dale told them all to have a good Christmas, and that practice would resume on the 30th. At that point, he was sure nine days off would do everyone a little good.

After the others had gone, he sat in his office going over stats and packing up papers for his time away. He heard a loud banging sound from the locker room and rushed over to see what was it was, though he already knew.

Calvin Turner was alone kicking the living hell out of his locker. He stopped when he saw Cooper come in. He stood in front of the dented locker with his eyes down and said, "I can't take it anymore. They don't give a damn about winning, and I'm tired of playing with them." He looked up just enough that Dale could see his eyes were wet.

Dale seethed. He had been living with a simmering rage for weeks now, but had tried everything to quell it. It was too much for him to see the young man defeated by the ignorance, cruelty, and apathy of his peers.

He sat down on the bank of benches in front of the locker. "I'm sorry, Ten. I thought when we agreed to bench you that they'd see we were getting worse, not better. Now I realize they just don't care. They all expect that any day now they will just turn it on and have their magical .500 season. They deserve to lose every damn game the rest of the year. I almost want to let them."

Turner thought that was funny. He actually laughed. "We lose too many more games, and they'll start freaking out. Four or five more losses, and we'd have to win some games in the tourney to even sniff .500."

Dale chuckled too. "Yeah, if we drop the first fourteen games, we'd have to win state in order to…" His voice trailed off. He stood still for a moment as threads of the last several weeks wove themselves together in his mind. He said it again, "If we lose the first fourteen games of the season, we'd have to win the state title in order to finish .500."

Turner smiled sadly, "Yeah, it's too bad that can't

happen."

Dale picked up right on top of Calvin's comment. "No, we are good enough. If we could get Tom to play ball, we could be good enough. Putting you on the second team has developed our depth. No, we could be good enough…" He trailed off. He knew the truth. He had known it for some time, but until that moment he lacked the courage to say it out loud. He looked at Turner who had sat down on the bench in front of his mangled locker. Dale knew what he had to do.

"I'm going to tell you something a coach shouldn't tell a player." he said to the younger man. "You're the best there is. You are one of the best players I've ever seen. In high school basketball, one dominant player on a decent team is enough to win state, and if Denton would pull his head out of his ass and play the point for real, we could take anyone." Then, as if convincing himself, he added, "They just have to *want* to win. They have to believe it's their destiny to win."

"What are you talking about?" Calvin was in no mood for jokes.

"We have to make this team believe they can't lose. We have to give them something to play for that is more than just a will to win. They don't have that. We can't give it to them. But if we go 0-14 and they absolutely believe they have to win every game in order to satisfy their fate, they might just give everything they have." He was talking nonsense and he knew it, but the presence of hope in his heart felt so soothing that he refused to let the idea go.

"Are you saying we have to go out and lose the next seven games in order to win the state title? You're crazy, man." Calvin said.

"No, it could work. We have to get them to try. We have the talent. They have to find the will."

"Look, Coach. Even if you did get every guy on the team to give his best, it wouldn't matter anyway. There's still one thing you can't fix. We could lose thirty games and it wouldn't make Denton pass me the ball."

Dale did not enjoy having reason spoil his dreams. He

liked how he felt and was not about to surrender the emotion so easily. Calvin was right. Tom would be a problem, but he was not one that had to be solved right at that moment.

"Yeah, don't worry about Tom for now. I'll come up with a plan to deal with him," he said projecting an unwarranted air of confidence. He chose to focus on a more pressing problem. "You know, it won't be easy to lose seven more games. We have some real cupcakes coming up, and even though we aren't playing well as a group, guys are improving. We can't stop that because we'll need them later. Sooner or later, we'll catch a break and accidently win one exactly like the one we dropped tonight. We are going to have to *try* to lose these games."

Turner paused before speaking. Coach Cooper was clearly serious. The ferocity of Dale's belief troubled Calvin. Rather than accept the plan, he searched for loopholes. "Won't the town get mad at you? They could try and fire you. People take this team seriously. You saw those shirts tonight. They want to go 10-10. "

"Yeah, 10-10. That means we lose in the first round of the sectionals. This team is 0-7, and even so, I say that for a group this talented, that would be a humiliating finish. Screw what this town wants. The board won't fire me. I probably shouldn't tell you this, but Coach Denton all but told me they pushed for my hire expecting a losing season. They are as sick of the .500 record as much as I am, and they figured a losing season would open the door to the town embracing class basketball. They don't care if we go 0-20; they just want change. No, don't worry about my job. I'll be all right."

Hope is contagious. Calvin wanted to embrace it, but life had taught him that hope was not to be trusted. He had only just resolved himself to give up thinking things could get better. Part of him wanted to embrace the freedom that comes with accepting fate. Dale could make out the struggle on his face. "If ever there was a player who could pull this off, it's you Calvin."

Those were the magic words. For all his politeness and military bred manners, Calvin Turner was young and proud, proud enough to believe that he could do anything he wanted on a basketball court. He was faced with a choice: he could accept that he would be a good player on a losing team, or he could accept his coach's insane plan and believe that winning was possible.

In the end, it was no choice at all. Calvin chose to believe.

"If you want to do this, I'm with you," he said. "I don't care how we do it. All I want is to win."

Dale smiled. "Thanks, Ten. But if we are going to pull this off, we'll need help."

Chapter Eleven

Throw it Away

Dale was pleased to find a message on his machine at home. Greg Denton wanted to meet him for breakfast before Dale left town in the morning. Dale was glad for it, as they had barely spoken since the ugly phone call. First thing on Saturday, they met for breakfast at Pam's and sat in the same booth they had a few months earlier. Out of respect, Dale waited for the older man to speak first.

"I want to apologize to you, Dale. I should not have called you when I was upset. I hope you can forgive me." His tone was clear and apologetic. He gave no hint of another shoe to drop.

Dale recognized honesty when he saw it and said, "Greg, I understand. You were defending your son. That's every father's responsibility. I accept your apology."

"I-I've never been that upset about sports before. I pride myself on keeping perspective, you see? But somewhere in the middle of last week's game, I lost track of my job as a coach, and could only see through a father's eyes. The last few nights have humbled me. I was ashamed of my son when he belittled his teammates. I know that Tom's attitude is a big part of the reason this team isn't winning games. I'm worried about how he acts at home. He gets upset easily and storms off to his room. His temper has gotten worse. I never would have thought he could be violent, but sometimes he's so filled with rage, that I can't be sure anymore."

"Where's it all come from? What does he have to be so angry about?"

Denton was at a loss. He lowered his head. "I don't know." He stopped to collect his thoughts. "He resents my job. When he was younger, I worked too hard. I started coaching ball a few years ago to try and get more time with him. I should never have sent him to my father's in the summers. The man poisoned him. I didn't realize how bitter and twisted my dad had gotten after mom died. Beyond all that, I've made other mistakes too. It's hard for a 'pastor's kid.' People always expected Tom to be perfect, and they held it against him when it turned out he was just like any other kid. Basketball was his way of being his own person, and I didn't see that until it was too late. He played ball to get away from me, and I just followed by coaching."

He continued, "I didn't want to admit it before. As a father, it's scary to realize you are losing your influence with your son. If I blamed you and your coaching at first, it was just because it was easier than admitting that maybe I was failing him."

Greg Denton was a good man. Dale had known that from the start of their relationship. The tension between them was a bigger burden than the losing. There was something raw and terrifying in his confession that chilled Dale's heart. If a father this attentive and involved could worry that he was losing his son, then what chance did anyone else have? He had no advice to offer his friend. Anything he said would surely be so trite as to sound insulting coming from someone so young. Instead of speaking, he simply reached his hand across a table filled with Risin' Rooster platters and offered it to his assistant coach.

Denton shook it warmly. He did not expect Coach Cooper to have any insight into his situation. He only shared his feelings because he knew that confession really was good for the soul, and because he felt like he owed Dale something. The young man was under tremendous pressure, and though he was handling it admirably, there were signs that he was ready to break. It hurt the pastor to know that he had wounded his friend with his behavior, and privately he swore he would make it up to Dale. By voicing his deepest fear aloud in the presence of a friend, Denton felt that he had gained some ownership of it. It was no longer inside, consuming him. He had shared it with another person, and with the handshake, he felt a swell of courage. There were a lot of people who cared about Tom. He was determined not to lose his boy.

"Now, Coach Cooper, what are we going to do about this dumpster fire of a team?" he said to change the subject.

"It's funny you should ask me that, because there's an idea I've been kicking around. How would you feel about winning the state championship?"

Greg laughed.

Dale did not.

The break gave him time to think. A few days with his family and a quick two days on the beach helped Dale find perspective as he debated whether or not to follow through with his plan to throw the next seven games. He lay in the sand and sun and tried to find some peaceful center from which to make the decision. Greg Denton told him the plan was dangerous, though he promised to support the coach in whatever he decided. Dale suspected that he felt too guilty over the behavior of his son to object.

No matter how much Dale tried to give up on the idea, a nagging sense that this could be a special team gripped him. He could not let go of what he knew: the team was good enough to make a run at the state title. Unfortunately for his players, the red and gold of the Invincible Indians might as well have been a jersey of black and white stripes. The kids were imprisoned by the idea that they could not be anything better than mediocre and that being average was some special form of excellence.

"I just can't accept that," he said aloud to himself more than once. He knew that if they were from any other town, they would be title contenders.

He was certain that throwing the games was necessary. The team was improving in spite of itself. One of these nights, Calvin Turner would take over a game and win it by himself unless Dale stopped him. It was Turner's future that bothered him the most. He should already have been getting attention from top programs, even looks from NBA scouts, but no one even knew he existed. Turner was buried on the bench for a team that never won. It was tempting to forget the team entirely and structure the whole season around what was best for his player. After all, he had earned it. Calvin's reputation and future as a basketball player would be jeopardized by helping his coach lose games; maybe it was too great a risk.

Ultimately, it was Calvin who made the difference. Dale knew he would do whatever he was ordered. He had a keen sense of authority and discipline. He carried the expectations and training of his dead father with him like an invisible talisman warding off the demons of sloth, idleness, and rebellion that plagued most kids. He had been baptized in the spirit of victory and was willing to take any risk to achieve it. He wanted to win.

It made Dale's choice simple. Calvin Turner was an incomparable player, but to realize his dream of winning, he needed the support of a motivated, unified team. What Dale owed him as a coach was a chance to be spectacular. It was his duty to give that young man a stage where he would get noticed. By the time this season was over, his name would be on the lips of every recruiter and scout in the United States.

All it was going to take was losing the next seven games.

Short trips can be masochistic. By the time Dale finally unwound enough to start having fun, it was time to head back to the great frozen north. He was so bitter about leaving the Bahamas that he considered making the team lose *all* its remaining games as a punishment for making him live in Indiana.

The winter of 1997 was cruelly cold, and trading white beaches and sunshine for hardwood floors and florescent lighting was a loser's swap. On the drive from Indianapolis to Invincible, he almost turned around five times. He imagined buying a one-way ticket to some place warm and never looking back. He was not sure if he was too brave or too cowardly to do it though, and before he knew it, he was back in the gym with a whistle around his neck, running his players from baseline to baseline.

He had made his decision to "challenge his players' expectations of themselves through a series of well placed obstacles." It sounded better to him than "dumping games." It was amazing what temporarily laying down the burden of winning did for him as a coach. Before, he had thought he was coaching with the end in mind: a strong finish and a good run in the tournament. Now he realized that the pressure to win each game had eroded his patience more than it should have.

He was a young man and the immediate call of pride during each contest had pulled his focus off of teaching and instructing his players to prepare them for the real tests ahead. Knowing the back to back games on Friday and Saturday did not matter and that he was going to ensure the team lost them if necessary freed him to run practice and teach basketball more purely.

After practice, he called Turner and Greg Denton into his office. "We're on," he told them.

Denton played it cool, but his eyes were worried. "Okay, how exactly is this going to work. We can't make it obvious."

"Agreed. The first step is to stay with the A and B team

set ups. Ten, I want you to play your best at all times. Forget that we are even attempting to lose the games. I'm only telling you we are doing it so that you can understand when I don't play you. If I think we need something to happen to cost us a game, I'll take care of it. It's important that no one ever knows you are in on this. Do you understand?"

"Yes sir." His support went beyond words.

"Greg, you are the second part of the plan. I may have to get myself tossed from a game. First, if I do, you have to be sure to do whatever you can to make sure we lose. Can you do that?"

"I think so

"There's more. Even if we drop the games, it won't matter if we can't get your son to screw his head on straight. He can be an exceptional player, and if he can embrace his role, I believe we can win it all. I don't know what you have to do to get through to him. But, it has to happen. Lecture him, reward him, ground him, do whatever you have to do to get him going the right direction. Without him, this doesn't happen."

"I'm praying for him for an hour a day, Coach. I'm serious."

"Yeah well, it might just take divine intervention, so I can't argue with that strategy. Listen guys, we have twelve regular season games left. It takes nine wins in the tournament to take the state title. That means we have to win our last five regular season games. The magic date is February 7th at Tippy Valley. That's the first game we have to win. We have a big game on the 21st at Plymouth. They have a great team. I think we can skate for a couple of games, but if we aren't firing on all cylinders by then, this is not going to happen. These kids believe it is their destiny to finish .500. They believe it's their right and obligation. Those are powerful motivators, and that is the only thing this team needs to really take off."

"Coach Cooper," Denton said, "You know this is totally insane, right?"

"Yes. Yes, I do."

Denton slumped back in his chair resigned that Dale would not change his mind. After a moment, he slapped his hands against his thighs and said, "Ok, then. Let's…go lose some games!"

Downtown Invincible was not Times Square. The only ball dropping occurred in the backyard of the Miller house where the kids had a yearly game of snow football. Other than the dozens of rifle shots at midnight, there is little in town to mark the passing of the calendar from one year to the next. No one would ever it say it out loud, but the New Year is an outsider in the small town. He is not an adorable baby to be welcomed, but rather a suspicious stranger moving in.

Dale was glad to be rescued from another night alone by Samantha's phone call. She and her fiancé, who was on leave for the holidays, were heading to Fort Wayne to party with her sister. They invited Dale to come along. Fort Wayne was no great party town either, but at least there were bars.

He was ambivalent about Sam's barely disguised efforts to match him up with her sister. Nancy was a nice enough girl and they had all had a good time when they hung out in the fall, but she was too chatty for his tastes. It was a minor complaint. Anything was better than spending the night re-watching the game tapes from the first seven weeks of the year.

Tim Garn, Sam's boyfriend, was about what Dale expected. He was friendly in a polite way and engaged easily in conversation during the ride to the city. It was strange for Dale to sit and talk so comfortably with the guy. Over the course of the year, Dale had forgotten he even existed. Sam was as close to a confidante as he had managed to muster since he arrived.

Seeing her with her fiancé, he was reminded of where he stood. He checked out of the conversation for a moment as his mind wandered. There was no room for him in the picture. He was an outsider. People had to invent roles for him; even Sam was doing it. She had a boyfriend, so the only slots available in her life were 'work pal' or 'potential love interest for her sister.' They were too friendly to be just work pals, so if he was going to be a part of her life, it was going to be in some other way, no matter how forced.

She was not the only one who could not figure out how to relate to him. Dale realized that no one else in town knew what to do with him either. The reason he had so few friends was because no one in Invincible knew how to make new friends. Most people there had never developed the ability to integrate new people into their lives. They rarely had to. Most social circles had no openings for new members. Newcomers perpetually remained outsiders. There were families that still received sideways glances fifty years after arriving in town. Sam was trying to unnaturally wedge him into her life, but he gave her credit for making the effort.

As he crystallized in his mind how she saw him, Dale was taken with a sudden empathy for Calvin. He was not only new but profoundly *different* from everyone else, he had little hope of gaining acceptance. Obviously, race was going to be an issue with some people, like Tom Denton. For them, he was the 'young black male,' a symbol of 'everything that was wrong with America.' Even those who could see past his skin color would not necessarily like or understand the content of his character. The values he held, the way he carried himself, the goals he set might as well have been from another world. Whereas Dale could at least find a level of belonging as 'the new basketball coach,' Calvin Turner was never going to be more than 'that black kid' to everyone he met. Outside of his aunt and uncle, Dale guessed he might be the only person in a thirty mile radius who treated Calvin like someone worth knowing.

They arrived in Fort Wayne and the four of them went to a bar. He was glad to be included, and knowing his place helped him relax and have a good time. He drank some beer, threw some darts, and made out with Nancy Lawson just to make her stop talking for five minutes. He counted down the New Year glad to be someone other than Coach Cooper, at least for one night.

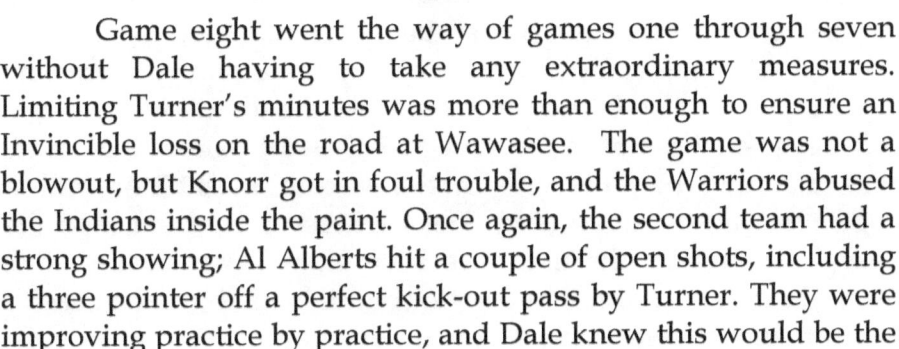

Game eight went the way of games one through seven without Dale having to take any extraordinary measures. Limiting Turner's minutes was more than enough to ensure an Invincible loss on the road at Wawasee. The game was not a blowout, but Knorr got in foul trouble, and the Warriors abused the Indians inside the paint. Once again, the second team had a strong showing; Al Alberts hit a couple of open shots, including a three pointer off a perfect kick-out pass by Turner. They were improving practice by practice, and Dale knew this would be the last time he would be able to count on the team losing without his intervention.

He also noticed signs of angst from the players. It did not translate into desperation or even extraordinary effort, but frustration was brewing. Knorr picked up a technical foul in the first half, which was stunning because he normally played like he was half asleep. Dale even heard a "You suck, coach!" coming from the visiting bleachers. It made his night.

His only regret of the evening came when he noticed a scout in the stands. It was a guy he knew from his days at Butler. Turner had a nice game (twelve points in eight minutes), but knew that he was putting the young man's future at risk. If Calvin were allowed to roam free, he would be a lock for a D1 scholarship.

He rearranged practice the next week to account for the team having to play three times. They had a Wednesday night home game, followed by a Friday and a Saturday night game on the road. They would then have a break for finals week, so he did not want to push the kids too hard. Practice was more important than ever. If the team was going to develop the last skills they needed to become championship caliber, the work would have to be done outside of game time.

That week, he went back to all the fundamental drills from the first practices, and added a series of new sets to the offense. They were plays that could only be effective with

Denton and Turner together, but of course, it did little good to pair the two of them. The other guards were not skilled enough to run them correctly, so Dale would often step in while running them to give Denton and Turner the right kind of looks.

Dale enjoyed practice because he loved teaching basketball, but also because he could feel the town's eyes on him whenever he was not at the gym. "10-4" had become 10-2, and it was dawning on everyone that the team might not pull it together. Dale received dirty looks wherever he went, and the easygoing joviality he had once been shown was evaporating. Greg Denton told him that people complained about the coach's performance to him at church on Sunday.

It was all going miserably according to form.

"The natives were restless" may be a cliché, but in the case of the crowd at Invincible High for the mid-week tilt with the Bellmont Braves and Squaws, it was appropriate in a literal sense. The students showed up to the game in red face paint and feathers. The mascot, Big Chief Wannawin, was expected to do his typical gesticulations at center court before the game. The band would weakly attempt to play the Seminole War Chant music, and whichever 98 pound freshman who volunteered that year would stumble around center court riding a broomstick pony and wearing an obscenely large headdress.

This night, however, the young man took it to a new level by recruiting several classmates to participate. They wore 'squaw' outfits and white T-Shirts that had BELLMONT emblazoned on the front with PC iron-ons. Big Chief Wannawin then took turns "scalping" the Bellmont squaws. It was a horrifying mix of racism, misogyny, and school pride that was offensive enough to upset most of the home fans over the age of sixteen. Some of them started to boo the kids performing the act, which only made the student section cheer all the louder. The game had not yet tipped off, and the crowd was already threatening to revolt.

The action on the court did nothing to calm the furor in the gym. It was tight from the go, and neither team managed more than a four point lead. The crowd was surly and rode every mistake hard. The ugliness before the game put everyone in a bad mood and they were ready to take it out on both teams. The game moved to the fourth quarter and the home fans showed no signs of tiring. As the clock wound down to under a minute to play, Steve Thompson rebounded a free throw with Invincible down two, and Dale called for a time out, wondering all the while if his plan was about to go up in smoke.

He called for a play he had only incorporated in the offense two days before. It was a special back door screen which set the shooter up for an outside/inside option. The point guard would have to correctly read the intent of the cutter and either feed him for a layup or a three in the corner. It took precision from the passer, speed from the cutter, and a special sort of telepathy between the two for it to work. With Adams playing instead of Turner, he knew it would have little chance of success. Even if it did work, the odds were strong it would only result in a game tying layup.

As the play unfolded, he was surprised by his own calm detachment. After all, the worst case scenario would be a win and a season-long struggle to get his team to meet their potential. As Thompson and Knorr set their screens, Dale was pleased to see both of the big men grasp the nature of the play and do their thankless jobs well. Roger Adams was lost and aimlessly running the baseline. Denton looked at Stevens who was set up near the left wing, but wisely did not pass him the ball. Stevens was a reliable enough shot but had terrible hands and could not be trusted to corral the ball in this situation. Denton made a subtle head-fake to Stevens and drew one of the help defenders from down low. Adams had a clear path to the basket; all he had to do was lay the ball in. He cut to the hoop.

As soon as the ball left Tom Denton's hand, presumably speeding toward the cutting player, he wished he could reach out and grab it back. Roger Adams had chosen that exact moment to pointlessly fade out to the three point line, despite having a guaranteed deuce. His move to the inside served only to fake out his point guard. He had misread the defense and was nowhere near the ball when it sailed past the end line and out of bounds. Bellmont successfully inbounded the ball after the turnover and the game was over.

Dale felt sick. He knew that in the long run, his players needed to learn humility and to work for wins. He knew that with time, they would learn to run that play, and it would be unstoppable. He knew that he had to coach with an eye on the future. But he still felt sick. He had intentionally put his players in a position to fail. Acceptance would come in time, but for now Dale was glad that it bothered him. It assured his throbbing conscience that he was doing this because he cared about his players and not because he wanted to punish them.

The loss was heartbreaking and deflated the crowd. It also saved the students who put on the floor show from suspension. The adults were so upset over the team dropping to 0-9 that they forgot all about the shenanigans of the pep squad. By the time Dale's boys managed to lose both games over the weekend, including a humiliating double digit loss to a truly terrible team at Prairie Heights, all memory of the ugliness was erased, replaced by overt outrage at the new guy in town who had ruined everything.

Chapter Twelve

Final Exam

Sam stopped by the bungalow Sunday night. Dale had the football game on TV with the sound off. The bulk of his attention was on the game tapes from the weekend. He was surprised to see her, as she had never come to his place before. He invited her in and offered her a beer. She accepted and sat down on his couch with a nervous laugh. It sat about an inch off the ground, and she needed a guide rail of some sort to get out of it. She immediately regretted her reaction. The purpose of her visit was unpleasant, and she did not want Dale to think she was taking it lightly.

The couch was the only memorable feature of the house. It was small, with a living room and two bed rooms, one of which was filled with VHS tapes and basketball magazines stacked like cordwood. The house had a tiny kitchen and a space where a dinner table would conceivably fit, though Dale had yet to find a reason to purchase one. He ate most of his meals on a green trunk which served as a combination coffee table/storage unit in front of the couch in the main room and never had company. There was little by way of decoration on the white walls except for a large framed poster of the RCA Dome that served as a constant reminder of Dale's real goal for his team.

She took a sip of the Budweiser, and decided to just come out with it. It could not be a surprise to him. "Dale, I'm not actually here as your friend tonight. I mean, I'm your friend, but that's not what I'm doing here…" She briefly trailed off and tried to start over. He knew what she was going to say but enjoyed watching her struggle with it. She was not the most compassionate woman on earth by nature, and it was amusing to watch her wrestle with a sensitive subject. Finally, she took a deep breath and said, "The town wants you out."

This time he laughed. "It took them long enough!"

She was put off by his bravado. "This is serious. A group was out collecting signatures after Friday's game, and they presented it to Ericksen. There's an emergency school board meeting at the gym on Friday night. They want to fire you."

He was not the least bit worried or shocked. He tried to calm Sam down. "It'll be ok, they can't fire me."

"You are damn right they can't fire you! I'm the union rep, and this is an outrage! We won't stand by and see one of our members…"

He cut her off. "No Sam, I mean they *can't* fire me. They'll never get another decent coach again if they let me go in the middle of the season. It doesn't work like that at this level. The town people can throw as big a fit as they want, but I'm not going anywhere."

She calmed down. She knew she was being more emotional than was necessary, but Dale was one of the few people in town whose world view extended beyond the county line, and she hated to see him pushed around. She did not have any other friends like him, and it made her take the whole fight personally. "That may or may not be so, but I'm here as your union rep to tell you that you have our full support. No matter what happens to your position as coach, you can't lose your job over this."

He wanted to laugh but suppressed the urge. He had too much respect for her. *I don't give a shit about my teaching job.* The year had taught him that much if nothing else. He kept working hard at it because it was his obligation, but if they did remove him as head basketball coach, he would leave town within a matter of hours, job or no job. Instead, he asked her, "Out of curiosity, who have they tagged to replace me? Kapler?

"Yeah, I think that's what the mob wants. The JV team has a great record."

He loved the irony. They had a great record because he had installed their offensive and defensive systems and got those kids to work their asses off all season. Kapler was just a caretaker. Dale refused to be insulted. He brought this on himself and had been expecting it for weeks. He said, "Thanks for coming to tell me. Do you want to stay and watch the rest of this game?"

She declined not because she disliked football, but because she knew her fiancée would not appreciate her sitting around drinking and watching TV at another man's house. She finished her beer and got up to leave. "All right, Dale. Just don't worry. We won't let this happen."

"Thanks, Sam. *You* don't worry. They can't fire me."

Invincible High was not the Harvard of high schools, but the administration did take finals week seriously. The athletic teams were not allowed to schedule any games that week, and coaches could only practice with players who had no finals to take the next day. They also had to have at least one team study table to start the week. For the sake of the students, they were fine policies, but obviously made it difficult for the coaches to maintain momentum. Dale was not a fan of forced study sessions. They were no help to struggling students and punished the better ones. He was lucky that academics were not a factor for any of his players. Because Invincible lacked the numbers to support a true jock subculture, few of the athletes could afford to slide by on talent alone.

Not surprisingly, his best student athlete was Calvin Turner who was as diligent about his studies as he was about everything else. He was pulling down a solid 3.5 with no fanfare. Dale doubted anyone at the school outside of the office and the coaching staff had any idea how well he was doing. He knew Turner did not need a forced hour and half study table and quietly let Calvin know that should he choose to skip the session his punishment would only be five laps around the gym to be completed sometime before the end of the week. Calvin came to the table anyway and worked silently until dismissal.

As he allowed the players to leave the cafeteria at the end of their mandated time, Superintendent Ericksen approached him. "MR. COOPER! MAY I HAVE A WORD WITH YOU?" He said it with the force that one would normally use for ordering the light brigade into the valley of death. The juniors and seniors had already filed out, but the younger players still hanging around froze, half-terrified by Ericksen's shouting. Among the students, the rumor that Coach Cooper was going to be fired was picking up steam but this was the first hard evidence any of them had.

Cooper eyed them wryly. "Alberts, McNichols, Tyson, get out of here." He said, picking on the three closest to him. "Go home and try not to fail World Civ, Tyson. I know you need a B on the final to stay eligible. Mr. Snyder and I are good friends. I'll know how you did on that test before you do. Go on, clear out, all of you." His voice was calm and reassuring, and he submissively raised a finger (though not perhaps the one he wanted) to Ericksen, gesturing for a moment to let the players exit.

"YES, YES! OF COURSE. GOOD LUCK ON YOUR TESTS BOYS!" Ericksen boomed encouragingly to them. Poor Ben Hanagan was so terrified he actually sprinted from the room. It made Dale smile to think that if the kid had showed that much speed in tryouts, he might have made the squad as more than just the stat guy. Dale hoped the players had actually left the building, but he knew he could not count on that. Unless they all made the parking lot before Ericksen started to talk, that half of the conversation would soon be public knowledge.

After a minute wait, Dale addressed his superior. "Yes, Mr. Ericksen. I am at your service." It was a bit of a suck up thing to say, but faced with unemployment, some modicum of humility was necessary. He was nervous about the conversation, regardless of his confidence in the ultimate outcome of the ordeal. He had not spoken with Ericksen since the town meeting fiasco in October. He did not know if Ericksen was the kind of man to hold a grudge, or how that might affect his future.

"DALE, I HAVE SOME BAD NEWS. A PETITION HAS BEEN SIGNED CALLING FOR YOUR IMMEDIATE RELEASE. A GROUP HAS OBTAINED ONE THOUSAND SIGNATURES ASKING THE SCHOOL BOARD TO REPLACE YOU AS HEAD COACH. THIS IS A SMALL TOWN, SON, AND THAT'S A LOT NAMES. IN FACT, I'M NOT SURE HOW THEY EVEN FOUND A THOUSAND PEOPLE TO SIGN ANYTHING." If Dale's performance at the open forum was still bothering him, Ericksen did not let on. Granted, at full volume, it was impossible to accurately gage any subtleties in his emotional state. "THE BOARD HAS AGREED TO HOLD A PUBLIC HEARING ON THE MATTER FRIDAY NIGHT AT EIGHT. YOU SHOULD ATTEND."

Dale saw no reason to play coy, so he asked Ericksen directly, "Do I have your support?"

Ericksen looked straight at him and said, "I ALWAYS SUPPORT MY PEOPLE," but gave him no indication at all as to how deep that support went.

"Let me be frank, Mr. Ericksen. I need to know who it is I am trying to convince on Friday. If I'm going to argue for my job, it helps to know who is on the jury."

"IN ALL MATTERS OF SCHOOL OPERATION, THE BOARD DEFERS TO ME. IN ALL MATTERS CONCERNING INVINCIBLE HIGH SCHOOL, I DEFER TO PRINCIPAL HERSHEY. THE BOARD WILL NOT OVERRULE ME. I WILL

NOT OVERRULE HIM. I'M SURPRISED, MR. COOPER. I THOUGHT YOU KNEW HOW THINGS WORK AROUND HERE." And there it was. Ericksen's ultimate revenge. He was entrusting Dale's fate to the most hapless man in town. It did not matter what was said on Friday night by either side. Jim Hershey would weigh the facts using some rubric all his own and render whatever decision would cause him the least amount of work.

"Well, thank you for informing me, Mr. Ericksen. I will certainly be there on Friday. And sir, for the record, I believe I'm doing a good job teaching these kids to play basketball. This team has a lot of wins in it."

"YES, I BELIEVE IT DOES," he said as he turned to leave. "AND COACH, FOR THE RECORD, THE BOARD IS QUITE PLEASED WITH THE JOB YOU'VE DONE. I WISH YOU THE BEST." He was either being ominous or encouraging. Dale had no idea which.

Most people fail to realize that finals week is actually a great week for teachers and students. There are always the kids on the bottom rung that are desperately trying not to fail some classes, but most kids' grades are so firmly entrenched that unless they suffer from massive test anxiety, they cannot radically affect their final standing. Invincible, like many schools, operated with an adjusted schedule all week long. Students had one test period on Monday and two a day from Tuesday to Thursday, with Friday off. They were given an hour and a half from the start of school to study, followed by an hour and a half for an exam. This was repeated in the afternoon.

Few tests required an hour and a half to complete. Many teachers did not give true final exams at all. Though they were supposed to offer a comprehensive test of a semester's worth of knowledge, more than a few just handed out normal end of unit or even end of chapter tests. This meant the students spent most of finals weeks not doing anything at all. A lot of classes reserved an A/V unit and showed movies after tests. The Spanish classes ate Doritos and salsa and wore sombreros while watching *La Bamba.*

Dale's own preparations were modest. His predecessor was not known as the finest educator in the Hoosier State, but he had left him one gift: a beautifully written comprehensive final exam. Marvin Anderson, a man who could barely be bothered to even take attendance, loved tests. Long before he left the dreary Indiana winters behind for the sirens' call of Boca Raton and its cheap greens fees and early bird specials, he devised a nearly perfect exam. Maybe he figured that by giving the kids a good test, he would have some hard evidence of what he had been doing as a teacher. Maybe he had residual guilt over scarcely trying day in and day out. Maybe he just stole it from some other teacher. Whatever the reason, it was a sound evaluative tool, and Dale had no guilt at all over kipping it.

During one of his free periods on Tuesday, which seemed endless thanks to the prolonged schedule, he slipped over to Samantha's class room. "Ericksen stopped by to talk to me last night."

Sam turned on her advocate mode. "Tell me everything he said. Did he say how he was leaning? Seriously, Dale, anything could be helpful if we have to take legal action on your behalf."

He smiled, wanting to make some crack about her being cute when she was worked up. He decided against it, mostly because it was true. "No, he told me it would be up to Hershey. He said the board would back him, and he would back his principal…only he said it way louder than I just did."

She relaxed and even smiled at his weak attempt at levity. "Okay, that's helpful. Jim Hershey hates conflict and hates acting on conflict even more. I'll stop by his office and let him know that the union is prepared to file a grievance on your behalf. Maybe if I mention that it will probably involve him having to give protracted depositions, he'll be less likely to fire you just to keep from having to leave his office."

Dale looked at her steadily. "Sam, it means everything to me that you've been my friend this year. I don't have many here.

I want you stay out of this. I know you can save my job as teacher, but it's not worth the effort. I don't love teaching, and if I'm not going to be the coach of the basketball team, I'm not going to stay in town and burn five more months off my life. If I'm done as coach, I'm done as a teacher, and I'm done in Invincible."

As he watched her consider this, he realized why outsiders stay outsiders. Sometimes, they never want to belong. Like an infection attacking a cell, they often stick around just long enough to do damage, and then they leave. Maybe everyone was right to not accept him.

Samantha Lawson was angry. She was angry at the stupid town of Invincible, Indiana for being too slow to change and grow. She was angry at her principal for being so weak and ineffectual. She was angry at her boyfriend, Tim, for spending the last two years in goddamn Germany instead of with her. She was angry at her mom for getting cancer. She was angry at Dale for being smart and funny and utterly committed to all the wrong things. She was angry at herself because she might start crying without knowing why.

Without ever betraying for a moment the churning she felt inside, she said, "I'm your union rep. My job is to help you keep your job…whether you want it or not."

He understood. He nodded and left.

He was angry about a lot of things too.

At eight P.M., the gym was packed to the rafters, as it had been for scores of Fridays in January stretching back longer than anyone could remember. The atmosphere was no different than it had been for the last town forum. The setup was identical. Dale was flanked by Ericksen and Hershey with the board to their right at center court. Only this time, sitting in front of what promised to be an angry mob gave Dale the distinct impression that he was facing a firing squad.

He prepared himself for what was coming. He informed

the team of the meeting after Thursday's practice, the only fully attended one of the week. Of course they already knew about the hearing, but he specifically asked them not to speak in his defense. He was not sure any of them would, but just in case, he wanted to keep them out of it. His advice to the players was for them not to attend at all. He did not want any of them to be hurt by things people might say about them. He knew that would not stop any of them, but it was his obligation to try. Sure enough, that night he saw Calvin standing at the back of the gym, and noticed several other players scattered among the crowd.

The meeting began as Dale anticipated. Ben Gordon dutifully opened the meeting with a brief welcome and then invited Walter Knorr, Sean's grandfather, to speak on behalf of the petitioners. Knorr was a lean, fit man in his late sixties. The Knorr family had lived in Invincible since its founding in 1845, and Sean represented the fourth generation of Knorr men to play basketball at Invincible. Mr. Knorr strode to the microphone and addressed the board.

"Gentlemen, I have seen every basketball team in Invincible for the past sixty years. I remember what basketball was like here before the Champs came. I played through several of those seasons myself. I believe I speak for a great many here tonight, when I say that I have never seen such an embarrassment to this town and its fine tradition as I have this season. Mister Cooper, a man with no experience and evidently little skill, has brought our team from a respectable record last year to the humiliating state of having no wins in eleven games. No one here will dispute that our boys are talented. In some cases, they are obviously more talented than the teams they are playing. Still, they do not win. The only logical explanation for this is that the coach is at fault. Meanwhile, our youngest players have a sparkling record of 7-2. It's clear that Coach Kapler knows what he is doing, and would be a vastly better choice to lead our boys into battle. We urge the board to make this switch while there is still time to save the season!"

There was universal agreement with his declaration. The board opened the floor for discussion, and the line to speak stretched from the microphone on the floor clear to the top of the bleachers. The arguments ranged from the historical (forty-nine seasons!) to the tactical (he sat the Denton boy for three whole quarters!) to the petty (Coach Cooper sucks!) to the incoherent (Melvin Anders blamed President Clinton for Dale's performance, though no one was entirely sure as to why).

Dale did have his defenders, as well. Samantha Lawson, as promised, made a public statement of support on behalf of the teacher's union. She threatened a lawsuit and possible strike if he was dismissed without cause. Her case was weakened when she was immediately followed by Mr. Snyder's long winded discourse about how Dale Cooper had no respect for history and was failing to teach the boys their heritage. A couple of the parents of players came down and said that their boys enjoyed playing for Cooper, and they saw real improvements. That was as far as anyone seemed to be willing to go for him.

As the night wore on, patience wore out. The speeches grew longer, more rambling, and more personal with time. Finally, as Gordon announced there would be only five more speakers, Dale noticed Barry Kapler push his way toward the front of the line. He was posturing for the final word of the evening. For the first time in the entire process, Dale Cooper was nervous.

Gordon saw the assistant coach approach the mike and announced that he would be the final speaker. It seemed fitting to everyone, and the rest of the line dispersed back to their seats. He stepped forward, and looked straight at Dale. All the other speakers had looked at the board.

Dale was filled with regret. In truth, he did not think much about Barry Kapler. He was a capable assistant but not the brightest man in the world. He took orders well and did his job. He was dedicated to the kids and hard working, traits which had barely registered with the younger man. He was not much of a talker, and Dale knew nothing about him. They had shared a few beers at the bungalow as they discussed team strategy, but he never took it upon himself to worry too much about Kapler or what he thought. Now, as Kapler was about to address the town,

Dale regretted his arrogance in not taking him seriously. Kapler had deserved better from Dale, and now Dale would reap what he had sown. The team was Kapler's to take if he wanted it. All he had to do was say the word, and Dale would be finished.

Kapler spoke in a clear, low tone. He was wearing a school sweat suit, one that he often wore to practice, and was holding a pair of index cards from which he read. "I'm not going to say much this evening. I appreciate that so many of you think I've done good work with the JV squad. They are fine young men and learning to be a good basketball team. I also understand and share your frustration with the varsity squad's lack of wins. There are three things I need to say before the board makes its decision. The first is that everything I do with the JV, I do because I was instructed by Coach Cooper. He designed all our offensive and defensive sets. I believe our younger players have taken to them more readily than our older players because they have less experience and less to unlearn."

He paused nervously. "The second thing I want the board to know is that I am convinced that Dale Cooper possesses one of the finest basketball minds I have ever seen and is an excellent teacher of the game." The crowd began to boo. Gordon banged a gavel on the folding table and demanded silence. Calling for order was easily Gordon's favorite part of his job.

Finally, with the crowd still muttering uneasily, Kapler finished his statement. "Lastly, Pastor, uh, I mean Coach Denton and I want you all to know that while we love this team and the school, if you fire Coach Cooper, we will also resign as assistant coaches. It's his job. He's the best man for it, and I won't take it if you give it to me. Thank you."

Dale stared at the man in disbelief. He vowed to never underestimate someone like Kapler again. After an entire evening of public vivisection, praise from one of the only men who actually knew the truth of how he coached was sweet.

Not that it would help. The crowd turned on Kapler too and began chanting, "Throw 'em all out! Throw 'em all out!"

Gordon happily whacked his gavel again and announced that the board had authorized Superintendant Ericksen to decide the matter. Ericksen stood up and in his normal tone of voice easily shouted down the crowd, saying that he had full confidence in Principal Hershey. Hershey stood up to say that he would take the matter under advisement and would render a decision by Monday morning. No one actually heard Hershey because they were still too busy yelling. Gordon adjourned the meeting, and Ericksen, Hershey, Cooper, and the board all exited quickly.

No one in the stands knew what had happened. Confusion dulled their ire and they hurried out of the gym hoping to find anyone in the parking lot who could explain what had been determined. The anti-climatic truth that nothing was decided filtered through the crowd, draining their energy and scattering them to their homes. Nothing quiets the passions like the bureaucratic chain of command.

Not withstanding the drama the night before, the team practiced on Saturday. When the players arrived on the floor, Dale addressed the uncertainty immediately. "I saw most of you at the meeting last night. Thanks for listening when I told you not to show." He paused while they laughed. "Just so you all know. I am your coach until someone tells me otherwise. I know you heard a lot of things last night, but I hope you were listening when Coach Kapler spoke. It's important that you understand that the three of us, your coaches, are 100% united in our mission to see this team become great. We will not rest until we accomplish that. I've spoken with Coach Denton and Coach Kapler, and I want you to know what I told them. First I thanked them for their friendship and loyalty to me and to all of you. Then I told them that if for any reason I can't continue as your coach, I need them to finish what we started. They have agreed to do so. Today, we are going to practice hard and put in some good floor time. As we do our work today, know that no matter what else happens these men will be with you to see this season through to the end."

Practice continued as normal, but there was hangover from the night before. Lack of urgency was a hallmark of the squad, but the uncertainty about their coach's fate added a melancholy aura that never lifted. As practice wore down, the players saw Principal Hershey slip in the side door and sit in the bleachers. They did their best to appear to work hard for the final ten minutes.

Not all the kids loved Coach Cooper. A couple actively disliked him. Their support of him had more to do with the sense of family that develops around a team. The boys felt attacked personally. When the community expressed their outrage, they could not help but feel responsible, no matter how hard everyone tried to convince them otherwise. They were the ones missing the shots and blowing the assignments on defense. They were pulling for their coach to validate their own efforts, not that they could have expressed as much in words.

The players finished the workout and were herded off the court by Kapler and Denton as Hershey approached Dale. "Mr., um, Cooper, can I have a word with you?" he asked unnecessarily.

"Certainly, Mr. Hershey. I hope you slept better last night than I did," Dale said.

Hershey failed to catch his meaning. "Yes, yes, I slept fine. I have one of those new, um, Serta sleep systems. It does wonders for my sciatica."

Dale was careful not to laugh.

Jim Hershey gathered his thoughts, having been unexpectedly sidetracked by Dale's question about his sleeping habits. "Yes, I need to speak with you about the meeting last night, Mr. Cooper. It has, um, come to my attention via Miss Lawson that should I remove you as head basketball coach, you will resign your post as government teacher as well?"

Acid welled up in Dale's stomach. Hershey was going to pull the plug. "Yes, sir. Effective immediately. I want to pursue a career in coaching, and finishing the semester would be detrimental to my ability to find work with a college program. I'm sure you understand."

"What I understand, Mr. Cooper, is that you have put me in an, um, extremely difficult position," Hershey sounded like an angry canary. "The people of this town are quite upset with you, and I find it difficult to deny they have some degree of, um, cause. However…" To Dale, his pregnant pause stretched out for nine long months. "I cannot very well replace one of the finest government teachers in Indiana on two days notice, can I?"

More unlikely words had never been spoken. Dale had no response adequate for the moment. Had the principal any ability to detect vocal nuance, he would have easily identified the mix of incredulity and suspicion in Dale's voice when he repeated, "Finest government teachers in Indiana, sir?"

"My job, Mr. Cooper, is to oversee the educational state of this school. I could not possibly make any decision about you based on something, um, so trivial as your record as a basketball coach. If I am going to lose a teacher, I want to know what I'm losing. I reviewed your final grade reports for the, um, semester. I must say I have not seen such a fine teaching job in many years."

Dale stared at him slack jawed and silent, so he continued. "The scores on your final exam were 15% higher across the board than what, um, Anderson submitted last year. That's a remarkable improvement. High test scores are the backbone of a strong school, Mr. Cooper. It is obvious to me from seeing the numbers that you have a, um, true passion for imparting the intricacies of our government to the impressionable minds of my students. If you are firm in your, um, decision to leave the school if I remove you as coach, then you leave me no choice at all. Are you quite sure you won't, um, reconsider?"

Dale did not fully believe this. He looked Hershey in the eyes, and with no hint of humor said, "Yes sir. I will resign as a teacher if you remove me as coach."

Hershey was displeased with the answer; he was honestly hoping to avoid upsetting the town. He shook his head and said, "Well if that's the way it must be. I absolutely cannot lose such a gifted teacher. Fine, Mr. Cooper. You will remain as, um, head coach for the rest of this year. I will hear no more on the subject. I will inform Mr. Ericksen of my, um, decision. Have a pleasant weekend, Coach."

"Thank you, sir. I appreciate your…encouragement." Dale said as Hershey shuffled off to whatever kind of activity such men do for fun on the weekends. Dale stood at midcourt alone and stared at the basket at the south end of the gym.

It was official.

This was his team.

Chapter Thirteen

Losing it

The assurance that their coach would not be replaced lifted the team's spirits, and it showed in practice. The boost in energy level made Dale believe they were ready to install the final piece of the defense, the full court press. The press is a devastating and disruptive tactic when executed well, but requires true commitment on the part of the players. It is a high energy defense and not one that can be easily employed by a lackadaisical squad. Up to this point, he was hesitant to break it out because his players could not be counted on to give a consistent effort for a full thirty-two minutes. The team had been working on the press all year, but had yet to employ it outside of the last couple minutes of a game.

Invincible had back to back weekend games, which gave Dale a full week to work with his club. He was convinced that the best chance for an undermanned team to pull a big upset was to attack with a vigorous press. Especially at the high school level, where ball handlers are at a premium, it is an excellent way to generate turnovers and help wear down bigger players. In an effort to add more bodies to the team, Dale informed Jared Henderson, Mike Mann, and Sean's brother Carl Knorr they would scrimmage with the varsity. The three sophomores were playing well for the JV. Dale wanted them to keep getting court time. They would start with the JV while being familiar with the varsity come tournament time. An up tempo style meant that a steady flow of fresh legs would be critical in March.

Practice was a chess match for Dale. Because he still could not work with his ideal lineups, he had to improvise. He moved players around, playing lesser guys out of position so he could keep Turner and Aldrige in the same roles they would have when they rejoined the A squad.

Whereas most of the players were relieved that the coaching crisis was over, the one player disappointed was Tom Denton. Tom's father rode him constantly, and Cooper spent most of practice yelling at him. Meanwhile, Turner could do no wrong in their eyes. Tom tried to make everyone understand that this was his team, it had been for a long time, but most of the underclassmen responded better to Turner. He was stealing Tom's team, and Tom was not going to let him get away with it. Dale intentionally separated the two seniors during scrimmages, running plays and rotations that kept them away from one another as much as possible. Still whenever he could, Tom would rotate over to Turner and foul him just hard enough to remind him of his place.

Tom hated getting hassled at practice, and time at home with his dad was insufferable. He kept trying to talk to Tom and ask what was bothering him. He had obviously been talking to his mom too, because she just stared at him with a sad look all the time. When Tom told his folks he wanted to go to Auburn and live with his grandfather for school the next year, they threw a fit.

He grew increasingly bitter toward everyone, but especially Coach Cooper and Turner. He thought about quitting the team but did not want to give them the satisfaction of being rid of him.

He had no idea that Dale Cooper saw him as the key to the entire season. If he had, he probably would have quit out of spite. As it was, he channeled his rage at the world into his play on the court, as if by his play he could convince everyone to shut up and leave him alone.

The stands were only half full for Friday's game. Many of the protestors vowed they would not come back to the gym until Cooper was fired. Even the students and players' family who did show were subdued at best. Hopes for a fiftieth straight .500 season were all but gone. Some fulfilled their Friday night ritual out of habit but took little delight in showing up.

Those that stayed home certainly felt justified when they heard the final score the next day. Harding stomped the Indians by twenty. Dale unleashed the press for the entire game, and the results were disastrous. The team had little spark, thanks in part to the miniscule crowd, and multiple blown assignments meant multiple transition layups for Harding. The team had kept other games close, thanks to Turner's production off the bench. That night, however, he smacked his wrist hard on the bench diving for a loose ball near center court just after entering the game. The injury was not serious, but he never got his shot going. He scored only four points, a season low, and without his production the second team was destroyed. The Indians dropped to 0-12.

Dale was miserable. The team was miserable. The fans were miserable. Any temporary bounce provided by the drama of the previous week was short lived.

The team had to play a road game the very next night, and came out so flat and discouraged that Dale had no choice but to call off the press five minutes into the game. Their legs were dead. So were their hearts.

Amazingly, Turner kept the game against Goshen close. His wrist was still sore, so he spent most of his floor time driving with his left hand. He was so astonishingly quick off the dribble that he was virtually unguardable. Since Goshen had already built a sizable lead, they did not exert enough effort defending him. Dale saw his team needed life; he did not want to destroy them irreparably. He left Turner in to play with the A squad, with Denton on the bench.

The effect was electric. Having Turner play with the best players on the team gave Invincible juice for the first time in weeks. An early fifteen point lead was cut to just three by halftime, and when Dale brought back the press to start the second half, Turner forced three turnovers in the first four minutes and scored ten straight points to give them their first lead in what felt like a month

He was hitting his stride, and for a few minutes Dale got caught up in the beauty of the moment. Goshen was just an average team. Turner was more than enough to carry any four people in the building to a victory. Giving him actual basketball players to play with was wholly unnecessary and a little unfair to Goshen. As the third quarter wore on, Dale shook himself and realized they had built a ten point lead. He gritted his teeth and waited for Turner to get fouled.

It was not a long wait. He was shredding the Goshen D with such regularity that the interior players had begun just taking random swipes at him as he soared past on his way to the rim. After a love tap resulted in a potential three point play, Dale called time out before his player could shoot the free throw. He called Turner over and asked him the question that would determine their fate that night.

"It looked like he smacked you pretty hard on the wrist, there, Ten. I know it's sore. Can you keep going?" He knew there was nothing wrong with Calvin, but he had no other choice. He had no idea how Turner would respond.

"No coach. I was just going to tell you. It hurts like hell. He smacked it hard. I don't think I can even take this free throw." He sold it. He was the most committed person Dale had ever known. Turner would not see any more floor time that night.

Merely taking Turner out of the game was not going to be enough. Dale called off the press, ostensibly because Turner was out of the game. Secretly, he hoped to give Goshen a chance to come back. Dale was going to have to get creative if he hoped to drop his team to 0-13. Fortunately, Goshen's two-guard got hot and hit a couple of threes to cut Invincible's lead to just four heading to the fourth quarter.

Throwing games went against every instinct in his body. There was nothing he wanted more than to win. This kind of end game was taxing. He glanced at Calvin who was sitting on the bench with his wrist wrapped in ice. He was fiddling with the wrap constantly, and Dale could see he was wrestling with the same questions. He wanted to come back in the game.

Watching the young man struggle with the decision was hard on the coach. If Turner waivered at all and asked to reenter, Dale knew he could not tell him no. He did not have enough strength for the both of them. He would not be able to pull it off alone.

The Indian lead hovered between two and five points for most of the quarter. Goshen could not make consecutive baskets. Denton played hard and made all the right decisions with the ball. Dale even called the backdoor screen option play, and this time the senior guard ignored the still confused Adams and took the ball to the rim for a layup. As the clock closed in on a minute to play, and his team was still up three points, Dale was conflicted. Winning the game would be disastrous. He knew his players. He knew they could make a little run, get some respect back in the community, and maybe even win the sectional. He also knew there would be a hard and fast ceiling to what they could accomplish without some extraordinary motivation.

They had to reach 0-14. A win now would be like scratching a poison ivy itch. It would feel good for a moment but would only spread the irritant. He nervously checked the clock and prayed to Wooden, Iba, Rupp, and whatever other hardwood deities might be listening for a miracle.

As it turns out, the spirit of Bob Knight must have heard him, because he got his wish. Thompson blocked a shot that would have pulled Goshen within a point, and the ball careened toward the side line. Stevens and a Goshen Redskin both dove for the ball right in front of Dale, with the Goshen player clearly knocking the ball out of bounds. The whistle blew, and the official awarded the ball to Goshen. Stevens leapt to his feet and shouted, "WHAT THE FUCK?" right in the face of the referee who immediately whistled him for a technical foul. Dale had his opening.

Free of worrying about the final score, he unleashed twenty years of pent up frustration from every bad call that had ever gone against him. Until that moment, he had never received a single technical foul at any level of organized basketball. His streak ended in fine fashion. He wove several of the best techniques ever witnessed into a tapestry of histrionics and emotion that left the poor middle-aged man who had blown the original call devastated.

Knowing that he had to avoid a suspension, he deftly avoided using any profanity but immediately stormed the court and pushed Phil Stevens aside. He then used *The Finger Point* approach. He charged the ref and wagged his index finger angrily, "I CAN'T BELIEVE YOU BLEW THAT CALL! THAT WAS LAZY! YOU ARE LAZY, YOU HOME TOWN IDIOT! HOW COULD YOU POSSIBLY MISS THAT CALL!" He was immediately teed up by the other official who had rushed to their side of the floor. It was far from over.

He went with *The Louganis* next, diving to the floor to mimic the Goshen player who was still standing there in complete shock. "THEY TOUCHED THE BALL LAST! YOU COULDN'T SEE THAT PLAY! YOU WERE OUT OF POSITION! DID YOU ASK FOR HELP? DID. YOU. ASK. FOR. HEEEEELP?" He pointed at the other official. "ASK HIM! ASK HIM FOR HELP!"

He switched to *The Good Cop*. Turning to the second ref with an eerie calm he said, "Mike, you saw the play. He got it wrong. Tell him he got it wrong. He was out of position. You saw it."

The other official said what referees and umpires always say in such cases, "It's his call. I was watching the action underneath the hoop. I didn't see it. You need to calm down coach, or I'll run you." The fact that he did not immediately eject Dale meant both officials knew the call had been blown. They felt morally obligated to give the coach a little time to vent. After all, Goshen was already due four free throws and the ball, down three points with forty-eight seconds to play. He deserved a little rope.

As soon as the man in stripes said the magic words "I'll run you," Dale went to *The Lou Pinella*. He got right up in Mike's grill and insulted his intelligence, his salary, his integrity, his breath, his hair, and even the kind of car he drove. He made sure they had no choice but to eject him. The second T came about five seconds into his new outburst but did nothing to stem the tide. Finally, they gave him a third technical, which was enough to move him into the final phase of his demonstration, *The Helicopter*. He stormed back to the bench, grabbed his abandoned suit jacket, and waved it in circles over his head as he left.

The Goshen crowd booed and jeered in complete adulation of the scene. Though they feigned outrage and whispered to one another about how embarrassing Dale's behavior was, the truth is that the people of Goshen were unlikely to experience anything more entertaining than Cooper's variety show the rest of the season. After he made his way to the exit of the gym floor, he stopped spinning his coat. Turning to face the officials at the other end of the gym, he shouted for good measure "THAT WAS THE SINGLE WORST CALL I HAVE EVER SEEN IN MY ENTIRE LIFE!"

It earned him a completely gratuitous fourth technical.

Goshen had ten free throws and the ball with little time left. Dale could only hope he had done enough. From the locker room, he counted the cheers of the fans with each foul shot. Eight times they roared.

He had done plenty. Just one loss to go.

Dale knew there would be some consequences for his display. It started as the team headed back to the locker room. Every single player came in and immediately wanted to give their coach a high five. They giggled like five year olds at recess and mimicked every one of Dale's impressive array of protests. This was not the message he hoped to send to impressionable young minds. Though he privately found the whole thing hilarious, he knew he could not let the kids believe such behavior was at all acceptable.

"Settle down, guys. First let me say that you all gave a great effort tonight. I'm proud of how hard you played. I'm sorry that I cost you that win. You deserved it." It was the truth. Losing the game was for their own good, but it did not stop him from regretting it. "What I did was not excusable. I want you all to know that I behaved childishly. It was a selfish display that cost you the game. No matter how bad the call was, I should have treated those officials with respect. I want you all to know that I am going right now to find both men and apologize. Please forgive me. Get dressed and get on the bus. We'll talk about the game on the way home. It's a long ride. Let's get out of here."

He left the locker room and headed out to the parking lot where he knew the refs would be leaving. He managed to catch up to them both as they were getting in their cars, "Mike, Bob, hold up a minute!" he called after them.

The two men looked warily at the young coach but did not climb in their cars and speed away. "That was uncalled for tonight, Coach," said Mike Gino, the older of the two men, and the one who took the brunt of Dale's abuse, despite not having actually made the call.

Dale did his best to look chastised. "Yes, gentlemen. I know. I'm very sorry. You both deserved better than that. I apologized to my team for my actions, and I want you both to know that I am very sorry. I should not have insulted you. You were just doing your job."

His apology eased the tension somewhat. "That's ok, son. I appreciate that you at least didn't cuss. I'm not going to recommend any disciplinary action, especially because Bob here blew the damn call." Bob shot Mike a dirty look, but then shrugged and nodded to the affirmative. "Take it easy next time, kid. You won't get any latitude from me if I do another game of yours."

Dale thanked them both for understanding and watched as Mike drove off in a fine looking Mercedes.

Wow. *Beats the hell out of my ride home,* he thought as he climbed into I.H.S. Bus #4. It did not have heated seats or an all-leather interior.

"My sister is coming to town for the weekend. Do you want to come over for drinks?" Samantha's not at all subtle invitation caught Dale off guard. He swallowed hard on a bit of bologna sandwich. "That would be great, Sam, but I can't. I'll be exhausted after the game tonight, and tomorrow night I have to drive out to Mentone to scout Valley."

Sam stared at him in wonder. "I've never seen anyone work harder than you at anything. Remind me again why you haven't won any games yet?" The dig hurt a little. It was supposed to.

Dale wanted to tell her the truth, but the time was not right. There were a few other teachers hanging around the lounge during lunch. He swallowed his pride and said, "Work is the name of the game in coaching. It's the only way to get where you want to go."

Samantha shook her head. "What's the point of a job where you have no fun, no friends, no life?" She caught herself, not wanting him to misunderstand. "I mean, I'd like to think we're friends Dale, but I never see you away from school."

There was a reason for that, but there was no way to tell her. "What can I say? I love coaching. I love the competition. I love basketball." He tried to infuse his words with passion, but was painfully aware of how hollow they sounded.

"Is that enough for you? Basketball? Don't you want relationships? Do you ever think about a family or the future? I mean, aren't you lonely living like this?"

He was lonely. Before coming to Invincible, before meeting Sam, he had never stopped long enough to notice. The snail pace of life in the small town coupled with the fact that everyone hated him for ruining the fiftieth season pounded home just how isolated and alone he was. Even now, he did not want to admit that to Sam, but felt his defenses crack.

"Yes. I'm lonely. Yes. I think about the fact that I haven't had a relationship that lasted more than two months since college. Yes. Part of me does wish there was more to my life than zone defense and half court traps. On the other hand, I have this dream to coach college ball. Sacrifices have to be made."

She looked at him sadly. "Dale, come over tomorrow night. Nancy would love to see you."

The offer was tempting, but Nancy Lawson was not what tempted him. "I can't, Sam. I really just can't."

She nodded, almost as if she saw through him. "Well, I hope you get what you are after in the end."

He finished his lunch, relieved but a little disappointed that she did not understand him at all.

With an excited giddiness, Dale made his way onto the court for Invincible's fourteenth game of the season. No one could have known by looking at him that he was the coach of the team with the worst record in the state and that nothing would make him happier than dropping one more game without doing permanent damage to his team. Losing was no sure thing, as the Leo Lions were not an impressive team, but managing to intentionally screw up the last several games had given Dale a particular kind of confidence. He figured that no matter the situation, he would think of something, although with insane outbursts off the table, he knew his arsenal was somewhat depleted.

As it turned out, losing to Leo was harder than he thought. They were a small team, and Invincible looked like a band of ceiling scrapers in comparison. Dale stared at his 6′10″ center during warm ups and wondered what he could possibly do to neutralize him. Leo was going to counter in the middle with a 6′3″ kid who could generously be described as "a bit chubby." Thompson had no meat on his body at all, but even the lanky sophomore would be able move fast enough to be effective against a football offensive guard posing as a basketball center.

Dale's first step was to use his least effective line up, which happened to be his most talented one. For the first time in weeks, he started Turner with Denton. Dale had told Calvin not to do anything to alter the outcome of the game in a negative way but also knew he could trust Calvin to ignore that advice if he had to. Both of them knew the goal was within their grasp, and they only needed things to go right for one more night.

Turner proved brilliant in his ability to sabotage the game. He had such a fine understanding of both the offense and the defense that he knew exactly what to do wrong and how to do it in a way that no one else would notice. His first move was on the defensive end. He released his man off the dribble and fed him into Thompson who was supposed to double down and help. Turner had quicker feet and better foot work defensively than anyone in the state, so the rotation was designed to use Thompson's height to trap the dribbler on the baseline and force a turnover. Turner, however, played a step slower than normal, which allowed the ball handler to slither past him, leaving Thompson alone to stop the layup. Thompson was inexperienced and prone to reaches and slaps against faster players, and without Turner to help contain the guard, he picked up two quick fouls within the first three minutes of play exiling him to the bench for the rest of the half. With scarcely any effort Turner had neutralized Invincible's greatest advantage.

On offense, he helped the cause by hitting two tough jumpers to start the game. Denton loved to try and feed him the ball when he was double teamed or out of position for a good shot. On both of the first two possessions, Calvin merely took 'bad' shots over double teams and drained them both. In doing so, he ensured Leo was going to key on him all night. He spent the rest of the game subtly running the men shadowing him right through passing lanes. Denton struggled to find an open man, and the offense never found a rhythm.

Even so, Leo was not a talented club, and Invincible was. Calvin worked to keep Leo in the game, but Sean Knorr played uncharacteristically hard on defense and helped to shut down the wide-body the Lions were posting up on every play. Fortunately, the B team was a total mess thanks to Turner's migration to the starting lineup. The end result was another nail biter. Dale's stomach churned on every possession.

As Knorr collected his twelfth rebound and called timeout with just eighteen seconds on the clock, Dale was overcome with the sick realization that he had no tricks, no answers. As a coach and a player, he had spent his entire life learning to win, learning to stave off defeat and make the impossible, possible. He had already exhausted every trick he knew to lose a game. There were seconds to play; his team was down just a point, and he could not imagine anything that would guarantee a loss and not embarrass or wound one of his players. Too many times that season, he had watched them fail in the tight moments.

He would not do that to them. Not again. *These kids may not be winners yet, but they don't deserve this.* He could put it on Turner, knowing he was strong enough to bare the shame, but knew the repercussions down the line would undo whatever good was done by it. No, this time he had to give them their best shot. Maybe he was a coward. Maybe he was just too soft.

He called for the best play he could, the backdoor option for Calvin. He drew it up for them again in the huddle, knowing that Denton and Turner had never run it together. He looked hard at Tom. "Listen Tom, Ten is taking this shot. YOU WILL pass him the ball. Read the defense both of you. Screeners, you make the play happen." He turned his head to look at Calvin. "Hit the shot, Ten. Hit the shot." There was no flash of question on Turner's face, just a simple affirmative nod. He was a warrior, just as his father had taught him. He would follow orders. Dale did not notice that another set of eyes were also fixed on him. This pair burned.

Denton dribbled off the remaining seconds and waited dutifully for Turner to make his move. He seethed inside. The point was his. It should be his call on what to do with the ball. "Asshole," he muttered under his breath as the screeners set. He would show that idiot Cooper what would happen if he trusted Turner with the ball.

He read the defense perfectly, as did Turner. The play was to the inside, and a smart bounce pass would have easily found its way into Turner's hands for the game winning layup. Denton threaded the needle almost perfectly. Almost.

The pass had just enough extra pace on it that Turner could not field it cleanly. It brushed off his finger tips, and spun past the baseline. Turner flung himself toward the ball and corralled it in mid-air but behind the back board. In one motion, he secured the ball and flipped it up over the top of the board. It caught the rim, hopped into the air, and fell harmlessly to the ground.

Calvin Turner Junior crashed to the floor and lay in a heap near the wall of the gym in Leo.

He was not hurt. He was in disbelief.

He had expected to make that shot.

Chapter Fourteen

Thicker than Blood

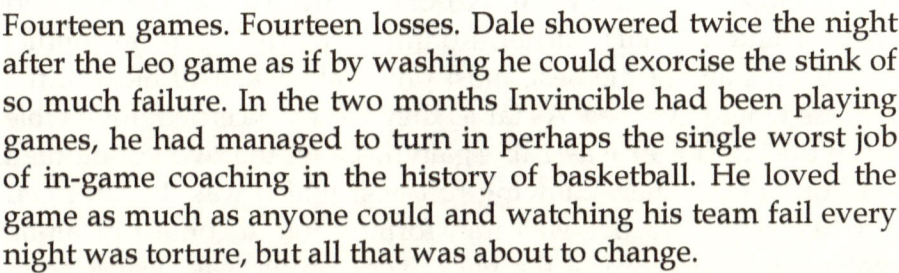

Fourteen games. Fourteen losses. Dale showered twice the night after the Leo game as if by washing he could exorcise the stink of so much failure. In the two months Invincible had been playing games, he had managed to turn in perhaps the single worst job of in-game coaching in the history of basketball. He loved the game as much as anyone could and watching his team fail every night was torture, but all that was about to change.

They only had two practices to prepare for the Wednesday night game at Tippecanoe Valley High School; Dale was confident it would be enough. His first move at practice the next day was to bench Denton. Alberts and Turner replaced Denton and Adams with the A team. Alberts was still far from being a deadly shooter but had improved enough to give the team a chance. Most of the team barely registered the change. Dale worried that he had let things go too far. They had accepted their fate as losers as easily as they had embraced their destiny to finish .500. Convincing them that they could be winners would prove challenging.

Tom Denton was visibly outraged by his demotion. His dislike of his coach and Turner frothed to the surface. Dale saw it. He knew Denton threw that pass to Turner at the end of the game too hard. He knew Tom wanted everyone to blame Calvin for the loss. At this point, no one was buying it.

The last, and most important, part of Dale's plan was almost in place. He just had to break Tom Denton's will. Dale did something in scrimmage that day that he had resisted for several weeks.

He let the two seniors guard each other in practice.

The result the first day was savage. Turner and Denton channeled months of mutual hatred into an epic closed-door war. Denton was an excellent player and a strong defender, but Turner was elite in ways that he could never hope to be. They banged bodies, slapped wrists and arms, and collided for every loose ball. Dale swallowed his whistle, stood back, and let them have at it. By the end of the day, both had bruises, but it was clear that Turner was the victor.

By the following practice, the malaise was gone. There was a buzz about the team. No one could wait to lace up and watch Denton versus Turner, Round Two. Their private conflict produced some of the best, most physical basketball most of the players would ever see. As far as they were concerned, Invincible wasn't 0-14; Turner was 1-0. Again, Dale let the two young men wail on one another, knowing full well which was the stronger. For two days, practice was transformed into a contest of alpha wolves vying to control the pack. The verdict was clear. Calvin Turner was the big dog.

The following night at Tippy, he left no doubt. Finally unchained from the bench and allowed to play with the starters, he led a vicious full court press and erupted for an astounding forty points on 15-20 shooting. His performance immediately injected life into his teammates, all of whom played with the same fervor as their new leader. Tippy had no answer for Turner who could have beaten them that night if he had played one on five. The Indians won by thirty points on the road.

The ride home was jubilant. The players were loose and happy for the first time in weeks. Even Calvin was smiling, laughing and having fun with the guys. It occurred to Dale that for once, he looked like a kid.

It was the first and last time he would get to see Calvin that free, that happy, that young.

The win felt wonderful, but Dale knew it would be short lived if he did not get through to Tom. He played limited minutes in the Tippy game, and his mood afterward was disturbing. He did not show his anger or his frustration outwardly after Calvin dismantled him Friday. His rage had gone from hot to cold, and Dale feared it made him dangerous. He vowed to keep a tighter rein on the two players at Monday's practice.

Nevertheless, he was committed to breaking Tom down. Whatever the cause of Tom's anger and resentment toward Calvin, they had to root it out and make him face it. His father could pray for him for the next ten years, but Dale doubted this had anything to do with God.

The players got some grief and a lot of Bronx cheers at school on Monday, but everyone took it good-naturedly. Even Calvin got a lot of pats on the back as word of his exploits filled the building. Few made the trip out to Mentone for the Tippy game, but word of mouth had made "Cal" Turner the most popular kid in school that day.

Most people had always wanted to like him, but could never figure out how to relate to him. He was handsome but barely spoke to the girls. He was one of the brightest students in the school but would never raise his hand or open his mouth in class unless expressly ordered to. He was clearly a superior athlete but had spent most of the season on the bench.

The other students did not care that Calvin was black, but they had no other category to put him in. In two practices and one game, he had finally carved himself a niche in the social hierarchy of the school, and everyone was relieved to include him.

Practice started out innocently enough that afternoon. The schedule was spread out now to allow players to enter the meat grinder of March with fresh legs. They would not play again until Friday night's home game against Luers. Dale appreciated the extra practice time, as it gave him a chance to install the rotations and assignments that would carry them through to the end of the season. Luers was not a strong club, and he knew his team should dispatch them with ease. On the horizon was the true test with Plymouth. He had just two weeks to get this team in top gear or it would be impossible to finish .500.

As the A and B teams scrimmaged, Denton was strangely subdued. He played hard, but his intensity was dialed down slightly. He was quiet and did not jaw with Calvin at all. Dale wondered if the fight had gone out of the young man. He thought briefly that Tom had finally broken, and it would only be a matter of time before he could start building him back up into the player they needed him to be.

Tom Denton was anything but broken.

In the end, it all happened so fast, there was nothing Dale could do to stop it. He was at the half court line when Denton went up for a rebound with Turner. Tom had good position and secured the ball cleanly. He then raised the ball to face level, and turned violently into Turner's face with his elbow. The crack was audible. Calvin staggered backward, blood streaming down his face. It looked like it could almost be an accident until Denton shoved him to the floor hard, then stomped on the boy's face. Everyone in the gym froze. The whistle dropped from Dale's lips as he took steps toward his fallen player.

Tom Denton looked down at the young man whose nose he had just broken and laughed. "All niggers have flat noses anyway."

The words caught Dale full in the face like a left hook. The severity of the bleeding, the premeditated nature of the hit, the vile words all fermented together. It mixed violently in his heart and he was instantly drunk with bitter rage.

He hated this kid.

He hated him in a way that he had never known hate. He looked at Tom Denton and saw evil, the kind of evil that makes someone believe for the first time that there really is a God. For an instant, he was no longer concerned for Calvin but was consumed with such anger that it could only be described as murderous.

He felt himself stride toward Tom Denton who was still standing over Turner, gloating. Approaching him, Dale cocked his fist to rain blows down on the teenager. He had crossed the line; he knew he was going to end his career and possibly go to jail, but he did not care. He could not live with himself if he did not teach this kid a painful lesson. Denton was too preoccupied with mocking his fallen teammate to even notice that his coach was about to beat him senseless.

Dale reached him and raised his hand to strike when an arm reached in front of him and grabbed him. Greg Denton bear-hugged him, stopping his momentum completely. He held tight to Dale, and said in his ear, "I'm the boy's father. This is my job. You take care of Calvin."

The appeal to Dale's concern for Turner was wise. As much as he hated Tom Denton, he cared about Calvin Turner more. He snapped out of the haze long enough to say, "All right, Greg. You deal with him."

The father released the coach and turned to face his son. With no hint of malice or anger of any kind, he simply said, "Tom."

Tom looked up at his dad; he was still flush with victory. Even so, he could not raise his eyes to meet those of his father.

"Son, I love you. I will always love you. But I have never been more ashamed in my entire life." With tears in his eyes, Denton calmly slapped his only son across the face, leaving behind the imprint of his hand. "Tom, I don't know who taught you to act like that or talk like that. It wasn't me. It wasn't your mother. You are an adult, son. You are eighteen years old. If this is the man you want to be, that is your choice. You can't be this person and be my son. Go home, pack your bags. If this is who you are, you can't live in my house. You've already abandoned us and everything we love. You might as well make it official. I love you, Tom. Goodbye." He grabbed the boy, and kissed the bruise that was forming on his face. He released him, and pointed to the lockers.

"Go on, son. You aren't welcome here anymore."

Tom Denton left the gym while the team wiped Calvin's blood up off the floor.

Turner was at school the next day. His face was swollen, and he had received a nice gash to go with his cracked nose, but his wounds would heal. Tom Denton was not at school, and no one knew where he was. The team did not talk about what happened. Rumors were flying that Denton had beaten up Turner and gotten expelled, but no one knew for sure. The kids who had seen it were too disturbed to have much to say.

Dale was disturbed as well. The incident left him sickened. He could not settle himself. None of the other players had noticed that he almost lost control. They had been too focused on Tom and Calvin. Still, he knew. And he knew that Greg Denton knew as well. There is a door in everyone that when opened reveals just how dark the heart of man can be, and he knew that his had been flung wide. He had always thought of himself as a good man. The loss of that conceit troubled him.

Later that day, he addressed the team at practice. "I know most of you are still upset by what happened yesterday. I am too. Yesterday, a member of our team chose himself over his brothers. He was jealous because he didn't care about what was best for you, only what was best for him. He acted in cowardice and ignorance. He failed every one of you. I'm sorry for that. Now is a moment for all of us to make a choice. We saw real ugliness here yesterday, and we have to choose whether or not we are going to rise above it. If anyone has any questions, or anything they want to say, now is the time."

Al Alberts, whose family attended Denton's church, spoke up, "Where is Coach Denton?"

Dale did not strictly know the answer to the question but felt comfortable saying, "Coach Denton is with his family. They have some things they have to work out."

He wished he knew the real answer. The night before, practice had ended abruptly as Dale accompanied Calvin to see Doctor Daniels, the local GP. Denton was in no condition to continue practice and gently waived the boys off the floor. That was the last time anyone had seen him. Dale had tried calling him but there was no answer.

The rest of the Q/A was a blur to him. Yes, Turner is ok. He'll take a few days off practice, but should play Friday. No, Tom has not been arrested to my knowledge. No, I don't think it will come to that. Yes, he has been kicked off the team.

Finally, Sean Knorr stood up and provided a natural close to the mid-court meeting. "Coach, can I say something? I want to apologize to Calvin. Tom's my best friend, and I've treated you pretty bad this year. What he did to you...I'm sorry man. I didn't want nothin' like that to happen. Sorry." He lowered his head slightly as he finished.

Turner just looked at him without answering. He let Sean stare at his deeply bruised and bandaged face before bobbing his head ever so slightly. It was as much absolution as he was prepared to give out just then. Knorr nodded back.

Practice dragged on like a sleepwalker's ballet. Calvin could not participate for a few days and would be fitted for a face guard for Friday's game. Dale told him he could go home, but he stood off to one side studying the action on the floor.

It was a difficult practice, but Dale was pleased. He suspected that the team would rally some once Turner could participate again. As he watched the team work out, it occurred to him that all his plans for the season were wiped clean.

Denton was never going to play with the team again or fulfill the role Dale had laid out for him. Without him, they could win some games, but the dream of making a run deep into March was dead.

He wondered if he should call or stop by the house. Dale knew no etiquette for visiting a friend who had recently exiled his son. He wanted to comfort the Dentons, but that was a task well beyond him. The events of the last twenty-four hours left him feeling lost, and subconsciously he understood that lost people have a better chance of surviving when they stick together. He pulled into their driveway, took slow steps up to the door, and rang the bell with leaden arms. He had no plan, no speech prepared.

Sue Denton came running to the door with puffy eyes. Her smile almost covered her disappointment when she realized who it was. Then she surprised Dale with a big hug, and said "Greg is in the living room. Come on in, please." She left the two of them to talk while she reflexively went to fix some coffee.

Greg looked up at Dale with a soft smile, and gave him his hand to shake. Dale took it. "Thanks for coming by, Dale. It's been a hard day for us."

Nothing he could say would sound natural or useful, so Dale tried to stick to sentences of less than five words. "Yeah, I imagine so."

Denton knew the questions he wanted to ask and spared Dale the difficulty of finding an appropriate way to ask them. "Tom isn't here. I don't know where he is. I've lost my boy." He sobbed the dry tears of a man who has already cried more than his eyes will allow. The soul has a greater capacity for sorrow than the flesh.

Dale said nothing. Anything he could say would only cheapen what the man was suffering.

"Are you wondering how I could do it? How could I send my boy away?" Dale had not been wondering that, but now he realized he should have been. He was so mad at the kid that the reality of his father's severe punishment never set in. Anyone less entangled in the situation would have found Tom's banishment draconian.

Denton answered his own question. "It was the hardest

thing I've ever had to do, but I'm not sorry I did it. I knew he was out of control. You know I've been trying to reach him for months in every way I knew how. He let hate get inside his heart and change him. He has always been such a good boy, but somewhere along the way I lost him. This was the only way I know to get him back."

Dale remained quiet. He let Denton continue. "He's convinced his parents are fools, that his teachers and coaches are fools. He's angry and violent. I have pleaded with him, begged him, punished him, spent time with him, and prayed for him. Dale, I saw his eyes when he hit that boy. There was murder in them."

The words burned. Dale spoke. "Greg, I think there was murder in mine too." Protestant ministers do not hear confessions, but to Dale it felt like an unburdening. As Denton sat and pondered his words, Dale wondered what penance was coming.

Denton's eyes were kind. "When we see something truly evil, it reminds us that inside we are grotesque. Every one of us has a warped morality in our hearts, and we find ways to pervert even noble things like justice. What Tom did was an offense against the soul of everyone there. He assaulted his brother and then murdered him with words. Your anger was only natural. That means, of course, that it was corrupt and wicked as well."

Dale did not want to make the Denton's pain all about himself, but he was too troubled to stop himself. "Well, I'm just glad you were there to save your son."

"No, Dale. I can't save my son. He's passed out of my hands. I was only trying to save you."

The swelling in his face had gone down enough to allow Calvin to play in the game Friday night. As Dale hoped, his return to practice on Thursday had a positive effect on the team. There was relief and restoration in the air. Whatever collective responsibility they all felt for what Tom had done and said,

Turner released by returning to the floor with the same intensity and flash that he had shown before.

Greg Denton also returned to the court after his brief absence. He pulled Calvin aside before the game and said something to him that Dale could not hear. Turner did not look at him and merely replied, "Yes, sir."

"What did you say to him?" Dale asked when Denton took his place beside him during the introduction of the team.

"I told him to play with love in his heart and not hate."

Dale gave him a quizzical look. Denton did not elaborate.

As the game got under way, the meaning of the pastor's advice became clear. Turner was a force of destruction on the court. His play was brilliant as usual, but it was altered somehow. He never got his chance to drop Tom Denton after he cracked him in the head. He laid there on the floor, woozy and bleeding while the bastard walked away. Now his fury churned inside and the unwitting recipient of all his frustration was whatever poor kid he lined up against that night. He was going to ensure they won the game, but he was also determined to foul out and make each one count.

His was a controlled burn. He would drain jumpers, steal passes, lead fast breaks, and then inexplicably body check his man into the first row of the stands. The kids wearing red and black were going to be black and blue by the time he was done. He had five fouls to give. Every one of them would be hard.

Early in the game it was easy to overlook, but as his play on the court stretched the Invincible lead out past twenty points, his motives became clear. Dale benched him in the third quarter and sat him down next to himself. "That's three hard fouls on you, Ten. Do you want to win?"

Turner looked angry but said nothing. The question was insulting.

Dale pressed him, "If you are going to be as great as you can be, you have to lead this team now. They may not have followed you before, but you are the new captain of the Invincible Indians, and you have to care more about your teammates than yourself. That's what a leader does. That's what a winner does. So let me ask you, again, Ten. DO YOU WANT TO WIN?" He grabbed the front of Turner' jersey as he said it.

Calvin smacked the hand away. "No one is ever going to lay a hand on me again. Not even you, Coach." His glared eased. "But yeah. I want to win."

Dale turned away from his player. "Then play with love. Love your teammates. Love your opponent for forcing you to be your best. Love winning because it's good and right that the best are recognized for their hard work. Love the game, and thank almighty God you were born in Indiana. Now, get out there on the floor."

He played Turner the rest of the third quarter and for two minutes of the fourth. By then, the lead was large enough that he sat the starters. Invincible was 2-14. Calvin Turner Jr. finished the game with thirty-eight points and three fouls.

Chapter Fifteen

Homecoming

There was a pounding on his door. He did not know how long it had been going on because, like most sane people, Dale liked to sleep at three A.M. Monday morning. It took him five minutes to rouse himself enough to go answer the knock. He spent the entire time cursing and yelling at the lunatic who wanted him awake. When he finally got there, he wished he had stayed in bed.

Tom Denton looked like hell. Dale debated whether or not to slam the door on the kid's face, but for the sake of his father, he left it open. Tom did not say a word; he just stood there with his head down. He reeked of nowhere else to turn.

"Come in." he said begrudgingly. He flipped on a light he was not quite ready for and stumbled half blind to the kitchen to make coffee. He did not plan on offering any to his guest. "What are you doing here, Tom?"

"Please, I just need a place to sleep tonight." It was significantly less satisfying than what he had expected Tom to say.

"You have a home, son. Go there. I don't want you in my house."

"I can't yet, sir. Look, I know you hate me. You've hated me from the start, and that's fine. I get it. I deserve it. But I just got back to town, and it's freezing out there. I have no money, and I'll die if I sleep in my car. Please, Coach. Just for a few hours."

"I'm not your coach. Go home. Your parents are worried sick about you. You broke your father's heart; you know? I have too much respect for the man to let you stay here."

Tom had no fight in him. "Look, I'm messed up. I hurt Turner. I know it. I want to set some stuff right, but I can't go home until I do. Please, Mr. Cooper. Please just let me crash here. Just for tonight. I'll be gone by morning. I promise." Tears were running freely down his face.

Dale was not a merciful man. It was not part of his makeup. He felt no pity for the kid. He had seen and heard enough sob stories to last him a lifetime. People get their chance. If they blow it, they should face the consequences.

"Your father is one of the only friends I have. If the police found your frozen corpse tomorrow, I wouldn't shed one tear for you, but he would, and I'm not going to do that to him and your poor mother. Sleep on the couch. I leave for school at 6:30. I want you gone before I leave. I don't want to hear your story. I don't care what epiphany you've reached. My guess is that you'd say anything for a warm bed and a hot meal right now, so save your tears for someone who gives a damn. You could have messed Turner up for life, wounded his vision, fractured his skull. Don't think I'm forgiving you just because I don't want you to die on a night when I could have stopped it. If you need sleep, you'd better get it now. I'm going to bed."

He hoped his words cut Tom across the face. He hoped they made him bleed. He hoped they left him crumpled on the floor.

They did not. The kid was all bled out.

He said, "Thank you, sir," and lay down on the couch. He was asleep in seconds.

Dale debated whether or not to tell Greg Denton his son had shown up. He figured that if the kid was serious about going home he would be there soon, and if not Dale would just cause his friend unnecessary pain by letting Greg know he'd seen Tom. Then he realized that the boy's parents probably just needed to know he was safe and alive as much as anything. He called Denton when he got to school in the morning and related the whole story of the night before.

"Thank God, he's ok," was all Greg said before thanking Dale for being such a good friend. Dale decided right then that he never wanted to have children.

Denton was at practice Monday afternoon but had not yet heard from Tom. "Honestly, Coach, at first I was happy just to know that he's alive. I started to feel hopeful that if he came to you, maybe his heart had really broken. But fear eats at you, you know? It tells you lies and dares you to hope while threatening to punish you if you do. I started wondering if he was on drugs. It had never seriously occurred to me, but that story you told…it reminded me of a junkie trying to score. I keep praying, but it's hard to beat back the gnawing feeling in my gut that this isn't progress, but only a step toward some worse revelation."

"The kid was upset, Greg, but I don't think he was high. I think he's been living on hate for a long time. That's about as strong a drug as there is."

He blew the whistle to start practice, working heavily on the full-court press, but his heart was not in it. Seeing Tom the night before had reminded him of the real life beyond the court.

Not that life on the court was much solace. Without Denton at the point, they had little chance to beat Plymouth on Friday night. Plymouth was an elite team, ranked in the top five in the state. Calvin would make the loss respectable, but deeply flawed teams do not beat top schools on the road. All those weeks Dale knew the team was going to lose, he kept his heart in the practices because he knew they would pay off. Now he could finally do everything in his power to help them win, but he knew it was a lost cause.

After practice, Turner approached him. "Coach, can I come over to your place to watch some tape of Plymouth? I know you got film on them, and I know it's going to be a tough game. I want an edge."

All season, Turner had asked little of his coach other than the chance to win. Dale did not particularly feel up to company that night, but he was not about to refuse the kid anything. "Sure. Come over about eight. I've got some film on them from last year, and a game tape or two from this year. I'll teach you how to break down film. It's more than we can do all in one night though, so don't be disappointed if we don't get far."

"Anything that will help us win, Coach. I'll be there."

Dale went home, cleaned up his place a little. He already had the tapes ready because he had started on them early Sunday morning. He was glad that Calvin was pushing him. He needed to be pushed not to take a night off.

Eight o'clock came and went. Calvin Turner never showed up. He never called. Dale was surprised, but figured something had come up at home. He was sure it was no big deal.

There was a soft rap on his classroom door during his first prep period. He looked up to see Calvin standing in the hall. "Hey, Ten. Aren't you supposed to be in class? Why didn't you show last night? I thought we were going to watch some tape."

"I'm out on a bathroom pass, Coach. I need to talk with you. Something happened last night." Dale's look gave him permission to continue. "Tom Denton came to my house after I got home from practice."

Dale was furious. "What the hell did he do? Did he threaten you? Did you call the cops? Where is he?"

Calvin spoke slowly, but not without conviction. "He's at my auntie's house. I told him he could stay there."

"Why in God's name would you do that? Are you crazy? That kid should be in jail for what he did to you. How could your aunt and uncle let him stay there?"

"Simple. I never told them he hit me on purpose. They know he's my teammate and the pastor's kid. They know he's in some kind of trouble. They were happy to let him stay. I told them it was ok."

Dale sat silently in total disbelief.

"There's more, Coach. I want you to let Denton come back to the team."

Shock displaced the rage. "NO!" He shouted before remembering where he was. "There is no way in hell I'm letting that kid back on the team after what he did, not only to you but to everyone all year. He's playing you, son. He's a punk who got scared out on his own and now wants to get his old life back. No way. He's done. How could he ask you to ask me that? Why the hell would you?" For the first time in their association he was angry with Turner.

Calvin was unfazed. "He didn't ask me to ask you coach. He said some things last night to me. Whatever was between us, I'm willing to forgive."

"That's fine for you Calvin. I applaud your generosity of spirit, but my job is to run a team. First, he should be expelled from school and face criminal charges. Beyond that, I'll never let him step foot on that court again, as long as I have anything to say about it. What kind of a message would that send to the team? No way. No."

"He's not asking, Coach. I am. He didn't say nothin' to me about the team yesterday. He said he knows he needs to get you to forgive him too. Says you are pretty mad at him. I don't think he wants to play, but I want you to ask him to come back."

"Why? Why should I do that?"

"Because I want to win. That's the only damn thing in the world I want, Coach. I want to win. We need him. We can't go far enough without him. I want to get into a good school, and I need a point guard who can show everyone how good I am. I want everyone to know that I'm the best player on the best team in Indiana. All I want is to win. Denton is different, Coach. He cried in my living room last night. He begged me to forgive him. I think he can help us now. Please, Coach. You owe me this."

Dale did not know what to say. Letting Tom come back was impossible. He sat quietly, and squinted at the back wall of his class room.

Turner pressed him. "Listen. At least let him come talk to you in person. If he asks to come back, say no, whatever. That's fine. But if he doesn't, and you think he's changed, ask him to suit up. For me. Please. Just let him come talk to you."

Dale had no interest in talking to Tom Denton ever again. He had less interest in forgiving him. Still, he knew that Calvin Turner had less reason to do either than Dale did. "Get back to class. Tell him to come by my house after practice. I'll hear the kid out."

"Yes, sir," he said as he left the room, and Dale thought he could see a grim smile on his face.

He ran the varsity practice that afternoon by himself. Denton called the school to say he would not be able to attend that afternoon. Dale assumed that meant that Tom had come home. He supposed that was a good thing. He was not looking forward to sitting down with him that night. It was too much for him to believe that in just one week Tom Denton was a different person.

He had never thought of Calvin as naïve, but he was still young, no matter how much maturity he displayed. People were too soft hearted, too quick to sweep things under the table and move on. Actions had consequences. It was fine for the boy's father to take him back. It was admirable that Turner would forgive someone who attacked him. They both had that luxury. Dale, however, represented the establishment, the school. He could not look the other way just because a kid got weepy with him.

He arrived home to find Tom standing in his yard. He looked to be in better shape than the last time he had seen him. He had been waiting by the coach's door in the February air for at least a half an hour. "Hello, Tom. Come inside," Dale greeted him.

"Thank you, sir. Thank you for letting me talk with you."

They entered the house. "Would you like some coffee, Tom?"

"Yes, sir. Thank you, please." His earnest politeness was repulsive.

Dale recognized that he had already softened toward the young man. Two nights ago, he would not even have offered him a cup of water. The realization helped him keep his guard up. It is always easier to be angry at a person who is absent. When someone seeks to make peace face to face, there is a natural tendency to relax, to seek a way to minimize the conflict. Dale promised himself he would not give in to that urge.

"So, Tom. Have you seen your parents? If you haven't, I want you to understand that we have nothing to talk about."

"Yes sir. I just came from home. My folks know I'm here."

Dale nodded. "I agreed to speak to you because Calvin asked me to. I respect him enough to do him this favor, though God knows why he'd ask it. So, if there is something you want to say, you had best say it. I'm a busy man." *So far, so good.* He was keeping his defenses firmly in place. Whatever scam this kid was pulling would not work on him.

"Coa…Mr. Cooper. I just wanted to come and tell you that I'm sorry for how I've treated you. I didn't respect you. I undermined you as coach. I'm sorry I hurt Calvin. My dad told me that no action has been taken against me at school yet since I disappeared. I just want to let you know that I will be back at school tomorrow so that you can do what you need to do. I expect to be expelled; I won't cause any trouble over it."

Dale masked his surprise with cynicism. "Expelled? You should be prosecuted."

Tom lowered his head. "Yes sir. I should. I went to see

Calvin last night and told him I would turn myself in. He told me he's not going to press any charges. He was nice to me. I don't deserve it."

"Tom…" He could not finish the sentence at first. Against his will, Dale felt his suspicion crack a bit. Curiosity was creeping in. For now, he held his ground, but he could feel it giving way beneath him. "Frankly, I find your change of heart a little sudden. What happened to you?"

Chapter Sixteen

Restitution

Tom Denton hated Calvin Tuner. He saw him as a threat. His grandfather warned him about black people time and again every summer. "They steal!" the old man said. Tom had never personally known any black kids growing up. Turner's arrival in Invincible upset the natural order of things.

All his life, Tom had been waiting to play for the varsity squad. Like most Indiana kids, Tom dreamed of leading the team to victories and scoring all the important baskets. Calvin Turner moved to town, and old Coach Anderson just let him join the team without trying out; he even put Turner right in the starting lineup. He could not stop talking about how this new boy was going to really change things. Denton was a team captain as a junior, but he was immediately forgotten in the enthusiasm over the 'athletic' player. From their first meeting, Tom had pegged Calvin as a rival, a thief, someone who would steal what was rightfully his.

When Coach Cooper came to town, Tom's worst fears came to pass. The new coach clearly favored Turner, and his decision to bench Tom cut deep. Anger filled him. He'd already hated Calvin Turner, but now it had grown much worse and that anger went far deeper than he realized. Tom held Calvin personally responsible for humiliating him in front of his own team.

On the day of the incident, Calvin had been delivering such a beating to Tom on the court that something in Tom snapped and all his buried rage rushed to the surface. After breaking Calvin's nose, Tom stared down at him, watching him bleed on the court. His only thought was to stomp, kick, and crush his enemy. His attack was not premeditated or calculated. He was a wounded animal, and he lashed out.

His father's slap cleared his head a bit. He had never laid a hand on Tom before that day, but that blow carried with it a lifetime of discipline. All the lessons his father had ever tried to teach him were in the palm of his hand. Somewhere inside, Tom knew. He knew how far he had gone. He knew how far he could go but was nowhere near ready to admit it. He was cast out, cut off. Sanity seeped back to his awareness, and he could do nothing but run.

So he left. He fled the gym, got in his car and drove. He went to the only place he could think of, to his grandfather, to Alabama. He drove all night, arriving 12 hours later. On the way, he did not even stop to eat. He got gas and kept moving. His heart pounded as he tried to imagine out a new life free from his parents. He had fantasized about it many times, but now that he was facing the reality of independence, he knew his dreams were sickly and false.

When he made it to his destination early the next morning, he did not receive the welcome he had hoped for.

"You on drugs, son?" was all his granddad said when he opened the door. Tom explained that he had "beat the shit out of a nigger" and that his dad had thrown him out of the house. Those were like magic words to the old man, who eagerly invited him in, crowing that his grandson had finally become a man. He made the boy some eggs from his hens, which Tom ate greedily before collapsing on the filthy couch.

Old Man Denton took Tom out on the town that night, parading him around the bars and showing him off to his old drinking buddies and Klan brothers. His courage was acclaimed by all the toothless old drunks in town. They were all the same kind of men. Angry, ignorant, bitter do-nothings rotting their remaining years away, eagerly hoping to drag anyone else they could grab down to hell with them. They were a sad and despicable lot.

Tom took no delight in their praise. For the first time, he saw his grandfather for what he was. He was not the kind old man who taught him to hunt and fish, gave him copies of Playboy and told him racist jokes. He was a lonely old wino that no one respected. As the night staggered on, Tom realized there was no future for him there. The town stank of slow death, and Tom was determined to run from it.

Tom had no money and nowhere to turn. He wanted out, but had nowhere to go. Home was not an option. He was too proud, too stubborn to own up to what he was, though in his heart, he already knew he was no better than those old men. He was ugly and evil and had beaten and mocked a better man. Knowing it was true was one thing. Facing it was another. He stayed the next day with his grandfather before slipping out and heading west.

The west was big and open and vast in Tom's mind. He was sure there would be a place to go and a plan to figure out. Cash was thin, but he guessed he could make it to Dallas. Maybe there he could find a job and…he never had much of a plan. He was just running until he could not run any more. He wanted to get lost somewhere where no one knew him.

He never got as far Dallas. Just as he crossed over from Louisiana, he hit a terrible storm. He tried to pull off the road, but skidded out into a ditch. It was the middle of the night, and his only recourse was to march through the mud and rain to a service station about a mile from the next exit. He knew his car was in bad shape, and fear consumed him. He had no money for repairs. He was stranded and alone. He even tried praying for a moment, but it was no use. He knew God was not listening.

He was a pitiful sight when he made it to the station. He had slipped on the embankment and was covered in mud, bleeding slightly from a small cut on his nose. The clerk called a wrecker, openly worrying about how filthy Tom would get his store.

The driver arrived, took one look at the mud soaked kid and shook his head. Harold Jones, the owner of the rig, was a kind man. He was an old man. He was a black man.

He asked Tom if he had anywhere to take the car. Tom, exhausted from the walk, the drive, and from his life, did not answer. He just broke down and cried. Whatever conceit and self respect he had left drained out on to the floor of that East Texas Gas N Go.

Jones looked at the young man, shook his head and said, "Jesus lives, boy! It wasn't that hard a question!" The pitiful mess left him no choice but to respond with charity. "Let me take you to my brother's shop."

Tom did not know why the old man took pity on him, but he was grateful for it. They towed the car to Jones' brother's garage in the middle of the night. Instead of asking the boy to pay for the tow, he asked if he had a place to stay. Tom had less than twenty dollars left and was forced to admit that he had nowhere to go.

Harold Jones invited him home.

For two days, Mike Jones, Harold's brother, went to work on the car while Harold and his wife Linda took care of Tom. They knew he was in trouble, and a long time ago, they had been kids in trouble. They asked about his parents. They talked to him about Jesus. They stuffed him with fried chicken and Dr. Pepper. The Joneses knew he could not pay for the repairs on the car.

To Tom, none of it felt like salvation. It felt like one more lie. These people took care of him, loved him, and Tom knew they would never have done any of it if they knew the truth about what he had done and why. They were trying to help him, but each kindness was an ember burning on his head. Their mercy was as irrational as his hatred had been. The difference was that the mercy went down easier.

When the car was ready, all they asked him to do was to go home because his mother was probably worried about him. They handed him a bag of sandwiches and a hundred dollars, making him promise to use it for gas to get back to Indiana.

He could not refuse them. He still had a soul after all, and after all they'd done for him, he could do the one thing they asked in return. He left their home in the same clothes he had arrived in. Linda had washed them clean.

Tom swore he would send them a check when he got home but was never sure they believed him. For all he knew, they were angels. It was the only explanation he could find. Never in his life had anyone treated him like that. He admitted that before the Joneses came to his rescue, he had never believed in God, but on that long road home from Texas the two of them came to an understanding. This time, Tom was sure He was listening.

Just seven days after leaving Invincible, Tom Denton came home broken and whole at the same time.

Stories are easy to invent. In and of themselves they mean nothing. Dale knew that Tom Denton might well be lying but believed him anyway. He had to believe him. The regret mixed with joy in the young man's face witnessed on his behalf. He meant every word he had said, Dale was certain. Tom Denton was still deeply ashamed. He knew that everyone condemned him; he did not blame them. He was willing to come home anyway.

Finally, after a long pause to collect himself, Dale said "So you spoke to Calvin last night."

Tom looked at him and said, "I don't want to talk about what I said to him. He didn't say much to me, but asked if I had some place to go that night. I honestly didn't, so he let me stay with his family. They are very nice people. I don't think he ever told them what I did to him."

"So your folks? They are glad to have you home, I'm sure."

"Yes sir. My mom just cried a lot." There was an awkward silence. Tom was acutely aware of the pain he caused his family and his eyes pleaded with Dale to not ask him any more questions on that line. When it finally became apparent that Dale was willing to grant him that small mercy, Tom spoke again. "I've taken up enough of your time. I am sorry, sir. I'll come by your room tomorrow so you can take me to see Principal Hershey. I do have one request, though."

"What's that, Tom?"

"Please allow me to come and apologize to the team. I'm done with basketball, but I owe it to them to look them all in the face and own up."

Dale did not want to allow it. The team had been through enough. Tom's problems were Tom's problems. He heard the boy out but did not want him anywhere near the team. "Tom, I respect that you are trying make things right. Just don't expect me to forgive you. Tomorrow, we go see Hershey. We'll take it from there."

Calvin had asked too much of him. Dale did not want to let Tom talk to the team, let alone rejoin it. Even so, he did more than wrestle with the decision. He went a full fifteen bare knuckle rounds with it. It was impossible to reconcile his own desire for justice with his firm belief that the boy was sincere in his change of heart. He could not resolve his need to maintain order on the team with the encroaching realization that in three days they were about to play an unwinnable game. He wanted to protect Calvin, but it was Calvin who was pleading with him to bring Tom Denton back to the team.

Before the first bell rang that morning, Tom arrived at Dale's door. Turner was with him. Dale stared at the pair and could not decide which was more striking: how different they were or how alike. He took a deep breath and, still unsure of what would come out of his mouth, said, "Tom, we aren't going to see Mr. Hershey. I want you to come back and play on the team." He was surprised at his own decision.

Denton looked confused and said, "No. No! I can't do that. I don't deserve that."

Dale cut him off. "What you don't deserve is to be forgiven for what you did. Playing for the team isn't a blessing. It's a penance. You owe Calvin more than just words. You owe him all your skills and as much hard work as you can give him. Look at his face. It's still bruised. You owe this young man. You have to come back. He needs a real point guard to show everyone just how great he is. You want to show everyone how sorry you are? Well you don't do that by being a martyr of your own making. You do it by hitting the floor and undoing everything you did this season."

Tom turned to look at Turner, "Do you want me to play?"

Turner was expressionless. "Let me talk to the team today, Coach."

That afternoon Turner spoke to the players without the coaches present. Tom Denton was with him. Dale had no idea what he said to them, but when the team emerged to start practice, Turner came up to him with everyone else in tow. "Coach, we've voted to let Denton back on the team." There were no objections.

Dale nodded and for the first time in months, the five best players on his team practiced together.

Over the course of the next two days, the team was transformed. The biggest problem Dale had was figuring out how to help his second string deal with the first team. Finally, he had to send them six on five just to slow down Denton and Turner. There were two nights left before they faced off with Plymouth, and Turner spent the good part of both of them at

Cooper's house watching film. Tom wanted to come too, but had missed more than a week of classes. His parents had called him in sick, but he had a mountain of make up work.

Plymouth was bigger, longer, and deeper than Invincible. They were a seasoned club that already knew how to win, and they were playing at home. The only thing going for Invincible was the element of surprise. It is difficult to convince a group of high schoolers with one loss on the season to take a team with fourteen losses seriously. Dale knew going in that this game would be pivotal for Turner's scholarship chances. Plymouth had a highly recruited guard named Foster, and there would be scouts present. If people were going to start noticing Calvin, it would have to start that night.

From the tip, Plymouth was flat, and Turner was hot. That was just the recipe the Indians needed. With Denton actually setting Calvin up for open shots, Turner was unstoppable. Plymouth's best player, Marcus Foster, picked up two early frustration fouls as Turner abused him offensively. Every made bucket gave the Indians the chance to press the home team, and each forced turnover raised the confidence level. The Pilgrims tried collapsing on Turner on every possession, but Denton destroyed them by draining open jumpers. By half time, they were hopelessly behind, having been washed under by a confluence of their own overconfidence and Invincible's talent and game planning.

Dale left his first team on the floor until late in the game, despite a sizable lead. He had no desire to humiliate Plymouth, but it was his chance to showcase his star. Turner scored thirty-one points against one of the finest teams in the state. Denton finished with twenty points and twelve assists.

Dale knew the game was a breeze only because they snuck up on Plymouth. He also knew that this would be the last time that could happen. With a minute to go, he called time out, and pulled his two senior stars. He smiled as they walked off the court together.

Tom stopped in front of the bench before taking a seat. "Coach? He's great isn't he?"

"He's the best," was the only possible reply.

Chapter Seventeen

Fired Up

Three wins were not enough to make Dale any more popular around town. If anything, the stunning upset of Plymouth only served to frustrate people. There were just two more games until the tournament, and no one had done the math yet. Most people were still stewing over the loss of the Fiftieth Season and watching the team suddenly roll off a few wins only cemented the opinion that Cooper could have done more to save the season. After all, if the Indians could knock off a powerhouse like Plymouth on the road, surely they could have managed a record better than 3-14.

Now that he was confident of his team's ability, Dale was able to relax enough to find the angst amusing. Walking into school with Samantha, he let her in on his private joke. "We're going to win the sectional easily, Sam. What's funny is that I don't think anyone around here will even feel good about it.

How messed up is that?"

She laughed. She was glad he was able to laugh about the town again. Other than New Year's, they had not seen each other much. He was a fun guy to be around when he felt free to be sarcastic. But looking down on everyone requires a place to stand, and the losses had robbed him of his perch. Now that he was back on top, he was his old joking self. It was nice. She felt like she had her friend back.

"Oh, I don't know. I bet if you took home the state championship some people would forgive you…though not everyone. That old Mr. Knorr is determined to hate you no matter what. You know he's still trying to get you fired?"

He grinned. "I suppose we'll just have to finish .500 then"

She stopped. Ever since childhood she could not walk and do math at the same time. She grabbed his arm as she added up the record in her head.

"Wait…Did you…?" She laughed out loud. She could not decide what was more hilarious: that he set the whole season up, or that he thought it would work. "Dale, you are crazy," she said.

"Oh, right. Everyone in this town believes that destiny guarantees them a .500 record, but *I'm* the crazy one? Listen. You told me yourself that people here are convinced they are meant to go .500, right? So, maybe I engineered a circumstance where that belief will work in our favor. A team has to have talent to succeed, but they also have to believe in themselves. I couldn't have my kids going into the state tournament *convinced* they were going to lose because it was their destiny. Trust me, by the time I'm done with them, this team will face every game certain that God Almighty Himself has ordained them to win. And you know what…they are good enough to pull it off."

Her lingering smile faded. She said, "My God. You really mean it. You really think your kids can win state."

"Can you imagine what that would do to this town?" he said.

She had never considered it before. Now that she did, she was troubled. What if they did it? Winning a state title that preserved the Invincible Myth would encase the attitudes of the town in granite. People that were already slow to accept change would feel perpetually justified in believing that God or fate or George Washington or whatever minor deity they accepted was looking down on them with approval for their every action. The thought made her sick to her stomach. "Wow…that would be…huge for Invincible."

He was thrilled to finally tell someone what was going down. Everyone else in town still thought he was a terrible coach, but at least she would know the truth.

"I'm going to start pushing the idea on the team after Wednesday's game. We should take out Marion with ease, and that's when I'm going to tell them that they can't lose, that their destiny is to live up to the name on their jersey, that they can be great."

She was put off by his enthusiasm, but did not want to be unsympathetic. "Not to be too negative, but is another season of .500 ball really greatness? I mean, sure winning the title would be amazing, but something about this doesn't feel right. This team might have what it takes to win it all, but aren't you just dooming future teams to live down to the…myth?"

It upset him that she chose this moment to raise a moral quandary about his decision. "Listen, I don't care about the future of this town and this school. I'm done here after this season. Win or lose. I'm not built for life in a small town. My job is to teach these kids to play basketball and to try to win a title. That's what I'm doing. That's all that I care about."

Sam was aghast. "That's bull. Your job is to be a coach and a teacher. You have to show them there is more to life than living down to the expectations of a dying town. You are supposed to help them be great. Confusing greatness and mediocrity is… well, it's just wrong. Weaving an incredible accomplishment in with the backward attitudes of this place…that's not greatness. That's not teaching. You can't…" She wanted to cry, but did not. There were tears behind the anger in her eyes.

He did not know what to say. This was not the reaction he had expected. The first bell rang and she broke the silence by saying, "I've got to get to class."

He let her go with a nod, wondering at what point the conversation took a turn for the worse. He concluded that being friends with a woman was a bad idea after all.

Dale's words about Marion were prophetic. Invincible won comfortably by ten. The margin could have been greater, but the same lack of focus that had plagued the team all year crept in. Turner and Denton were unstoppable, but several of the others failed to give their best effort. Dale knew it was time to give the team something to believe in. They had to know they were not just playing out the string.

He asked Greg Denton to meet him for an early breakfast the next morning before school. They had not spoken privately since Tom's return.

"Your son seems like a different person, Greg," he said.

Denton just smiled and said, "Yeah. He does. Thank God."

Any more discussion of the subject was going to lead to tears; Dale may have had no clue when a woman was upset, but he did know enough not to press a buddy about his son in public. Denton's face told him what he needed to know. Details would have to wait. For once, Tom was not the reason for their meeting. Dale was still bothered by his conversation with Sam the day before, and wanted to talk to Denton one more time before springing the plan on his team at practice that afternoon.

"This is awkward. I'm going to ask you a religious type question, but not for the reason you might think." He had no desire to get into the whole "God-thing" with Denton. He had been to his church a few times and knew where the pastor stood. He respected him but was not ready for a 'come to Jesus' chat with the local minister. "I want to know if you believe in destiny…you know, fate."

Greg looked at him quizzically. Dale could see him trying to discern his intentions before he answered the question, so he clarified. "I don't. I believe we all do what we do. Each one of us is running his own ship. Tonight, I'm going to lie to my team. I plan on telling them that it is their destiny to finish .500 and win the state title. I don't believe that for a second. I believe they are good enough to win the title. I believe if they work hard and if they believe they can win it, they will have a great shot. But I will be lying to them when I tell them it was 'written in the stars' or whatever. Personally, I don't mind telling that lie, if it helps. I just want to know what you think about it. Is there such a thing as destiny?"

Denton was thoughtful. "Well, Coach, you know I believe in God. I believe he is sovereign and has decreed all ends for man. 'A man's heart deviseth his way: but the LORD directeth his steps', says the Proverb. So yes, I think God knows where all this is headed. He's the author of life. Surely the author knows the ending to the story he is telling."

The answer was what Dale expected, but it irritated him anyway. It was a bit preachy for his philosophical tastes, which typically dealt with such weighty matters as zone versus man to man. "Yeah, but can't the author ever change his mind and alter the end of the story if he likes the characters?"

"Oh, I think He'd probably like to, but in the end, God knows what is best, and always chooses the best ending over the easy or the happy one. Listen, do I think it is our team's destiny to win State? I have no earthly idea. I don't believe in witchcraft and divination, Dale. I don't know what God's plan is for our boys. I know he has one, but he hasn't seen fit to fill me in on any of the details. If you feel uncomfortable using the word destiny, then don't use it. You don't need to lie to them or tell them anything you don't believe. Just lay the facts out there and let the boys put them together. I'm sure it'll work out."

"Because you believe in God, and He always works things out?"

He laughed. "Well, I do and he does. But that's not what makes me so sure."

"What then?"

"Because I believe in you, and you are a great coach."

He positioned a wipe board at center court. As the players came out for practice he huddled them up around it. On the board was written the number fourteen. Everyone knew what it meant without having to be told. Then he asked them, "How many games do we have left?"

The first answer was "One!"

"WRONG!"

Then Aldridge said, "Two! We have the tourney too."

"WRONG!"

Sean Knorr said, "We don't know how many games we have left. It depends on how far we go."

Again, Cooper shouted down the answer. When it was apparent that no one was going to hazard a guess, he took a red marker and wrote "10" underneath the large fourteen on the board. "We have ten games left. We are going to win ten straight games and take the state championship. We are going to win fourteen games this year. Nothing can stop us. We are going to win FOURTEEN games." He let the words hang in the air as he team processed the implications of what he was saying. "From now on, we have one goal: to win fourteen games."

There was a race in the mind of every player. Two competing ideas sprinted for supremacy. In lane one, the impossibility of winning the title got off to a strong start. In the other lane, the knowledge of what fourteen wins would mean to the school and the town quickly caught up. Dale could see them working through it. One by one, they bought into hope even though it was ridiculous. The players started to murmur amongst themselves, and still Dale said nothing. He let the idea soak in. Finally, he caught Turner's eye. Convincing the team was a two man job.

Calvin got the message and said in a clear loud voice, "We have WORK to do. Everybody in!" The team huddled around him and put their hands in the middle. He started to chant. "TIME TO WORK! What time is it?"

The team responded as one, "TIME TO WORK!." Again, "Time to work! What time is it?" and they responded. Again, **"TIME TO WORK! WHAT TIME IS IT?"**

The huddle was bouncing; belief is contagious. They answered his call, and he closed the circle by saying, "FOURTEEN ON THREE. ONE, TWO, THREE: **FOURTEEEEEEEEEEN!"**

Wipe board math and chanting would not be enough. There was a missing element to the equation that only Calvin Turner could supply. As the team broke the huddle, Turner unleashed the full scope of his desire and talent at practice. He always worked hard, but that afternoon, he was possessed. He flew across the floor, animatedly shouting encouragement and instruction to his teammates. Every time a player made a nice shot or hustled for a ball, Turner charged over to him, bumping his chest and yelling, "You are going to be a champion!" Before long, every player on the court believed it. They were going to be champions, and Calvin Turner Jr. was going to make it happen.

The team had already been playing well since Turner's promotion back to the starting lineup and had been playing at a championship level since Denton's return, but in the history of basketball, perhaps no team has ever had two practices like Invincible High did before their last regular season game. The elite skills of Turner began to synch with a ferocious dedication by the rest of the team. Every loose ball was met with at least three bodies flying across the floor to corral it. Every drill was crisp and efficient. Every player ran the lines with abandon.

Snaking through the halls on Friday, word that the team was going to win fourteen games spread first as a rumor, then as a suspicion, and by the end of the day, it was a generally accepted fact that Invincible High was going to win the state title.

By the time the game rolled around on Saturday night, the animosity of the town was replaced with elation. The gym was packed for the last home game of the year. The temperature in the building topped ninety degrees as bodies were pressed into every corner. Principal Hershey could be overheard worrying that the county fire marshal was going to shut the school down, but he did not know that Fire Marshall Gary Marshall was already at the game wearing his red and gold sweater and cheering on the team.

That night, the come-what-may attitude of the fans was replaced by total confidence and supremacy. Carrol was an average team playing a school some ten games under .500. As far as the crowd was concerned they were but sacrificial lambs.

Their faith was rewarded. Turner shot an ungodly fourteen of fifteen in the first half, and Invincible never trailed. Their press was so suffocating that Dale called it off before half time because his team was already up twenty-five points. Turner, Denton, and Thompson did not even play in the second half, but the B players extended the lead out to forty points by the end of the game. Even Al Alberts had a good shooting night, finishing with eighteen points off the bench.

His team was as complete and ready as possible. It only took nineteen games, but in the last home game of the year, the Indians finally showed that they wanted to win as badly as their coach.

After practice on Monday, Dale stopped by Jack's Barber Shop. He was greeted enthusiastically by the patrons. Sectionals started in two days, and the town was gearing up for a last minute bonfire/pep rally on Tuesday. The confidence of the locals ran high, but more than a few felt that repeating the great bonfire of '77 only made good sense. Everyone in town was asked to come and bring some basketball related item to throw in the fire. It was hokey but harmless, and even Dale had to admit that it was nice to have the town behind him again.

Ben Gordon was in the chair when he arrived. Oddly enough, though Dale had suffered through two school board forums, including one in which Mr. Gordon had the power to decide his fate, he had never actually spoken to the man. Gordon was a political animal, or at least as much of one as Invincible could muster. He was the kind of fellow who relished the power that came with being president of a quasi-public educational oversight committee. He knew full well the coach was popular at the moment and was happy to let everyone in the shop know how he had supported him all along. Of course, if the team failed to win state and finish .500, he would have his ass fired. It was good to be king.

"Coach Cooper! Nice to see you! How was practice today? Do you have the troops all fired up for sectionals?" He was jollier than a tipsy mall Santa.

Dale cared little for general socializing, but he especially detested a schmoozer, and Gordon was clearly one. "Practice was great, Mr. Gordon. I think the boys are ready for Whitko. You know, they took us in a close game to start the season, but I think we are a much better team now. I like our chances." The two carried on as if they knew each other, but it was all pretense. Gordon did not think enough of Cooper to even bother being formally introduced to him. He had always expected Dale to fail, and Dale knew it.

"Well the boys certainly are playing well. It's too bad the new tournament didn't go into effect this year, we'd have the title all but won if we were playing at the A or AA level. As it is, it'll be a tough road. But I have to believe this is a team of destiny. I'm tossing in a photo of the '52 Indians tomorrow at the ceremony. That was my senior year. I'm praying these boys can live up to the legacy their dads and granddads left for them." It sounded like a board meeting speech; Dale wondered if he was carrying his gavel under the barber's smock.

He knew he should just let Gordon's comments pass, but he was incapable of doing so. "This team deserves its chance to face the best talent. Winning an A or two A championship would be demeaning to the talent of this team, or any team. The point of sports is to set yourself up against the best and see where you stand. The new tournament will be a disaster for the state."

In the corner, the checkers players looked up from their game. In unison they said, "Right, Coach!"

Gordon was displeased. As Jack applied the hot shaving cream to his neck, he scowled and took up the fight. "Don't you think as many kids as possible should know what it feels like to win? It's only fair that small schools should play each other. Under the new system, Invincible will be competitive for years and always have a chance at the sectional title at least."

"At what cost? If kids want to experience winning, I'll set up a game of Candyland here in the shop and let them beat me. Winning only matters when it means something. Why do the kids at small schools deserve a trumped up title just because their school is small? In all other sports, school size and the big money tilt the playing field. But in this game, it's five kids, ten sneakers, two hoops and a ball. The new system celebrates the average and tells kids it's ok not to be competitive if they are out matched. I think that kind of thinking is killing America. We are a society that would rather have trinkets than greatness." He knew he needed to check himself soon, but then again, he had no plan to hang around town past the end of the school year.

Gordon was at a disadvantage because his was the unpopular view; he did not want to risk alienating the other patrons, but nonetheless remained unmoved. "There's nothing wrong with wanting everyone to have an equal chance. Small school kids deserve to feel like they can be winners too."

Dale gave no ground. "They have the chance. They just have to earn it. This whole mess is really about segregation and money. Small rural schools want a chance to compete without having to worry about not having any black players. Private schools want to buy championships so they can raise more money. Nothing in this debate has anything to do with kids or with basketball. Small school kids deserve to feel like winners? No, they don't. They deserve to have the chance to take the floor like everyone else and prove they are winners. Everyone deserves the chance to lace up with the best and take an accurate stock of himself. That's the only chance we deserve as Americans. Nothing is handed to us. We ask for no advantage. If someone else is more talented, smarter, or harder working, then he gets the job. Whining about 'disadvantages' is un-American, and it is wrong. No, sir. I would trade a dozen Class A titles for just one shot to line up against the best team in Indiana just to see if we could beat them. We're supposed to teach these kids that courage is to look at themselves with honest, open eyes. Just because someone gives you a trophy doesn't make you a champion."

Jack was brushing the hair off the back of Gordon's neck, signaling the end of the hair cut. Dale had the room, so Gordon chose his final words carefully. "My concern is for this town and the kids of this town. You went to a big school. You think you know something about life here, just because you've coached here for five minutes and won all of five games? You don't know what it's like going up against bigger schools every year for ten, twenty, thirty years without having a prayer to even win your sectional. Your big talk sounds great, but not having hope is un-American too. This system has taken our hope, and I can't wait to have it back. Next year, things will be different." With that, Gordon paid Jack, tipping him well as always, and left.

The bonfire pit was located behind the school, adjacent to one of the soybean fields laying fallow in the February frost. The weather was cold but clear, so the volunteer firemen in charge of starting the blaze had no snow to deal with. The fire would soon take the edge off the night air. The 'Ceremony' as it was called around town drew almost everyone, though some of the older, more religious types did not participate because "it smacked of witchcraft."

Despite their fears, the evening had more in common with the last night of summer camp than with a scene from *The Coven*. The town was small, but people came not only from Invincible but Arland, Gilded Lake, Bolivia and the other small towns that surrounded them as well. The total crowd swelled well past two thousand, spilling out into the parking lot. As principal, it was Jim Hershey's responsibility to emcee the rally, but all the local 'dignitaries' insisted on standing on the portable bleachers the custodian had dragged out near the fire. The coaches and players were joined by Hershey, Ericksen, the school board, and for reasons no one entirely understood, Mr. Snider the history teacher.

Under a new moon and illuminated by lights from the parking lot and the yellow glow of the bonfire behind him, someone handed Hershey a microphone. "Good evening, ladies and, um, gentlemen of the Invincible Consolidated School District, We are so glad you are here with us for tonight's, um, 'ceremony.'" He actually made the little quotation marks with his fingers as he spoke. Dale suspected that Hershey was trying to make a joke.

Too bad there was no punch line.

"Tonight we celebrate together the fine young men who play basketball for our school, and show our commitment to them as, um, they begin sectional play tomorrow. Sectional play, as you all know..."

Ericksen, sensing that Hershey was about to deliver an elaborate history of the tournament, unceremoniously grabbed the mike from him, slapping him on the back gregariously. "THANK YOU SO MUCH, PRINCIPAL HERSHEY! FINE JOB!" he bellowed into the microphone. Hershey was confused, but not offended by the quick hook. He merely assumed he had not gotten the final memo with the updated order of ceremony for the evening. He appreciated Ericksen's compliment on his oration and contentedly hung near the back of the small army assembled on the bleachers.

Ericksen proceeded to introduce every member of the team and staff present. Finally, he announced the school board members and passed the mike to Ben Gordon to start the ceremony.

Gordon said, "I'm so glad you are all here tonight! In just a moment we are going to begin the 'Ceremony of the Flames.' Some of you younger folk may not know the story of how twenty years ago, the town imitated an old Indian rite of sacrifice on this very spot. The result was the '77 miracles which ran our streak of seasons without a losing record to thirty. Now tonight, we will attempt to invoke that same spirit of unity and encourage our boys to make it an even fifty!" The crowd cheered.

Dale found the speech ridiculous, especially the completely made up part about Indian sacrifices.

"Now, there's nothing spooky about what we are doing tonight. We aren't going to chant or anything like that. In a few minutes, each person will pass by the fire and throw in some item about basketball. Maybe it's an old school program, or just a note to your favorite player. It's our way of showing that we are all in this together."

Thaaaaat's right, Benny. Explain the hell out of it. Dale thought. The town finally did something original and meaningful, but instead of letting the moment hang in the air so everyone could enjoy a hint of something mystical, Gordon dissected it for them. Dale was beginning to regret that he had to be there at all until he saw the line forming near the fire.

People tossed in more than just scraps of paper. Old sneakers, knee pads, rims, backboards, anything they could find was set upon the flames. It took more than an hour for everyone to filter past the fire, and the entire time no one spoke. There was a solemnity to the process that not even a pontificating blowhard like Gordon could kill. Finally, after nearly everyone else passed by, the team took its place at the back of the line.

One by one, Dale watched his players walk up to the fire. Several threw in old trophies. Sean Knorr tossed in a poster of Michael Jordan from his wall. They put pieces of themselves into the common flame. They affirmed that they belonged to the community, some of them for the first time.

Dale was last in line, behind the two coaches and Calvin. He saw Turner clutching a photo of his dad with a basketball. Greg Denton, who good naturedly laughed off anyone who claimed the Ceremony was evil, had a picture of his son playing pee-wee ball. In a sickening rush, it occurred to Dale that he had nothing to put in the fire.

At first he justified his oversight, rationalizing that he had nothing to sacrifice because he had already put in everything he had. He had put himself on the fire. He came here. His life and reputation were at stake based on how the team did in the next few weeks. Why should he give up anything else? They already had all they were going to get from him.

But he knew it was a lie. He had no stake in this night. If the team lost, he would be disappointed for certain, but his life would go on. He would leave town and never come back. He would coach again in another place more suited to him. He was a talented young man and a good coach. His best days were ahead of him.

For the people of Invincible, Indiana, these were the best days. With the way small towns were dying, they might well have been the last days. Their whole identity was wrapped up with their boys following in their footsteps. It went beyond basketball. Maybe it was mediocre. Maybe it was far from greatness, but it was their lives and their heritage, and each passing year put it a little more in jeopardy. Each class that graduated was smaller than the last, and when they left they rarely came back.

He could mock these people and belittle their values, but he had to hand it to them. In their own way, in their own minds, they did love this team. As he drew closer, he could feel the heat of the flames and the stink of the burning soles of old Chuck Taylors. There was no faking this moment. He could not just toss in a stick or a blank scrap.

He reached into his wallet and pulled out a business card with Coach Collins' number at Butler. He grabbed a pen out of his jacket pocket and quickly wrote on it. The heat of the flames hit him full in the face as his turn arrived.

Dale Cooper was the last participant in the 1997 Ceremony. He threw in a business card with a hand-written note on the back. It said:

If we win…I'll stay

Chapter Eighteen

Madness

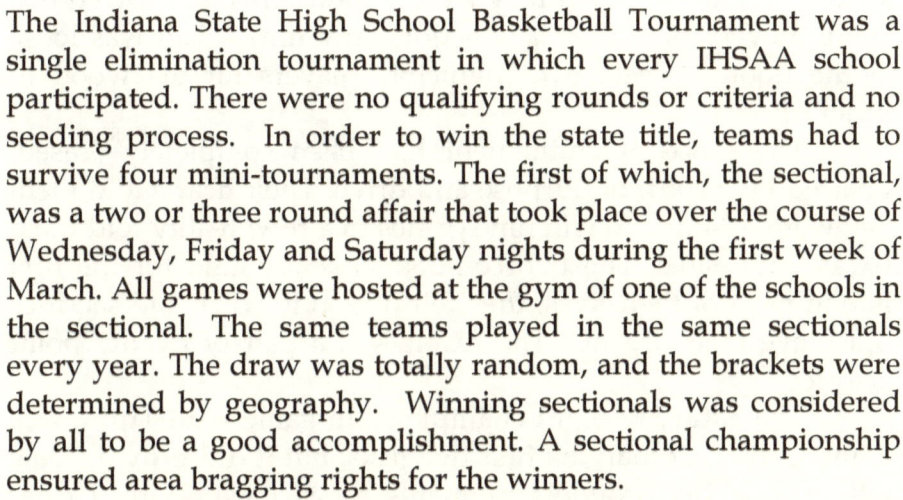

The Indiana State High School Basketball Tournament was a single elimination tournament in which every IHSAA school participated. There were no qualifying rounds or criteria and no seeding process. In order to win the state title, teams had to survive four mini-tournaments. The first of which, the sectional, was a two or three round affair that took place over the course of Wednesday, Friday and Saturday nights during the first week of March. All games were hosted at the gym of one of the schools in the sectional. The same teams played in the same sectionals every year. The draw was totally random, and the brackets were determined by geography. Winning sectionals was considered by all to be a good accomplishment. A sectional championship ensured area bragging rights for the winners.

Invincible drew Whitko in the first round. All three games were to be played at Tippecanoe Valley High School. Though he did not dare tell his team, Dale suspected that they would have an easy run through the sectional. They had already beaten Tippy, who was the best team of the lot. Moreover, he doubted many of the other schools would take them seriously. Whitko had defeated Invincible in the first game of the season, and had to like their chances against the small school with a 4-14 record.

In fact, the first two games of the sectional were significantly easier than Dale had even hoped. Turner played like a man possessed on both ends of the court, racking up huge scoring nights and accumulating healthy totals in all columns of the box score. The most impressive part of the first two nights was the turnout by the Invincible fans. The Wednesday game was completely sold out, and despite not having nearly the fan base of the other schools, the town made the drive out past Mentone and helped fill the seats from floor to ceiling. They were loud and enthusiastic, and the team repaid them for their dedication with inspired play.

Ever since Dale helped them draw the connection between their record and the number of games left to win the state title, several of the less driven members of the team had begun to play with abandon. Sean Knorr set crushing screens to free Turner for open shots; the three juniors who had spent most of every practice wishing they were somewhere else showed real emotion every time they saw action. Any time a ball was loose on the floor, at least two Invincible players hit the wood to retrieve it.

The sense of entitlement had been completely erased, replaced by a spirit of purpose and drive. Their hearts told them they were destined to win nine games in a row; reality told them it was impossible. The two collided violently, and for the first time in most of their lives, they felt driven to work and sacrifice to achieve their dreams. The result was a pair of twenty point victories.

The Saturday night championship game with Tippy was no more difficult than the first two tests, but it did provide Dale with one of his proudest moments as a coach. With Turner dissecting the Valley D to the tune of eighteen points before halftime, one of the Valley players showed his frustration. He fouled Turner hard on a drive to the basket, knocking him to the floor, and dislodging the facemask he still wore. As Calvin made his way to the free throw line, the young man who knocked him to the court muttered something inaudible as he passed. Turner stopped cold and turned to face the kid. At that moment, Tom Denton stepped in front of him and got in the face of the offender. Dale could not hear what he said to the player, but the official quickly separated the two, shooting a look at the coach, warning him to control his players.

Dale took the hint and substituted Denton out of the game. "What just happened out there?"

Tom's attention never left the court where Turner was draining his free throws. Without making eye contact with his coach, he said matter-of-factly, "I told Jethro over there that if he ever called Ten a 'darkie' again, me and the rest of the team were going the beat the holy hell out of him."

Dale's eyes widened a bit. "Oh. Good."

As it turned out, the only whipping administered was on the scoreboard. The Indians crushed Valley by twenty-eight points, easily winning the sectional title for the first time since 1947. Their record stood at a sparkling eight up and fourteen down.

After the game Saturday night, the team was greeted with universal acclaim in Invincible. Dale had assumed the whole town was at the game, but when they arrived back to the school parking lot, there were scores of cars. The gym was full of people, many of whom left the game right as it ended to race back to Invincible ahead of the team. When the players arrived, Ericksen noisily ushered them inside to meet their adoring fans. People took pictures with them; kids asked for their autographs. Like astronauts returned to earth, they were marched through a canyon of heroes. Nine of the original "Champs" from 1947 still lived in town, and lined up for photos with the boys.

The scene moved Dale. If the town was this excited over a sectional championship, he wondered how they would top it if they brought home the regional title the next weekend. People congratulated him in masse. Old man Knorr hunted him down and grabbed him from behind. He spun Dale around, and clutched his shoulders. There were tears in his eyes as he said, "Thank you, Coach."

Dale looked at the man who just weeks before had tried to run him out of town, and said, "We're not done yet." The title had purchased him a full pardon after all.

He grabbed a microphone that had been set up and called his players together. In front of the whole crowd, he told them, "Remember this night and this feeling, boys. This is what hard work and sacrifice do. They bring joy to the ones we love. Tonight, we share our championship with everyone else in Invincible. We play for them. We owe them greatness. Promise me something guys, with the whole town as witnesses. Promise me that tonight won't be the greatest night of your lives. We still have a lot of work left to do."

Calvin Turner stood up. He called to his teammates, "WHAT TIME IS IT?"

They responded in one voice, "IT'S TIME TO WORK!"

Wearing dress clothes and shoes, they took their place along the baseline, as if to run a suicide. "We are ready to work, Coach. Clear out the crowd, and we'll practice right now."

The cheers were deafening.

Samantha Lawson grabbed Dale Cooper in the hallway on his way out of the gym. "Big night, huh, Coach?"

Something about her tone reminded him of his first day in the building. He was flummoxed by her then and had not forgotten how that felt. His response was eloquent. "Uh, yeah. Big night."

She had a guilty look as she continued. "Listen, Dale, I just...I just wanted to say thanks for tonight. It makes me happy to see so many people that I love this happy."

Something was bothering her. For once, Dale could tell. He said nothing, letting her work it out on her own. Silence was his only hope to avoid saying something stupid anyway.

She looked away from him as she continued. "This year was rough for me. Tim's been gone. My mom's health is bad. It's made me do a lot of thinking about my life. All that time, you've been here every day. You're the first person I've ever been friends with who lived in Invincible, but wasn't from Invincible. I've watched you struggle so much with this town and these people. All year, it forced me to take a step back and ask myself what *I'm* doing here. Why would I want to stay here? You know?"

Honestly, he did not know. He had no idea where she was going with this. The hallway was dim, and he thought she might be crying a little. She went on, "I was mad at you for your little plan. I was mad for all kinds of different reasons. It made me mad that you were manipulating people's beliefs and emotions. It made me mad because I was afraid you might let them all down. Then I was mad because I was afraid you might actually pull off your little stunt, and that would set everyone's mind on being average forever. To be honest, that still bothers me. But that's not even the point. The point is that I realized what was really making me angry. When this tournament ends, no matter how it ends, you are leaving Invincible, and I am staying here. I think maybe I hated you some for that."

Where is she going with this? Where do I want her to be going with this? he thought.

"Tonight, though…tonight was like every Christmas and every fourth of July I've ever spent here rolled into one. I've known some of these people all my life, and I've never seen any of them this happy, certainly not all at once. There has never been so much joy in this place. Not even the time that squirrel was electrocuted."

She laughed just enough to reveal she was crying. "I think that so much had gone against us all for so long, that we forgot what it meant to win. This town has been dying since before I was born, and each year they managed to hold the line was a victory. But not dying isn't the same as living, is it? Tonight, we all *won* for the first time in a long time. It showed me something. I love. I love…" She sobbed a little bit.

He held his breath while she caught hers.

"I love this town," she finally finished as tears tumbled freely down her face. "I love these people. Seeing them happy reminds me who they really are. I think I had forgotten that, if I ever knew it at all. I forgot how beautiful it is that every old lady on Main Street held me as a baby. I forgot what it means to me that my kids will swing on the same swings in the same park that I did. I forgot what it means to belong to something old and delicate. I forgot what it means to share joy with hundreds of other people who all know precisely what a thing means to you. I forgot what it means to want to live here without having to." She paused and smiled. "You brought this to us. You gave this to me. You gave me something I didn't even know I wanted. Thank you, Dale." She kissed him on the cheek.

"You're welcome, Sam." It was all the response he had to give. She smiled and left him.

He stood alone in the darkened corridor, and prayed silently just in case God might hear him, "Please don't let us win State."

Cooper spent the week of the Huntington North Regional hammering home to his players that Saturday's games would not be as easy as the sectional games. They were matched up against Northfield in the morning game, but Dale knew the real challenge would be Plymouth, their likely opponent that night if they won. This was Regional play and there would be no sneaking up on anyone. Every team in a regional is already a champion, and no one is looking to wrap up their season early to enjoy a long summer off.

He drilled the team hard in the full court press through Wednesday but tried to save their legs in the last two practices.

Cooper's biggest challenge would be to meter out his substitutions effectively. For his team to have a chance to advance to the Semis, they had to commit to the press for the entire thirty-two minutes in both games. The fact that all the rounds from this point forward would be played in double same day sessions worked against the Indians. He would have to expand his rotations enough to secure the first game win without wearing out his big men so much that they would be ineffective in a second game later that night.

In terms of atmosphere, the regional was not much of a step up from the sectional. The games were still played in a gym, and the schools involved were not appreciably further away than the ones in the sectional were. Other than having to play Saturday morning and Saturday evening, no other special preparations were required.

As expected, Northfield represented only a modest test. As a team, they were no better than Tippy Valley, but they were more focused and had been coached about Invincible's press. They were overconfident coming in, and it was the last time a team would be blinded by their record. Turner and Denton played a ruthlessly efficient two-man game on offense, combining for fifty of Invincible's sixty-five points.

Their defense was what actually sealed the victory. Turner blanketed Northfield's best player, a 6'6" power forward. Dale made sure Turner covered him despite the height difference. Calvin's superior speed and hands gave the bigger man fits. Denton played physical with the point guard, picking up four fouls but intimidating him in the process. Invincible controlled play from start to finish, and cruised to a twelve point win. The lead was larger at one point, but Dale rested his starters for the final four minutes of the game to save them for the nightcap.

The format of the tournament forced a complicated postgame decision for Dale. Huntington was about fifty minutes from Invincible by school bus. He wanted his players to watch the second game but knew that doing so would make for a crowded afternoon. Instead, he and Denton stayed to scout the game between Plymouth and Warsaw, while the team went back on the bus. The second game would tip at eight p.m., and this allowed the players to go home and rest and eat instead of having to down fast food. As he watched Plymouth slug out a grinding 36-32 win, he felt good about his team's chances. Warsaw tried to slow the game down and succeeded in bruising the Pilgrims, though not in toppling them.

The two men drove back to Invincible after the game, because Dale wanted to be on the bus ride with the team later that night. They chatted about matchups for a few minutes before Greg asked him, "So, Coach, do you think we can win it?"

"Sure. It's our destiny right?" They both laughed.

"That's the prevailing opinion in that locker room. Those boys don't realize they aren't supposed to be winning these games."

"Tom and Ten are keeping everyone loose right now. Your boy played a hell of a tough game today. He almost took the head off of that little number twenty-two when he tried to drive on him."

Denton smiled weakly and kept his eyes on the road. "He still has a lot of anger in him. That hasn't changed."

"Yeah, how are things at home?"

The pastor set his jaw resolutely and nodded. "Things are good. Tom came home shattered, you know? Really shaken to his core. He's been very teachable, and I'm trying to spend as much time with him as I can, but I can see he's still upset about a lot of things."

"I don't have anything to worry about, do I?" Dale asked.

"Oh no. He'd take a bullet for Calvin now, but he's trying to figure out who he is supposed to be. Turner is the captain now, and everyone follows him, but Tom's a natural leader. He's not used to being the second banana. That part is still hard for him. We are working through a lot of things as a family. It's been good. I just thank God that He's given me a second chance to fix some of the things that were my fault."

It was all beyond Dale's ability to comprehend. "I never realized having a son was so hard."

Greg Denton laughed. "Yeah, neither did I."

Dale changed the subject. "Sam Lawson said something to me the other night that is bothering me."

Denton's interest piqued. "Yeah, what?"

"She implied that this plan of ours might be bad for the town. She mentioned it awhile ago, but I didn't really think about it until she repeated it. She thinks that we might doom the town to confusing being great with being average forever."

Greg smiled warily. "I think that the town's fate was sealed in that respect a long time ago."

Dale was unsatisfied. "Could we make it worse? Could we be hurting these kids by doing this?"

Denton shook his head. "Let your conscience rest. What's wrong with Invincible is bigger than basketball. We have a tendency to make sports more important in our minds than they are in reality. This town needs more than basketball to save it. It needs a time machine. It needs the world to roll backwards for a hundred years. No Dale, we aren't making it worse. Life is short. We have to find and give joy while we can. Right now, this team is bringing a lot of joy into everyone's lives. In my book, that's holy work."

The team arrived back at the Huntington North gymnasium with a massive caravan in tow. Every car was decorated with red and yellow paint and streamers. They filed into their seats loaded down with crazy hats, horns, cow bells, and signs that said everything from the predictable ("We are Invincible!") to the disturbing (No Thanksgiving for the Pilgrims! Scalp 'em!). The crowd arrived early, and their energy superheated the building. From the moment he stepped onto the sideline, Dale was swimming in his own sweat. His only consolation was that his counterpart on the Pilgrim's bench looked no more comfortable.

This second game between the two teams followed the script Dale had expected the first time they played. Plymouth had several advantages that they had failed to capitalize on in the previous meeting but operated much more efficiently in the rematch. They ran innumerable screens for their star guard, Marcus Foster, and made it difficult for Turner to stay with him. The Indians did a nice job on their switches, but every time Turner was forced off Foster, Plymouth's chances of scoring increased.

They still struggled with the Invincible press but not as severely as they had in February. Part of that was due to the play of Foster. He avoided foul trouble this time because his coach wisely chose to play him off of Turner. While it kept Foster off the floor, however, it was a green light for Turner to attack from every possible angle. He was a complicated assignment even for a team's best defender, but for a lesser player he was impossible to guard. By halftime, he already had twenty-four points and had managed to get most of the Pilgrim front court in foul difficulty. Invincible led by two at the break in a high scoring game.

Dale knew the third quarter would be the test of his team. Denton and Turner played the entire first half, and he had to give them a breather. He staggered their substitutions, giving Alberts and Adams three minutes of game time each. Turner glared at him every moment he was on the bench, his eyes demanding that his coach put him back in.

Finally, Cooper glared back at him and said, "Take your rest, Ten. You'll need it."

Three minutes to end the third quarter was all he could afford to rest Turner, though he tried to extend it by calling a time out with :45 to play. The end result was that Plymouth took control of a tie game and opened up a six point lead. It could have been worse, but Denton smartly worked nearly a minute of time off the clock when he was on the floor without Turner. They had only eight minutes to secure a spot among the sixteen best teams in the state.

Fortunately for Invincible, they had Calvin Turner. He played a brilliant quarter of ball, eschewing the drives, dunks and mid-range jumpers he had favored for most of the game, instead opting for three point shots. The Plymouth defenders had been giving him increasingly more space because they feared his first step off the dribble, and he abused that sliver of daylight to the tune of four threes in the fourth. He tallied forty-four for the game. Still, Plymouth hung tough, and with :25 to play, Marcus Foster picked up the fifth foul on Thompson for a three point play to tie the game.

In the timeout, Dale surveyed his players. He had already lost Knorr to fouls a minute earlier, and he knew that his team would not likely survive overtime with only Stevens and Aldrige in the middle. He drew up the backdoor option play, and looked straight into Denton's eyes. "Make the right play, son. You two have to be on the same page." Turner and Denton did not look at each other but only at Cooper. They both nodded.

There is only so much a coach can do. He can teach and train. He can draw up and call plays, but once the timeout ends and the huddle breaks, the ball is placed in the hands of a seventeen-year old kid who has to inbound it to an eighteen-year-old. Then five teen agers have to be trusted to do what they are taught to do. Dale was glad he had no more timeouts left because privately he started to panic. The play relied on screens by Knorr and Thompson who were sitting uselessly on the pine. He began to wonder if it was even the right call at all. It was out of his hands though, and that afforded him some peace.

As the clock wound down, his worst fears about the play materialized. Aldridge did not pose the same threat as the 6'10" sophomore he replaced, and his screen was not as tight. With the clock under :10, the entire defense began to converge on Turner as if he was exerting a special gravity on the court. Plymouth was not going to let him win this game, and as he made his cut, Dale could not tell which way he was going to go. There was a man waiting for him low, and two men high. His point and shooting guards made eye contact and instead of cutting, Turner stopped, planted and jumped straight up into the air.

The entire Plymouth team reacted to his movement and collapsed in upon him as Denton pumped a pass. His own defender's eyes followed the hypothetical flight of the ball, temporarily leaving his responsibility. Tom Denton pulled the ball in and put it on the floor. He easily drove past the Pilgrim assigned to him and let fly a soft floater in the lane. It kissed the glass and slithered through the net with ease.

His teammates buried him; Turner was the first to tackle the hero. The bench exploded. By a score of 66-64, the Indians qualified for the Fort Wayne Semi-State.

After the dog-pile lifted, the teams shook hands. Turner embraced Foster and congratulated him on a great game. Plymouth's coach took the time to tell him that his was the finest performance he had seen from a high school player since Scott Skiles graduated. There was no higher praise possible in his mind.

Greg Denton grabbed his son and wept on the court. He held the boy fast and repeated, "I'm so proud of you" several times. As the jubilant team finally cleared the floor after cutting down the nets, Dale pulled his point guard aside. "Hell of shot, Tom."

The young man smiled and let out one last "WHOOO," pumping his fists.

"How did you know the D was going leave the lane so open?"

"Ten told me, Coach."

Dale gave him a puzzled look.

"Just before the pass, he signals me with his eyes where he's going to go. If he looks back, he's cutting in. If he looks in, he's cutting out. He just looked at me, and then looked straight up. He knew he wouldn't get a look."

The coach laughed. "Enjoy this. When you come back from college some day, you'll never have to buy a drink in this town. You're the hero of the Huntington Regional for the rest of your life. Just remember, every year from now, that shot gets about two feet longer. When you're seventy, it'll be a full court desperation heave."

"No way, Coach. When I'm seventy, I won't even talk about this game. I'll be too busy telling stories about how much ass we kicked in the finals."

Chapter Nineteen

Highly Recruited

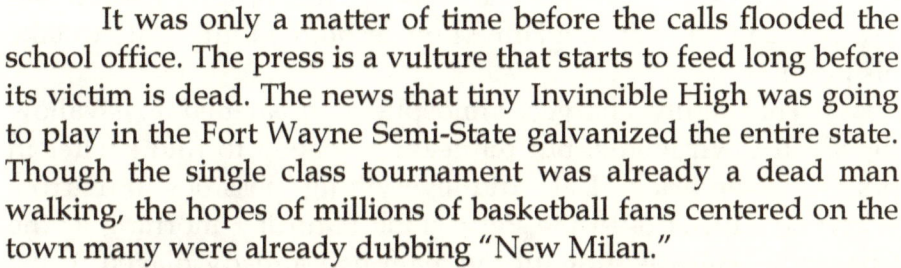

It was only a matter of time before the calls flooded the school office. The press is a vulture that starts to feed long before its victim is dead. The news that tiny Invincible High was going to play in the Fort Wayne Semi-State galvanized the entire state. Though the single class tournament was already a dead man walking, the hopes of millions of basketball fans centered on the town many were already dubbing "New Milan."

Superintendent Ericksen was so excited about the media coverage that he hired a substitute to cover all Dale's classes for the rest of the tournament to make sure he had time to fill as many requests as possible while still having a chance to game plan. Dale was no media hound himself, but he welcomed the attention. He used it to promote Turner, and to a lesser extent Denton, as much as possible. Calvin had quietly put together an unprecedented scoring run and had caught the eye of the press and scouts.

Turner was instantly the hottest commodity in high school basketball. Rarely is a blue chip senior unsigned just days before his final game. Universities typically push for commitments from kids as juniors or even younger. Turner was so completely beneath the radar that when he finally appeared on everyone's scope, the rush to sign him quickly became a crush. Coaches from Syracuse, Duke, Arizona, and Kentucky were already calling the school. Bob Knight himself was rumored to have called the Walker home personally on Sunday.

It did not take the scouts long to find Calvin's mother, either. Linda Turner was so hounded at work by press and recruiters that she was forced to come to town with her other son to stay at her sister's home. Anyone and everyone who knew Calvin Turner was a target for those looking to ply their influence on the young man.

Dale was popular among the college ranks as well. He was indirectly offered a pair of plum assistant jobs on the condition that he convince Turner to come along with him. It became increasingly difficult to maintain focus and think clearly through the din. He called his mentor, Coach Collins at Butler, for advice but did not get the answers he was seeking. Instead, Collins let him know he was leaving the program for a Big Twelve job and that he planned on recommending Dale to take his place.

The highly charged atmosphere threatened to swallow the small town whole, but the team managed to find shelter in practice every day. Dale did everything possible to narrow everyone's focus onto the Peru game Saturday morning at the Coliseum. He was grateful the team had already played in the building earlier in the year, because he knew they would not be intimidated by the setting. He encouraged his team that Plymouth was good enough to win it all, and that if they could beat them twice, they could play with anyone. As much as possible, he kept things normal in practice, knowing that fear was the first opponent that had to go down.

The Semi-State level was entirely different from sectionals and regionals. Teams were pitted against schools they rarely faced. The squads were only known to one another by reputation or by their place in the state media polls. The games were played at classic venues like Hinkle Fieldhouse or Mackey Arena and were usually televised locally. On top of everything else, the players became painfully aware of just how close they were to playing in the Dome in Indianapolis. The culmination of their basketball dreams was in reach, and it was easy for a team to get swept away in the emotion of the experience.

Meanwhile, the town itself was ablaze like a maple grove in the fall. Red and gold engulfed the windows and doors of Invincible. Every house in town sported streamers, and every car, pick up and tractor gave some indication of support for the boys. The banner was strung up across Main Street again with the message INVINCIBLE FOR FOUR-NINE. They were proud of their team, but no one was ready to tempt fate. It all fed into the media machine as rumors of destiny echoed throughout Hoosierland.

They were everyone's last, best hope for a happy ending.

With all the attention, Saturday came quickly. Oddly enough, the boys were calm. To them, the mere fact that they were playing in the Semi-State confirmed the miraculous nature of their mission. Reaching this level had been beyond most of their wildest dreams before the season started, but now they knew they were meant to be there. The team was loose and joking around as they entered the locker room to dress for the game. Only Turner seemed grim.

Dale noticed he was uneasy, even for him. He pulled him aside and asked, "You ok, Ten? Nervous?"

Calvin replied softly, "My momma is here." He looked up. "Coach, she's hasn't seen me play since I left Gary. It's been a couple of years."

Dale smiled, "I imagine she's proud of you."

The player looked down. "It's been a hard week for her. She's afraid she might lose her job because she had to come out here. She's also worried that all the 'nonsense' is hurting my grades."

His body language told the coach everything he needed to know. "Listen, Ten. I haven't met your mom. But I know this. She loved you enough to send you to Invincible. She loves you enough to worry about your grades at a time when a lot of parents would be looking at you with dollar signs in their eyes. It sounds like she's had a hard life and wants the best for her boy. Go play your best; she'll be proud of you…even if she won't tell you afterward."

Turner nodded. He always followed orders. His father taught him well.

Whether or not his mother was proud of his efforts that day, she never said, but she certainly should have been. Turner was again the dominant player, hitting five three pointers, thirteen free throws, and netting thirty-nine points in the morning game. The boys from Peru proved to be the nervous ones, and the Indians put them down early. Invincible sported a seventeen point lead going into the fourth quarter, and after Turner drilled two quick threes, Dale was able to pull the starters and make sure everyone was rested up for the night game. The humiliation of the Summit City Classic was a distant memory, and Invincible advanced easily to the round of eight, raising their record to 11-14.

The team had lunch reservations at the Olive Garden, along with their immediate families. Dale finagled the seating arrangements so that he snagged a spot alongside the Walkers and Turners. Linda Turner was a striking woman, but her face showed that the last seven years had been hard on her. She had none of the carefree charm that her sister Anita possessed in generous quantities. As they sat down to eat, Dale apologized for intruding on their table.

"I'm so glad to meet you, Mrs. Turner. I was hoping to have the opportunity to get to know the woman responsible for this remarkable young man." As a recruiter, he had always considered himself 'good in the living room,' but she was not a woman easily susceptible to charm.

She eyed him. "Thank you, Mr. Cooper. My son has a bright future ahead of him. His grades are good." Her sister rolled her eyes.

Dale caught the vibe and went with it. "They are excellent. I had him in government class. He got an A. I haven't seen his SAT scores yet, but his GPA makes him a likely candidate for the Academic All-State Team."

She hesitated before responding, "Good. His father would be very proud of that."

"I hope I'm not out of place in saying this, ma'am. I know I never met your husband, but this young man is as fine a person as I have ever met. He plays better, thinks faster, works harder, and has more character than anyone I've ever known. Coaching him has been a true joy and a privilege. With his grades and his ability on the court, he will likely be able to attend any university in the country for free." Out of the corner of his eye, he saw Calvin smile.

"Hmmm. I'm all too aware. I had some bag man for one of those basketball factories offer me $10,000 on my way to work on Monday. I've gotten calls from agents, coaches, shoe companies, everything you can imagine. Everyone sees me, and they think I'm some dumb single mother who will sign her baby away for a song. My son could never touch a ball again and still go to college and make enough money to buy and sell scum like that."

Dale was disgusted by the tactics but not surprised. "That's terrible. You should report the men who did that. Still, basketball has a chance to make Calvin's life a little easier. He won't have to graduate with school debt." Trying to argue with her was a mistake.

"Easier? What makes you think I want my son's life to be easy? You said my boy has character. How do you think he got so much 'character' at his age? It wasn't from playing basketball, I can tell you that. That boy has had to work for everything! I'm glad for that, Mr. Cooper. His father didn't give his life for this country so that people would hand things to his son. He gave his life so his son could be free to work his behind off to be as great as he could. I love my son more than my own life, and that's exactly why I don't want him to have it easy. He's a special young man, and he's meant for better things than throwing a ball through a hoop."

The lunch was quickly jumping the rails. Calvin stared at his pasta. Anita Walker was sitting on his other side, and slipped her arm around him. Dale felt like he had to salvage the conversation, but feared anything he said would only set Mrs. Turner off again. Finally, he spoke up. "I understand. I wish all my players' mothers felt like you do."

He had her attention. He continued, "Your son is great at many things. It just so happens that he is possibly the best in the state at one of the least important of his talents. You have raised him so well, that while I know the rest of the world will look at him like a piece of meat, he won't lose himself in it. I think you can rest easy that Calvin is going to make good choices. Whatever anyone gives him, he'll earn. The basketball is just a tool in his hands, like a hammer or nail. With your guidance, he'll use it to build himself a life both his parents would be proud of."

She was the kind of woman who had no need to cry because her suffering was the kind that would not be assuaged by more tears. Even so, she let one tear escape. "Mr. Cooper, I believe he already has." With that admission, the tension at the table eased, and the talk turned to other matters.

More than in any of the previous matchups, the Indians were true underdogs in the night game. Kokomo had guard play nearly as strong as Invincible's and possessed a vastly superior bench and front court. Most importantly, they were a tournament tested team. They sported a 22-4 record, and had advanced to the Semi-State in each of the previous two seasons as well. They had paid their dues and legitimately felt like it was their turn to play in the Dome

Kokomo calls itself "The City of Firsts." Everyone else in Indiana uses one of its other names: "Not the Place the Beach Boys Sang About" and "The Giant Stop Light on the Way From Indianapolis to South Bend." The city had increasingly become a bedroom community of Indianapolis, but still remained part of the Fort Wayne Semi-State. It was curious because there was no reasonable route to drive from Kokomo to Fort Wayne.

Perhaps the only advantage for Invincible was the crowd. Though the entire population of Invincible and the surrounding towns barely made a dent in the Coliseum seating limit, the Indians' appearance in the final game drew huge numbers of fans from the Fort Wayne area. The drive from Kokomo to Fort Wayne was complicated, and the large turnout from Invincible and the neighboring communities meant that the overwhelming majority of patrons were squarely behind the little school with the superstar shooting guard.

The full court press did serve as an equalizer. Though Invincible had skated all year with sophomore Steve Thompson at center, his height was not enough to offset his lack of bulk against an equally tall senior center from Kokomo. There was no effective matchup that could contain the Wildkats' post play. By pressing the bigger team, Dale forced them to use energy running the floor. Because they were likely to score down low in the half court game anyway, giving up the occasional fast break was an acceptable trade off.

Their size complicated matters when Invincible had the ball as well. They patrolled the middle of the floor so well that Turner was forced to settle for outside jumpers. He was effective, but the bulk of his arsenal was limited. He found ways to get his points but mostly through steals and defensively generated lay-ins. Though the game stayed close, the team played uphill the whole night as they struggled to maintain contact with Kokomo who led most of the way by five to ten points.

There are all kinds of ways to coach a game. Some coaches stand passively aside and let their players play, confident that they have already done all they can. Others try to impose their will on the action, barking out plays and assignments every trip down the court. As a player, Dale had always felt he needed his coach to be calm and in control. Now that he had his own team, he understood how difficult that was. He was still learning to master his emotions and never look worried. Especially with high school kids, it was his goal to stay confident and positive at all times. It paid off that night. Outwardly he was upbeat though inwardly he was wasting away as the grim realization set in that his was not the better of the two teams.

Trailing by nine with just two minutes to play, Calvin Turner, the one thing Invincible had that Kokomo did not, finally broke through. He drained a twenty-four-foot three to trim the deficit to just six points. The Wildkats tried to wear down the clock, but with a minute to go Turner used his blinding speed to step in front of a pass, starting a quick outlet to Denton. Kokomo's guards recovered before Tom could lay the ball home, so he kicked out to an open Turner for another three, forcing a Kokomo timeout.

The rafters shook.

With no shot clock in high school basketball, Dale knew his team would be forced to foul. It would not be easy. The Wildkat guards were quick and well accustomed to running out the clock. He set up the press, instructing his players not to foul until the ball crossed the time line. Once it did, they were to trap the guards and force a pass to Reynolds, the big center. Thompson was to foul him, hopefully forcing a 50% free throw shooter to make a pair under pressure.

Knorr nearly forced a turnover on the inbounds pass, and Kokomo struggled to get the ball to half court, just barely beating the ten count. They killed about twenty more seconds before Turner finally deflected a pass out toward the middle of the court. It was retrieved by Reynolds who was quickly fouled. With just thirty ticks left, all he had to do was hit his free throws to turn out the lights on the Indians' season.

Dale hated these moments. It was unfair to force a kid to bear the burden of carrying his team. He was standing there on the foul line, asked to accomplish a task for which he was ill equipped, with all the pressure of his team, his school, and his community riding on his every toss. Dale knew what was going to happen and would not watch. He wanted to win the game, but it was torture to watch the young man stand there and brick two shots. After the first one clanged off the rim, he got Knorr's attention, and told him to call time out if he collected the rebound on the second shot. The final free throw was no closer than the first. Invincible had the ball and the chance to force overtime.

With thirty seconds to play, Dale called for a quick two if possible followed by a repeat of the same strategy as before. He made sure his players understood that they had to shoot before the ten second mark so that they had a chance for a rebound in case the shot was missed.

Denton executed the offense to perfection but entry passes to both Knorr and Thompson led to quick kick outs back to Tom. The clock sped down and soon it was too late for a layup. As the clock hit twelve seconds, he hit Turner with a pass deep behind the three point line. The ball was a bit low, and Turner had no chance to catch it in rhythm. In fact, as soon as he brought the ball up to his chest, he was bumped intentionally by the Kokomo guard.

They had a foul to give and intended to use it to disrupt the Invincible offensive set. Turner absorbed the blow as the whistle sounded. He took a quick dribble and calmly tossed in a twenty-two footer, just for the hell of it. The crowd erupted, but neither Turner nor Cooper even flinched. The whistle had blown well before the shot.

Dale turned away from the court so as to devise a quick inbound play when he saw his own bench leap up. He turned to face the action in time to see the Kokomo's coach in the middle of the court practically popping a vein. The official on the wing had blown the call.

Inexplicably, he ruled the shot good; the game was tied; Calvin Turner would have a free throw with nine seconds to play to complete a four point play and give Invincible the lead.

Dale suppressed the urge to dance. It was nothing short of the worst call in basketball history. He could see by the way the officials were tolerating the antics of the other coach that they knew it too. No one was going to overrule the call, but they were justified in giving the poor coach a long leash.

He controlled himself, knowing his team still had a chance to win. The officials called the players back to the line, and handed Turner the ball. He had hit thousands of free throws in his life, and as he spun the ball in his hands, his coach knew he was about to hit one more.

It was pure. Invincible led 71-70.

Out of the 'Kats timeout, they raced the ball up the floor. Turner played the ball handler, who was attempting to take the ball coast to coast. Knowing that a foul would likely send them home, he played the ball brilliantly, subtly encouraging the guard to go to his left. He stayed with him, steering him up the court. His aim was to get his man to take the last shot. As number twelve for Kokomo went up for the layup that would send his team to Indy, he never saw the lanky 6'10" sophomore coming from his left. He was too busy trying to keep the ball away from the lightning hands of Turner to realize that his shot was about to get thrown. Thompson batted the ball away just after it left the shooter's hands. It sailed harmlessly toward center court, and was not retrieved until the buzzer fired.

Hundreds of people who had never even heard of Invincible, Indiana before that week stormed the court. Turner floated along on their shoulders, adrift on a sea of joy and rapture.

Chapter Twenty

Every Team's Dream

The greatest champions in Indiana history are long remembered because of the remarkable players that starred for them. Milan and Plump, Attucks and The Big O, Plymouth and Skiles, Marion and Edwards, Bedford North Lawrence and Bailey, Roosevelt and Robinson. Winning a state title is an honor for everyone who hoists the trophy, but a select few parlay that glory into Hoosier immortality, guaranteeing their names are never forgotten.

After his scintillating four-point play carried the 12-14 Invincible Indians into a spot in the Final Four, Calvin Turner Jr's name was on everyone's lips. Whereas a month before almost no one outside the county knew who he was, he was now the talk of the state. There were even rumors circulating that NBA scouts were interested in the prospect.

At school, he was just as much an outsider as he ever was. He had gone from 'the black kid' to a god in a letter jacket. Every hour, every class, every eye was on him. Denton was the hero of the regional; Thompson had "the Block that Saved the Season," but everyone knew that Calvin Turner was a legend in his own time. Every time the bell rang and he stepped into the hall, he was surrounded by a crowd of students. Eventually, the other players set up posts outside his classes, and no fewer than four of them escorted Calvin at the end of each period, just to give him room to walk.

The town and school were in full shut-down mode. Friday had been declared an official holiday because everyone wanted to be in the parking lot to see the bus off for Indianapolis. The school asked that only family members caravan down to the Dome with the bus, but there was no chance of that order being followed. The stream of cars headed for Indy stretched for miles.

On the ride to the Dome, Dale called Calvin to the front of the bus where he was sitting. "How are you holding up, Ten?"

"I'm good, Coach."

"Ready to go tomorrow? Keeping your focus?"

Turner answered with no hesitation, "I want to win, Coach. That's all that matters to me."

"Good. Just shut out the world. Come Sunday, you can worry about all the other stuff. If you do your best tomorrow, it will all take care of itself."

Calvin nodded. He started back to seat and then stopped. "Coach? Do you think I could really play in the NBA?"

Dale was not surprised by the question, just that it had taken so long to come up. "Ten, you're the best player I've ever seen. I believe you can do anything you decide you want to do. Do you want to play in the NBA?"

"Honestly, Coach, I never thought of it until this week. I always just figured I'd go to some college on an academic scholarship and try to walk on the team. The NBA…that's crazy, right?"

This was not the conversation he wanted to have, but he knew that Calvin's future was bigger than the game the next day.

"Let me give you two pieces of advice. The first is this: relax out there tomorrow. This team is bigger than you, no matter what anyone says. Do your best, and the rest will take care of itself. The second piece of advice is that when the season is over, don't lose sight of the big picture of your life. Don't think about where you want to be next year, think about where you want to be in ten, twenty, thirty years. Do what's best for yourself and your family in the long run. Not worrying about now will take the pressure off and help things stay clear. You hear me?"

He nodded again. "Thanks Coach. For everything."

"Thank you, Calvin." Nothing more needed to be said.

The bus came down 31, passing under 465 and into Indianapolis. For Dale, the experience was surreal. He had lived in Indianapolis for twenty-seven of his twenty-eight years on earth, but coming to town with his team in tow, it felt foreign and huge. He allowed himself to see the city through their eyes. These were not wide eyed hicks gawking at three story buildings. Most of them had been to Indy before. After all, the Future Farmers of America held their yearly caucus there, and many often came with their families. It made them feel relevant and connected to the outside world they spent most of their time resisting. For the kids the city was normally a familiar and fun place.

Even so, they had never before come for a reason so important. The weight of the moment stretched everything out of proportion. The buildings scraped the sky; Monument Circle appeared majestic, and the Dome was like something from another world. No matter how many times they had been there, the city still managed to be an imposing force. The subtle message carved in the concrete was, "We are big. You are small. You do not belong here."

The Hoosier Dome looked as if someone parked his flying saucer in downtown Indianapolis and misplaced the keys for twenty years. Still, as incongruent as it was with the rest of the local architecture, it came to symbolize the entire city to millions of sports fans. It was built for football, but like most things in Indiana, it was marked by hoops. The largest crowd to ever watch any basketball game did so in the Hoosier Dome in 1984 as the Olympic team coached by Bob Knight and featuring Steve Alford and Michael Jordan took on a team of NBA stars led by Larry Bird.

The high school state finals had been held in Market Square Arena for some time, but moved to the Dome in time for the massive ticket demand surrounding the arrival of Damon Bailey, as well as Alan Henderson and Glen Robinson the following year. 41,000 strong assembled to witness Bailey fulfill prophecy.

The Dome saw Grant Hill pull a pass from the sky to thunderously bring Duke an NCAA title.

Until the rights were sold to RCA, the very name of the building evoked the essence of Indiana, and that essence was basketball.

Everything about the experience screamed that the boys from the small town had no business being there. They were dropped at a beautiful hotel downtown where they would spend the night. Even the upper classmen, now princes in the streets of their hometown, appeared small and childlike, dwarfed by the real world. Words like 'destiny' and 'fate' lost all meaning when juxtaposed with the grandeur of the city. 'Mistake' and 'lucky' were more apt descriptions of how they came to be included among the four best teams in the state.

They had a practice scheduled that afternoon in the Dome to give the teams a chance to acclimate to the enormous building. The RCA Dome was one of the smallest venues in the NFL, but for basketball purposes it was cavernous. The court was placed at one corner of the field with portable bleachers set up on three sides.

The shoot-around was rough as most players had trouble adjusting to the site lines. Shots sailed over the rim with regularity. The size of the arena played games with their depth perception, as nervousness mixed with frustration and began to snowball. The unwavering security of their preordained march to glory was shaken for the first time, and doubt filled the squad. Dale pulled them all together around the top of the key.

It felt like big speech time.

"This place is HUGE! Tomorrow morning there are going to be probably 20,000 people here! No wonder Delta is pissing their pants right now!" The team laughed. "That school doesn't even have 1,000 kids in it! They don't deserve to be here! This building is for the big time squads! You know, the legendary schools like…La Porte!"

He had their attention. "Listen, all anyone wants to do these days is talk about how small Invincible is, how few students we have, how we only have one great player. These people want and need you all to be scared. They think it matters that our school is small. That's why they are ruining our tournament. This is the last time a school our size will ever get to stand up and be counted as one of the best. They think kids from Muncie and Bloomington are better than kids from Invincible. I think that's crazy. You think you are any more afraid to shoot in this barn than some scared shitless kid from Muncie? No way. We have the best team here this weekend. We are going to win this title. Let everyone else crap themselves when they walk through that tunnel, because our eyes are going to be on that trophy sitting on the scorers' table. We have a destiny, boys. We are meant to win this tournament. Everyone who is scared of greatness can go home right now. We aren't going to shock the world, because the whole damn world knows we are the team to beat! We are Invincible. We are going to be the 1997 champions of the state of Indiana!"

Turner had been holding a ball throughout Cooper's pep talk. He squared up, spun it, and drained a bloodless three from the top of the arc.

Suddenly, no one was worried anymore.

Delta was the ideal matchup for Invincible in the first game. It was the next smallest school in the Finals and had not even won sectional in several years before making a run to Indianapolis. The crowd for the early game was good for a first session, but given the immensity of the building, 23,000 people were not nearly enough to keep the place from feeling empty. Dale overheard one of the tournament organizers say they could expect a record crowd for the night game if Invincible could win the morning matchup.

Invincible jumped out to an early lead and managed to maintain it. Delta featured excellent guard play, but had no answer for Turner. He crushed any aspirations of a comeback by the Eagles by relentlessly attacking the basket. He had a vicious dunk in traffic to punctuate the first half, and by the fourth quarter Dale could empty his bench as the Indians waltzed to an authoritative sixteen point win. Turner dazzled the crowd with thirty-eight points and before their eyes he stormed the pantheon of Hoosier legends.

Dale's speech the day before and the convincing win in the semi-final matchup worked their magic. Before the tip off of the final game against Bloomington North later that night, the Invincible locker room was brimming with confidence. Almost every man in it was convinced they were meant for victory. Dale was the only hold out, but he was not about to show the team any cracks in his confidence.

Greg Denton led the boys in prayer before they left for the court. "Most Holy God, we thank you for the opportunity you have given us tonight to honor you with our competition. We know that you are sovereign over heaven and earth, and hold all things in your hand. Tonight we ask you to help us perform our best. We pray for our opponents that you would protect them from harm and bless them for challenging us to excellence. We pray that our play will be a fragrant offering to You. Amen."

Dale followed his prayer with a riff on the same litany he had used at the start of every practice and before every game.

Now it finally meant something to them. "We worked hard every practice. We played hard every game. We have all kept our promise. We are great. Look each other in the eyes. We are one team, with one heart. We play with one mind. Our weapon is work. We have no enemies. We have one goal, victory. We have already achieved our reward. It is greatness! This is our destiny! WE ARE INVINCIBLE!"

Turner led the team out of the locker room, down the tunnel and out onto the court. Dale and Denton were to be the last two out, but Dale grabbed his friend's shoulder first. "Greg, do you think this is meant to be? Is there really such a thing as destiny?"

Denton laughed, "At this point, does it matter?"

"No, I guess not. I'll tell you one thing though, if we win this game tonight, I'll finally be ready to believe in God."

Denton slapped him on the back with a chuckle. "All that means is that you already do."

Whereas the size of the venue made the morning crowd look small, it only amplified the presence of the more than 45,000 people that paid for the chance to witness a miracle. The smallest school to play for a state title in more than forty years faced off against a school three times its size. To most Hoosiers, it was a simple David and Goliath tale, only this time with an orange rock. But to each man and woman of Invincible it meant something different.

For Phil Ericksen, it was vindication for hiring Dale Cooper as coach.

For the Knorrs, it was a son following his father and his grandfather.

For the players, it was their destiny.

For Samantha Lawson, it was love triumphing over cynicism.

For Jim Hershey, it was an administrative nightmare as he had to figure out how to schedule the make up day for the missed classes on Friday.

For Jack Jr., it was shop talk for the rest of his life.

For the Dentons, it was the fatted calf.

For Linda Turner, it was hope she had long left behind.

For her son, it was all he ever asked for.

For Dale Cooper, it was helplessness.

Ever since the Ceremony, he was eaten away, knowing his life was lived on rails. He knew how this would end. They were going to win this game. He was going to be the hottest coach in the state, and he was going to stay in Invincible. There was nothing forcing him to keep his word to the bonfire. No one but the flames knew what he wrote on that paper, but he wanted to win this game badly enough that he sure as hell was not about to back out on his promise. He knew full well there was a God and figured he was just the kind of mean son of a bitch that would condemn him to a life in Soyville, U.S.A. *You can make me live there God, but I swear, you can't make me like Mellencamp,* he promised himself silently.

The existential anxiety attack he suffered from lifted with the introduction of the starting lineups. His team was playing for the championship of the state of Indiana, and there was no time for introspection.

Invincible had a simple game plan. They were outmatched at four of five positions on the floor and at every bench spot. To win, they had to rattle Bloomington North and force turnovers that would lead to fast break points. On offense, they had to find ways to get Turner the ball quickly off of screens in the half court. They were shorter, younger, and not as deep as their opponent. Their only hope was to work harder and to get in the head of the other team. Dale convinced his club that they were the better squad, but no objective observer (including himself) would have agreed with that assessment.

Playing an accomplished team like the Cougars did not help. Bloomington was one of the cradles of Indiana basketball, a college town where every boy and girl grew up dreaming in shades of cream and crimson. In the battle for the right to represent the heart of what basketball meant to the state,

Bloomington had every bit as much claim on the position as Invincible did. They were a school just coming into its own as a basketball powerhouse and sought to establish a permanent foothold in the upper echelon of the Hoosier hoops elite.

The opening tip went to the Cougars, as did most of the first quarter. By now, the Invincible press was a known quantity, and North had drilled on it during the week before. They broke the traps with ease, flinging sharp diagonal passes up court, leading to effortless scores. Their defensive strategy was simple: two men on Turner at all times. Denton was left open, but struggled with his shot in the early going. The crowd groaned with each miss, desperately wanting to get behind the little school, but neither team was willing to cooperate with them.

Dale had no time to be stunned that his team was down by twelve points after just a quarter. He was too busy searching for the antidote to the Cougar defense. No combination of players could affect the steady slide. Turner continued to fight valiantly, chipping in ten points on just five shots, but did not get enough good looks to cut into the lead. By the half, the Indians limped off the court trailing 35-15.

The boys sat with their heads down. Dejection and resignation ruled the room. Dale's message to the team was brief.

"Heads up! How is it possible that a 13-14 team from a small town is playing for the title? How is it possible that we've won thirteen straight games? How is anything that has happened this year even possible? How is it possible that we are going to come back from twenty points down in the second half to win the state title? It's not possible. It's not any more possible than anything else that we've already done. I've got a new wrinkle they haven't seen yet. Just wait, if we go out and hit them hard on defense, they will fold. Watch for it. Watch for the fear in their eyes. The pressure is all on them. We are going to win this game!"

It was not his finest speech, but they needed more than just words to win the game.

The biggest conundrum for Dale was how to make his press more effective. North was simply too well versed in breaking it. They had to get faster if it was going to work. They needed the turnovers to get Turner open shots. He countered by going with his smallest line up, pulling Thompson and Knorr, and inserting Jones and Alberts to play with Turner, Denton, and Adams. He moved Calvin off the wing and put him in low at the post, knowing that he would still draw a double team in the middle of the floor. At the very least, the outside shot would open up. He let Alberts run the point and moved Denton to shooting guard.

Greg Denton asked the coach, "If we get caught in too many half court sets on defense, with this lineup…"

Dale cut him off. "If we get caught in too many half court sets in any defense, this game is already over."

At first the small lineup had only a negligible effect. Granted, the lead did not grow for the first couple of minutes, but that was because North unconsciously took their collective foot off the gas. Finally, Turner muscled inside for a brutal three point play over the North big men down low. He followed up his made free throw with a steal and a kick out to Denton for a three off the inbound play, and suddenly the Indians had developed a pulse. The crowd roused, anxious to participate in a game from which they had been systematically excluded.

The Cougars broke the Invincible press on the next possession leading to what appeared to be any easy dunk by one of their front court players. Al Alberts, the smallest man on the floor, used his unparalleled speed to race under the Cougar forward and planted his feet firmly moments before he went up for a dunk. The diminutive sophomore, outweighed by sixty pounds was blasted off his feet and past the end line as the North player thundered home a basket. The whistle blew.

The call was charging.

Through the thunder of 40,000 lungs breaking overhead, Dale yelled for a time out. Alberts was still down at one end of the court, with the wind knocked out of him. Dale ushered the entire team off the bench, and as one they arrived at their fallen teammate, helping him to his feet. He stood up and pumped his fist.

The response from above was deafening. As he soaked in the roar, Dale Cooper knew the game was back on.

Alberts stayed in the game, not seriously hurt by the collision. He followed up his heroics with an open jumper. His first points of the game cut the Cougar lead to twelve and met with the universal acclaim of the patrons.

The teams traded baskets, and the Invincible offense picked up when Denton found his stroke. As the third quarter closed, Turner managed his first long distance shot of the day, thanks to a bone jarring screen from Roger Adams who picked off two defenders. Calvin sank the three just ahead of the horn to cut the deficit to single digits for the first time in what seemed like months.

As he trotted back to his sideline, he looked into the eyes of the North players and saw exactly what he wanted. He saw fear.

Dale gave no instructions to his team to start the fourth. "Bring it home," was all he needed to say. Two quick baskets off of Bloomington turnovers affirmed that his boys had received the message. They were still down five points, but the building felt like victory. The crowd was having a real effect on the North players who were obviously unaccustomed to being treated like villains.

The Cougars took a time out, and it settled them. They answered the Invincible run with a couple of made shots, but each time they were matched. They tried to slow down the pace of play and take advantage of their size inside, figuring that Turner could not possibly guard their center, John Jeffords, who clocked in at 6'11." It was a mismatch to be sure, but not how they expected. Turner's speed and vertical leap made it difficult to get entry passes into the big man. With the Indians still trailing by five, Turner baited North into a bad pass which he stole, immediately breaking down the floor. He was fouled as he spun home an awkward layup.

His free throw made the score 52-50. He had twenty-one points, and was nine for nine from the floor. With just over three minutes remaining, North played for the stall. Taking the air out of the ball helped to calm both their players and the crowd. Dale ordered his players to back off. He knew that the shorter the game, the better chance they had of stealing it. The crowd became agitated as two full minutes ticked off without any court action as the Cougar guard stood with the ball on his hip, scarcely moving. Finally, when the time dwindled to under a minute, Cooper motioned to Alberts and Denton to begin the trap.

Fifty seconds. Dale hoped to avoid ordering a foul, knowing that North had their best free throw shooters on the floor.

Forty seconds. The passes glided from one player to another, as if on strings.

Thirty seconds. They were crisp and error free. He waved Jones and Adams to back court, daring the North guards to throw a pass forward to any of the three open men standing near the basket.

Twenty seconds. He was ready to call for the foul when at last the beleaguered point guard was overcome with the temptation to hit the small forward standing ten feet from the hoop. He rose up and rifled a quick toss into the open man, who instinctively turned toward the basket. He should have just dribbled out the clock, but ten years of basketball reflexes were too much for the young man to overcome. He went up for a layup, not stopping to think that the best player on the other team was the only one back on defense.

As the shot went up, Turner vaulted high into the teflon night and tapped the attempt back over the head of the stunned shooter. Calvin landed squarely and dove for the ball he had sent hopping idly toward the sideline. He hauled it in with and outstretched right arm, cradling it and seeking an official as he signaled for his team's final timeout.

It was granted with nine seconds on the clock.

Dale called for Turner to inbound the ball. Alberts or

Denton were to advance it past the half court line. Calvin was obviously the first option; he was to drive if he could and shoot as quickly as possible to tie the game.

Dale looked at his players as the official came to order them back into play. "This is greatness," was all he could say.

He knew what was going to happen even as it unfolded. He had ordered Calvin to drive to the hole, but that was unlikely. North tried trapping the tiny Alberts as soon as he caught the ball, but he slithered through with the dribble. He was out of control, but batted the ball ahead to Knorr, who entered in case of a rebound opportunity. Knorr hit Turner who was blazing down the right sideline. Jones set a perfect screen just in front of the bend in the three point arc. Turner let fly his tenth shot of the championship game as the final seconds spun in tenths.

Dale knew it was good. He had no need to watch it. The air from the lungs of the multitude pulled straight in to the ball like an orange star about to collapse in upon itself. There was doubt and wonder on the lips of everyone there that night, except the coach and the shooter. They both knew it was pure.

There are dozens of reasons why a shot does or does not go in the basket. The angle can be wrong, and the ball will still tap off the glass and go. The rotation can be perfect, but the air compressor in the gym, triggered by the heat from the fans, can click on at the wrong moment and cool the air just enough so that a shot that would have found the bottom of the net just minutes earlier spins off the rim and out. The shooter feels like he has control, but it is an illusion. At the moment of release, the ball leaves his hands and destiny takes over. The same shot that makes a hero on one court, on one rim, can glance harmlessly away on another court, another rim.

On that rim, on that night, the ball glanced off the inner cylinder. And rattled out.

Chapter Twenty One

Small Town

The buzzer sounded. Turner crumpled to the court as if shot. Dale's knees buckled, while the bile in his stomach leapt to his mouth leaving an acrid burn behind. The Bloomington North players piled upon one another as their bench spilled out onto the floor. Each boy from Invincible dropped to his knees in disbelief. Everyone involved in the game was openly weeping, but not all for the same reason.

No one could remember anything that happened the rest of the night. Eventually, all the players shook hands, but no one from Invincible could recall the look on even one opponent's face. There was an awards ceremony in which medals were hung around their necks, but at the time they felt like they were bowing their heads for a guillotine. They gathered in the locker room and cried together, hugging each other and listening as their coach spoke words of comfort. They could see on his face that he did not believe a word he was saying, so they forgot those too.

When a season ends too soon, it feels like the staircase was built a step short. The missing step haunts briefly before the climber realizes it was never there at all. When a season goes as far as it can and the team loses, it is wholly different. There is a spinning, twisting descent that can only be accepted by knowing that the fall may never end. Years later, all of the men who played on that team had moments of regret and loss whenever they thought about that night.

Dale was unable to help the boys. There was no help to be had. Life is full of cruel disappointments, and they would be stronger for learning that fact while they were still young. He had nothing to offer them but to take his place at their sides and cry along with them. Together they mourned the death of their dreams. Perspective would come in time, but that night it was an unwelcome visitor in the Invincible locker room.

The bus-ride home was cathartic for most of the players. Youth both adores and abhors misery, and will embrace it for only so long. As the black and yellow bus passed the limits of Kokomo, Sean Knorr shouted, "Suck it, Kokomo! We kicked your ass!" His exclamation met with cheers from everyone.

As they neared State Road 24, they passed Peru and someone in the back shouted, "Next year, Peru! Next year!" Laughter ensued. Approaching Invincible, the bus passed many of the schools they had vanquished. By the time they reached home, they knew the truth. They were not invincible, but they were champions.

They were great.

They had spoken several times since the game, but never more than a few words. After more than a month, Dale grabbed Calvin in the hallway after class to catch up. "I have to tell you Ten, I miss seeing you every day. How are you?"

Turner nodded. "I'm good, Coach."

Dale knew not to expect much of a response. "You dealing with the colleges ok?"

Turner had an almost guilty look. It did not keep him from speaking with his customary directness. "I'm going to enter the draft."

"Really? I guess I shouldn't be shocked; I heard the draft guys are talking like you'll be a first round pick. Still, I had you pegged for school."

The younger man was expressionless. "My mom made me sign a legal contract saying that I would save money toward my education every year, and that I would take at least three hours of class each summer. I wanted to go to school, Coach, but when I looked at how much time the big schools were asking me to give to basketball, I figured I was better off getting paid to play. Even if I wash out of the league in a year or two, I'll have made enough to pay for my own schooling, and I'll be able to focus on studying when I go. Don't worry, Coach, I got a plan."

Dale smiled. "I'm not surprised. Listen, anything you need, you know you can always ask me, right?"

Calvin looked down, and then back up at his coach. "I would appreciate if you would give me any notes or tips you have about how I can improve my game. What do I need to work on to make it at the next level?"

What could he say to the reigning Mr. Basketball and future NBA star other than the trite or obvious? Calvin Turner was a man with no holes in his game.

He thought for a moment and said, "Don't ever be afraid to take the last shot. You have to want the ball. If I was coaching a team and I had to pick one player to make one shot and the rest my life depended on it, I would pick you every time and sleep easy at night."

There was a long silence between the two. Calvin finally broke it. "I thought it was good, Coach."

"It was good, Ten. It just didn't fall."

Turner fought off a sob. Six weeks had not lessened the sting. Six years could not have helped. "Thanks, Coach. Oh, congratulations. You'll be great."

Dale Cooper hugged his best player. "We'll see how well I do without you around to bail me out."

Turner laughed and left. It was a short, awkward conversation. Dale knew he would stay close to the young man, but for right now this was all they could manage.

"So you are taking my son away from his poor mother?" Greg Denton said over The Overall Platter at Pam's.

Dale laughed. "It's not like Indianapolis is that far away, Greg."

Denton almost commented on the irony of that statement, but instead laughed his good natured laugh. "Well, we're grateful you've offered him a scholarship. Butler is a fine school. He'll do well there."

"It made me the man I am today!" Dale replied.

"Ha! In that case, maybe I won't sign that consent form!"

Dale had no wish to waste time small talking Denton. There was something he had been meaning to ask him for weeks, but every time he thought about that game, the sick ball in his stomach rose up his throat. This time, he came prepared. He popped an antacid and said, "Greg, I KNEW that ball was going in. I knew it. I never believed in fate or destiny or really even in God, but I knew that ball was going through. When it didn't…I…I don't know. I felt lost."

Denton took the matter seriously. "You felt like God was there one minute and then he was gone."

Dale did not like having it put that way but nodded. It was as accurate as any description of how he felt. "Yeah, I suppose it's funny, but I thought that if that ball went in, it meant that there was a God, and he was going to enslave me. When it didn't go down…it meant that I was free, but alone. I'm not sure I like either option."

"Dale, I look at everything that has happened to you, and to all of us, this year, and I know that God is good. He is just as good because that shot rattled out as he would be if it had rattled in. Destiny, fate, the will of God, whatever, it has nothing to do with silly things like who hits and who misses a basketball shot. I know he could do something about that if he wanted to, but I'm not sure he doesn't have more interesting things to worry about."

Cooper stared at him, not quite following the preacher talk.

Denton went on, "Sons coming home to fathers, orphans becoming heroes, towns learning to believe, outsiders figuring out how to belong. That's what destiny is made of, brother. That's where I see God."

He considered his friend's words. "Yeah, but would it have killed him to make that shot go in?"

"I don't know, Dale. He tends to die for weightier issues than even the state championship of Indiana."

Dale smiled. "Thanks, Greg."

"Anytime, Coach." He said the last word just a touch louder than normal. He wanted everyone to know who it was he was talking to.

She knew he was moving before the date but invited him anyway. "It's only a couple of hours. You can make it, can't you?" she asked.

He did not want to go to Samantha's Lawson's wedding. He could not tell her that. "Sam, I can't make it. I have an alumni function to speak at that night. I'm heartbroken." It was not *really* a lie.

Her laugh could not hide her disappointment. "I was

hoping to give you another crack at a certain bridesmaid!"

"I'm sorry, Sam. Some things are out of my hands. I'll send you a nice toaster though!"

"So this is it? You are just leaving. You're never coming back, are you?"

Yes. No. It did not matter how he answered. They both knew it was true. He wordlessly shook his head.

"They'll never forget you, you know. You're a hero here. You were the best thing to ever happen to this town." There was more that she could not say, so instead she said, "Other than that squirrel."

He packed up the Taurus with the last odds and ends. The moving truck already left for his new condo in Broad Ripple. Dale Cooper was not sad to say good bye to the pink bungalow, but the banner stretched over Main Street gave him pause:

THANKS COACH! GOOD LUCK!

He was the least successful coach in the last fifty years of Invincible, Indiana, but there was no one waiting to run him out on a rail.

He flicked on the radio as he pulled out onto the county road that would eventually feed him back toward home. *Hurts So Good.*

He punched the dial.

"I was born in a small town…"

He sighed and let it play.

1997 marked the death of the one class tournament.

The state legislature fought valiantly against the change, and pressured the IHSAA to adopt a "Tournament of Champions" that pitted the four class champions against each other. It was a compromise, and temporarily stilled the anger from most fans around the state.

The following year, AAAA champion Pike High School won the mini-tournament. The IHSAA resented the event, complaining that it was anti-climactic and unnecessary. Smaller schools whined that they did not feel like champions because they lost their last game. It was discontinued after just two seasons.

In the past fourteen years of the Indiana high school boys' basketball tournament, there have been fifty-six champions crowned.

In the fourteen years since the death of one class basketball, barely 400,000 fans have attended the finals.

In 2011, 28,655 people came to Conseco Fieldhouse in Indianapolis to watch eight teams play the four games of the IHSAA Boys Basketball State Finals.

In the fourteen years since the multi-class format was adopted, attendance has never topped 35,000 in any given year.

Seven times it has failed to draw 30,000 fans.

About the Author:

Nate Dunlevy was born and raised in Indianapolis where he currently lives with his wife Deborah and three children. A graduate of Pike High School and Grace College and Theological Seminary, Nate has a Masters degree in Intercultural Studies and spent most of the decade of the 2000s living and working in Argentina. He is the editor and head writer for 18to88.com. His first book was Blue Blood: Tales of Glory of the Indianapolis Colts.

For the record, Nate finished Invincible, Indiana in June of 2009 and watched in horror as Gordon Hayward's shot rimmed out against Duke the following year.

He may never recover.

About the Designer:

Raised in Indiana, Matt Hasenbalg now makes his home with his wife, Kellie, and their three children among the rolling hills and horse farms of Kentucky - the "other" basketball state. Matt graduated from Indiana University in Bloomington with a degree in Graphic Design. He is the executive presentation specialist and creative lead in corporate communications at a technology company in Lexington.

Matt and Kellie witnessed firsthand Indiana's 2002 tournament win over Duke at Rupp Arena, and he patiently awaits the return of Hoosier basketball to such prominence. It sure would make the annual matchups with UK easier to handle.

www.ingramcontent.com/pod-product-compliance
Lightning Source LLC
Chambersburg PA
CBHW031943240626
47153CB00003B/848
9780984762408